Dark Cloud on Naked Creek

"*Dark Cloud on Naked Creek* is an enjoyable and thrilling read. Cindy O'Quinn is an extremely talented author. I'm looking forward to reading more of her work."

—Annabella Gentile, screenwriter

"Cindy O'Quinn's characters are so well developed they come to life on each page. Will absolutely recommend *Dark Cloud on Naked Creek,* to others. Fantastic read!"

—Cathy Moriarty, Oscar®-nominated actress

Cindy O'Quinn's novel *Dark Cloud on Naked Creek* takes us into the disturbing, dangerous world of Appalachian lore and legend, and rightfully places her in the company of past Southern Gothic horror masters Jack Cady, Fred Chappell and Michael McDowell. Don't miss this one.
—Thomas Tessier, author of *The Nightwalker*

"The thing I love most about Cindy O'Quinn's work is the deeper-than-bone compassion for her people and place. Her horror is unflinching but never cruel, thoroughly grounded in its history and lore, letting the hills and the hollers speak through her to tell us what they know. This is horror with heart, rendering its nightmares with integrity, while still more than tough enough to kick your ass. That's why I love it. And I think you will too."
—John Skipp, New York Times bestselling author

"Dripping with beautifully written prose, and enthralling characters, *Dark Cloud on Naked Creek* is a profoundly emotional tale of family and the ties that bind us. A shining testament to Cindy O'Quinn's mastery of story craft."
—Candace Nola, author of *Shadow Manor*

Dark Cloud on Naked Creek

by Cindy O'Quinn

BRIGIDS GATE
PRESS

Edited by Candace Nola and S.D. Vassallo

Formatted by Stephanie Ellis

Cover illustration and design by Lynne Hansen

New Edition: June 2025

ISBN (paperback): 978-1-963355-29-1

ISBN (ebook): 978-1-963355-28-4

Library of Congress Control Number: 2025936826

BRIGIDS GATE PRESS

Overland Park, Kansas

www.brigidsgatepress.com

Printed in the United States of America

Dedicated to Thomas Tessier and Ronald Kelly

Introduction

Reading the work of Cindy O'Quinn is like going home again.

I must confess, I've never had the pleasure of visiting West Virginia, but I reckon it can't be that much different from my home state of Tennessee. The mountains, wooded hills, and hollows, the music (folk and bluegrass, if you want the purest kind) and, of course, the backbone of the land itself—the people who dwell there. Folks you've grown up with or gone to church with all your life, as well as your kin. Mothers and fathers, siblings, cousins, and grandparents—the glue of DNA that binds us and holds the family together as strong as seasoned hickory.

Speaking of kinship, I felt that way about Cindy the first time I read her story "Quondam," which earned her a Bram Stoker Award for Best Short Fiction. As far as her prose was concerned, she struck me as a kindred spirit. I felt that even more so the first time we met in person at Authorcon in Virginia earlier this year; it was like staring into the face of a long-lost sister. Since then, she has often told me that she was drawn to my Southern-fried fiction as well because "we shared the same voice." I wholeheartedly agree. Our brand of down-home, rural storytelling is drawn from the same well: creative waters that are sometimes mystical and rejuvenating, while at other times bitter and tainted with strife. Country life can be blessed with treasures of the heart and soul, but it can also be wrought with hard times, tragedy, and disillusionment. I believe in our own separate ways, Cindy and I have experienced our share of both

When she asked me to read *Dark Cloud on Naked Creek* and appraise its storyline and characters honestly, with "a fresh set of eyes," I jumped at the chance. What I found between the first page and the last was a blessing within itself.

I grew up at the knees of storytellers: my mother, my uncles, and most particularly my maternal grandmother. From an early age, I listened, mesmerized, as Grandmama Clara Spicer imparted family history from before the War Between the States, through the Great Depression, and the decades afterward, as well as local ghost stories and rural folklore. In turn, I myself craved to carry on the storytelling tradition, by creating worlds and enabling characters with flesh and spirit of their own, upon the written page. I'm sure Cindy O'Quinn also had storytellers in her early life that molded her desire to tell engaging tales and instilled the love and skill of writing that has served her so very well over the years.

Within these pages, you will enter the world of Afton Sullivan. You will walk her pathways—sometimes sunlit, while other times shrouded with shadow—and experience her joys and fears. You will also encounter the strange folk who dwell in the mountains of West Virginia: Appalachian Grannies, skinwalkers, and benevolent beings known as the Cunnin' Folk. It was when I entered their world through Cindy's prose, that I truly felt that I had reclaimed a bit of the home I had known as a younger man. I had, on occasion, visited the herb-laden kitchens of granny women who concocted medicinal potions and conjured poultices for everything from migraine headaches to gout. I had also witnessed the healing of an infant's thrush as an old man breathed five times into the baby's mouth; a seventh son in his late seventies who had never laid eyes on his father, who had been a seventh son before him. So, many of the characters in this book revealed themselves to me naturally and with little effort, since I had encountered their true life counterparts before in my own past.

Dark Cloud on Naked Creek is a journey that will set your feet upon earth you have never tread before, and in some ways, may just return you to the trails you strayed from in years gone by. Without a doubt, it is a story that will surely draw you in and keep you entertained throughout its narrative. It is definitely a story worth reading and one worth telling. Cindy O'Quinn has done that quite masterfully, rendered by the pen of her creativity, primed from the inkwell of a storyteller's soul.

Ronald Kelly

Brush Creek, Tennessee

September 2024

Part One: Afton

Chapter 1: Back to Prison

Driving north on route 340, Afton Sullivan couldn't help but notice the dark clouds gathered over the bridge at Naked Creek. They were thick, surly, pregnant with the potential for rain or worse. Just seeing them made her want to turn tail and head back home. But there was no doing that. She had been gone long enough.

Today will be different, she told herself. Today I'll be able to go in and do my job and there won't be any episodes. No horrible visions of what the inmates have done in their past. Even worse, what some are planning to do when they get out.

She had been off from work for six weeks, recovering from surgery. After wrestling with the issue longer than she should have, she finally got up the nerve to have breast reconstruction. Many years ago, something bad had happened to her. Something she had never talked about to anyone. Only Grandma Ruby had known the truth about it. She never brought it up because she knew it was too painful for Afton to discuss. It was a secret they had both kept locked tightly away; from curious friends and neighbors with wagging tongues and no tact to hold them in check.

Afton was healing fine physically, but mentally the damage ran far deeper. The surgery had done wonders for the scars. At least she could look at herself in the mirror now without that wild rush of emotion setting in or feeling sick to her stomach. But so much tissue had to be removed that it had diminished what curves she previously had up top.

She couldn't have been more wrong about her first day back … about it being better or even different than it was before.

The prison was an all-male facility. The first patient of the day was a fifty-five-year-old man named Mit Daniel. He was brought into the medical unit in a wheelchair, complaining of chest pain. It was his third trip to Medical for the same reason. The other two times had been stress-related chest pain, not cardiac. Nevertheless, Afton went to work and started the protocol.

"Help me get him on the gurney," she instructed the guard who had brought him; a big rawboned fellow named Byler. Together, they wrestled him from the chair. The inmate was lost in his distress and no help to them; no more than dead weight. Never assume when it comes to chest pain, thought Afton. It was one of the main lessons she recalled from nursing school. The first time you did, it was guaranteed to be a myocardial infarction, otherwise known as a heart attack for folks who weren't familiar with the technical jargon.

There were times when Afton Sullivan hated to lay hands on an inmate. She never knew what she would see, and no matter how many times it happened, she was never prepared. This time was no different. The moment her hands touched his chest to remove his shirt, searing pain shot into her fingertips and up her arms. It felt like jamming the tines of a fork into an electrical socket, or what she figured that might be like.

It began. Afton could plainly see him at yesterday's visitation with his granddaughter. Her long blonde curls, the frilly short dress, appropriate for a six-year-old but not for a prison known for its high occupancy of pedophiles. His hand on her back might appear innocent to the unknowing correctional officer, but not to Afton. She knew what he felt and thought as he touched her; the sick and twisted plans he had in store for her in one short month when he was due to be released. She couldn't allow that to happen … not to her, not again. Afton hoped the electrocardiogram would show that he was having a massive myocardial infarction. But no such luck. Instead, the EKG was normal.

This wasn't the first time the nurse had been faced with such a dilemma. The last time had been a close call, but she understood that she had a duty to help this man if she could. Afton focused on the rhythm of the chest compressions. Soon, she realized that nearly ten minutes had elapsed since his arrival and her hands continued to pump. One, two, three … one, two, three.

The guard watched closely as she worked. The inmate, Daniel, stared up into her eyes with an expression of sheer terror. What's happening? she thought. Afton opened her mouth to question him but the words wouldn't come. Was it possible that the disgust she felt for him could be transferred through her touch? Something was happening to him, that was for certain. She glanced at the heart monitor. The EKG showed only a flat line.

Byler looked to her for direction. "Notify Control and have them dispatch an ambulance," she told him. Of course, she couldn't stop. She was obligated to continue trying to bring that monster back from the brink of death—or at least give it her best shot.

His eyes were open wide and focused directly on her. That was the worst part of it. They seemed to be staring directly into her soul, searching for forgiveness. It was not her forgiveness that he needed. His pleas for forgiveness should be to his poor granddaughter. He could stare at Afton all he wanted. No pity would come from her eyes or from her hands as they continued to administer CPR. No one dies in prison. It's an unwritten but well-known rule. So, she did her job until the medics arrived and took over. Soon, he was wheeled out of Medical and loaded into the ambulance.

Inmate Mit Daniel was gone from there. He was now headed to the nearest hospital. Considering that the prison was located in rural West Virginia, it would be over an hour's drive. By the time they reached the medical facility, there would be nothing else left to do but for a doctor to pronounce him dead.

It took longer to write up the reports than the duration of the entire episode itself. After that, it was time for her to seek shelter in the break room and figure out exactly what had just taken place.

Before opening the locked doors that kept the medical unit safe from the inmates, she heard, "Afton. Afton, could you please come here?"

Dear God, not now. She was in no mood to endure the third degree from that overbearing, dot-all-the-i's, mouse of a man that was their so-called nurse manager.

"What is it, George?" she asked. Her wrists ached from the compressions she had delivered for nearly half an hour. "I really do need a break after what just happened."

He stared at her with his less-than-knowledgeable eyes and informed her that Officer Byler had just left a copy of his report.

"And?" she asked, a little too impatiently.

"Well," George began, "he thought you handled the situation like a true professional and I just wanted to say, good job."

"Oh." Afton tried her best to clear the catch in her throat. "Okay. Thanks for letting me know, George."

Alone at last, she slumped into the chair closest to the window in the tiny break room. It was only mid-morning, and she was already exhausted. She felt bad that she had snapped at George, but the feeling was brief. You just had to know George Samoht. He had a way about him that could make a saint cuss a blue streak.

Her mind began to drift back to her sixth birthday. It had fallen on a Friday.

Momma had wanted to surprise her with a cake and a dress she had made for her. Afton already knew about the dress because she had been working on it for weeks, and she had been hinting around about cakes. Her parents were good, hardworking people. Momma had sent her to Grandma Ruby's to get her out of the house for a little while. Grandma insisted on walking her home that day. Afton had just played along like she didn't have a clue about the surprise. Then, she and Grandma saw the thick, dark smoke before they had reached the top of the ridge. Her family's little two-room house was fully engulfed in flames …

An alarm sounded in the background. Back to reality. Routine prison alarm check every Friday at noon.

While standing in the medical unit, you could look out any of the six-foot windows and believe you were at an old country resort. The massive building was surrounded by beautiful mountains. The inmates would be scattered across the grounds like ants. Some would be playing baseball. A few would be jogging on the track. There might even be a handful playing croquet. If it weren't for their prison clothes, it would be easy to forget where you were. Of course, there were always the eight-foot chain-link fences and razor wire for anyone who needed reminding.

Afton remembered the day she came there for her interview, a little over two decades ago. She was impressed by the building, but in a sad and uneasy way. It had a powerful presence with its massive size and all the huge windows that seemed to look down on you as you approached. Most modern prisons were on one level because it just made more sense. This one had reminded her of a medieval castle in one of the picture books Grandma had gotten from a bookmobile that came to the ridge the summer after the fire.

Once the officer in the control box had pushed the button to open the gate, it made its warning buzz and Afton had entered. The gate automatically slammed shut behind her, causing her to jump. It was that sound. The metallic clang of finality. Whether you left that place or were destined to stay depended on who you were and whether or not you were a free citizen or an incarcerated felon.

Once inside the building, she had signed the visitor log and waited for the nurse manager to come down to escort her to Medical. If she had tried to find her way to the medical unit the first time by herself, she probably would have never gotten back. Again, the image of a castle had come to mind. Inside, it seemed more like one from an old horror movie—one wrong turn and who knew where you would end up.

Finally, George Samoht had arrived. He had given her the two-cent tour and a brief history of the place. It had originally been built in the late 1800s as a sanitarium for "colored people afflicted with tuberculosis," as he put it. That explained why the place was so off the beaten path. None of the local townspeople had wanted to be reminded of the hospital full of dying and contagious people just fifteen minutes outside of town. The sanitarium had remained open until 1965. It sat unused for one year and then reopened as a medium-security prison.

Afton had never even heard of the small community of Duck, West Virginia, until she saw the help-wanted ad in the newspaper. It was an hour and fifteen minute drive on a crooked country road from her home. Some said the place was haunted, either by the patients who died there or by the handful of overworked nurses who had dedicated themselves to taking care of them.

It was no wonder the pay was more substantial than most positions offered: they couldn't seem to keep staff for very long. They either got tired of the drive or they were just plain scared of the place.

Break was over far too quickly. Afton made her way back up the three flights of stairs to Medical.

She could feel their eyes on her. They looked at her differently today. She was more uncomfortable than usual, walking near them in the hallways. After all those years, it still seemed strange to her that the inmates were allowed to roam about the place unescorted. Inmate movement was announced and then monitored via camera, and head counts were done around the clock.

It's my surgery, she thought self-consciously. They can see the difference. She had always worn such baggy scrubs that she didn't think anyone would notice. Most men were drawn to women with large breasts, but these were far from average men. These monsters liked little girls and boys. What was left of her breasts, along with her five-foot-four-inch frame, resembled the body of a twelve-year-old girl or boy more than a mature woman in her late-forties.

She felt the heat rush to her face as she realized their thoughts. Afton picked up her pace to get back to Medical as fast as possible. She was so distracted, she forgot to count the steps. She had made that mistake one other time and ended up in what looked like the basement. This time, she went up one extra set of stairs and came out on the end of the hall where their rooms were, not the end where the officer's desk was.

Her feet had the sudden urge to run, but she didn't want to give them the pleasure of her anxiety. Some of them really fed on the fact they had a talent of striking fear into others. She quickly walked down the long hall, not daring to look into any of their rooms. Finally, she could see the officer's desk and hear him talking to someone. She allowed herself to breathe again, attempting to settle her nerves.

Afton went straight into the pharmacy to get ready for pill call. She felt someone staring at her, but knew it wasn't an inmate. The overly sweet smell of Red Fox chewing tobacco told her that it was Sergeant Dawson. Before that day, the guard had seemed harmless. He was always eager to lend a hand if she needed it. His willingness to help usually came across as an innocent gesture. But that day, his glare felt like it was burning a hole through her clothes. He said he was glad she was back and commented that she somehow looked different—younger or that she had lost weight. Once again, the heat started to rise up her neck and into her face. That was always a dead giveaway of Afton's emotional state. She told him it was probably because she had gotten a much-needed rest while she was off and left it at that. She turned her back to him and continued her work. Eventually, he got the hint and left the medical unit.

An older nurse named Joetta came into the pharmacy. She had started working there part-time when she was out for her surgery. Afton didn't know her, but she felt oddly familiar. Joetta stared at her the way little kids would stare at a crippled person. She could feel her eyes looking at her or, rather, into her. Afton wasn't the social type, so she didn't bother to look up or stop working.

Finally, when Joetta had waited long enough, she spoke. "I know you."

Afton sort of half-laughed. "I doubt that." She opened a sleeve of white paper cups and laid them out on a stainless steel tray for the medication.

Joetta frowned. "I don't mean that I know you personally … but I definitely know you."

This piqued Afton's interest. "What do you mean, you know me? It's not like we went to school together. Aren't you like eighty years old?"

"Eighty-three, to be exact," she said proudly. "You know, one other time in my life, I met someone like you."

She went on to tell her that, when she was about twelve years old, she had lived in McDowell County, West Virginia. "An old woman came to our house—well, it was more like a shack, really— when my mother fell ill. That woman made me feel afraid, made me feel like she could see into the very depths of my soul. As though she could see every bad thing I had ever done."

"Well, you were only twelve. Surely she didn't see much."

"Funny," she said, "you didn't question the notion that this woman had the ability to see into my life."

"Look, Joetta," Afton said, growing a little impatient. "I'm not judging you for what you obviously believe happened when you were a child, but what does this story of yours have to do with me?"

It seemed as though Joetta would stare at her for all eternity before answering. Finally, she said, "I get the same feeling when I look at you."

She then turned and walked away.

For as long as she could remember, Afton had made a painstaking effort to never grow close to anyone. Never let anyone into her private space. Everyone knew her as the quiet, but knowledgeable, nurse who took her job seriously, did her work well, and never talked about anything very personal. She had made it a point to tell people only what she believed to be the safe and generic norms of life that they wanted to hear.

Who is this complete stranger who just stepped into my life, believing that she knows so much about me? she wondered. Had there really been someone else like me?

Afton never asked to see the things that she saw, but she always felt that the day would come when she would be called upon to do something about it. Joetta had told her that the old woman had been summoned when her mother fell ill. But if the old woman was like Afton, she definitely hadn't been there to heal her. She knew she should have asked about her mother, but Joetta had caught her so off guard she couldn't think straight. Had her mother done horrible things and the old woman was there to hasten her death?

The entire conversation had been awkward and a little disturbing. So many questions came to mind, but Afton was bone tired. She swept the odd encounter to the back of her mind and continued sorting the pills.

Chapter 2: Irish Eyebrights

Afton fell into her bed and drifted quickly into a deep sleep, which was very unlike her.

The dreams of her mother and father had been coming less frequently. Her parents had died in that fire on her sixth birthday. A fire that burned so hot, even their bones had been turned to ash, leaving nothing to be buried. Grandma Ruby took her in without hesitation and raised her like she was her own daughter. They seemed even closer than mother and daughter, if that was possible. They were connected, even finished each other's sentences and thoughts. There had been one person in Afton's entire life who had made her feel safe and normal, but somehow special at the same time. Her grandma, Ruby Shires, was that one person who could always make life better.

Afton knew she was asleep, but could feel Ruby near her, even though she had been gone for nearly a year. She remembered the night she had passed away. As she took her last breath, Afton had felt a gentle wisp of air kiss her face. Warmth washed over her like a hug, and she knew it was Grandma's spirit touching her. What a blessing! She was the one who pushed her toward nursing school. She had told Afton that she was special and that she needed to share that specialness with others, because there would be those who would someday require her to use her gift. Had she really said gift, or in her dream state was she just adding things she wanted or needed to hear?

When sunlight began to peek through the edges of the blinds in her bedroom, Afton opened her eyes and remembered her dream about her precious Grandma Ruby. Had it been an actual dream? She hoped not. She hoped that she truly came to visit her, and if she did, perhaps help her understand what was happening to her. She had called it a gift. If Afton was killing people, how could that be considered a gift? Maybe she wasn't killing them but simply helping them to transition into the death that was already going to take them and allowing them to see the things they needed to see.

What a lovely way to put it! But who was she kidding?

Afton felt an urgency to get to work that morning. She would ask Joetta a few questions about her mother and the old woman who had scared her. Once she was clocked in, she looked around, but didn't see her anywhere.

George stepped into the medical unit with a handful of papers and nervously sorted through them. Afton could tell that she made the man nervous. She wasn't quite sure why she had such an adverse effect on him, but secretly, she was glad. It seemed to keep him at a distance, which was exactly what she wanted.

"George, is Joetta working today?"

He visibly jumped at the sound of her voice. He almost dropped his paperwork, which made her smile. Shame on me, she thought. She quickly wiped the smile from her face before he looked at her.

"She's not on the schedule again until Monday," he told her. "Why? Did you have a problem with her yesterday?"

"Oh no, she did fine. I just wanted to talk to her."

He had the strangest look on his face. It made her wonder if she was really so unsociable that he thought she never talked to anyone unless it was strictly about work. It didn't matter; Afton went on with her day. Finally, a fairly quiet day. When her shift ended and she had given her report to the oncoming nurse, she hurried to clock out and get to her car. When she was finally in the seat with the door closed and her hands on the steering wheel, it felt like she could fully breathe for the first time in the past eight hours.

Afton knew very little about her ancestors, beyond her parents and grandparents. She was a Sullivan, which was an Irish name. Her mother was a Shires, which she believed was English, but some of the Shires had moved to Ireland centuries ago. Afton thought her mother's people were from that group. Her mother's mother was a Leary. That was Grandma Ruby. Ruby Leary Shires.

A sense of calmness fell over her whenever she thought of Ruby. That day it made Afton long for one of her home-cooked Irish meals, so she made a quick detour by the store and bought the ingredients to make potato-leek soup and soda bread. She lived in what was known as the Village of McKinley. It was a small community of people who lived off the land. When Grandma Ruby was still alive, she would drop her off at one of the widows' houses and they would put their old ways of canning and preserving foods to good use, and, most importantly, quilting. She had told Afton it was a dying art that needed to be passed along. She often wondered what other things they might have worked on.

Once she got home, Afton started dinner, and while the soup simmered and the bread was set aside to rise, she ran a tub of hot bubbly water. A long soak would help her to unwind; it always did. Her neck and shoulders felt like they were tied in knots. She lowered herself into the tub of steaming water, wincing at first because the water was a little too hot, but after a bit, it felt soothing. She rested her head on a folded towel on the back of the tub, and before she knew it, she had drifted off to sleep.

Afton could feel Grandma Ruby close by. She opened her eyes slowly for fear that she would disappear. She hoped it wasn't merely a dream. She could hear pots and pans being moved about in the kitchen, and smell the wonderful aromas she remembered from her childhood. Afton quickly put on a robe and hurried to the kitchen. The woman had her back to her while working at the stove. She set the lid down on the big pot of soup.

Without turning to face her, Grandma Ruby said, "Afton, you have really come a long way with your cooking skills. I guess you were paying attention during those lessons I gave you, after all."

Afton's cheeks felt warm and her eyes began to water. Ruby turned, and she looked into her grandmother's kind eyes.

"Don't cry, my dear," she said gently. Ruby walked over and wiped a tear away before it had a chance to make its way down her face. "My fair-eyed beauty, do your pale blue eyes still bother you on bright days?"

"Yes," replied Afton. "Even on days when it's not so bright, I find the need to wear sunglasses."

Her eyes were full of love and concern. "My precious child, you truly live up to the Sullivan name."

Afton didn't have to ask for answers; the question on her face said it all.

"Sullivan means 'fair-eyed,' and you are just that, my child. There's not been one as fair-eyed as you for many generations. Eyes as pale blue as yours are very special; they can look into the souls of others. When another looks into your eyes, there is no darkness, only light. This allows them to see in themselves what others cannot and what they themselves have sometimes buried deep. Even if they don't want to see, they have no choice. Please know, Afton, that you are not hurting those who look into your eyes."

Afton opened her mouth to ask a thousand questions, but a shiver came across her that took her breath away. She could feel coldness all around her. She opened her eyes and found herself still in the tub—but now her steaming water felt frigid.

A dream, she thought to herself. It had only been a dream. Disappointment, as cold and uncomforting as the bathwater, washed over her. She had wanted so badly to ask Grandma Ruby her questions. She was desperate for answers.

Afton slowly dressed in her gown and fuzzy robe, then walked into the kitchen. The bread she had left to rest was no longer on the counter under the dishcloth, but now sat fully baked and on her little kitchen table next to a piping-hot bowl of soup. A cold glass of milk sat next to the soup and bread. The wonderful aromas of home cooking were thick throughout the house.

A red gingham napkin was folded neatly with her favorite spoon on it. It had been a long time since she had seen that napkin. It was the only one left from a set of eight Grandma Ruby had stitched by hand. It was worn thin and patched in several places, but still held the simple, elegant characteristic of everything she had made. In the center of the small table was a simple blue mason jar. Could Afton's eyes truly be seeing what was in the jar? Three Irish Eyebrights in full bloom.

She had only seen those beautiful little flowers once before, and of course had heard in great detail about them from Grandma Ruby throughout her life. They were her all-time favorite flowers. When Afton was little, her grandmother would tell her that she was like the Irish Eyebright—she was small and dainty like the flower, and her eyes were as bright as sunshine in the center of the bloom. Even then, she had made many references to Afton's eyes, but she had never really noticed until that moment.

Before Grandma Ruby passed, she had said she only wanted Irish Eyebrights at her funeral; a single bouquet with three of the flowers in it. One for her special Afton, one to represent herself and all the brightness her life had been blessed with because of Afton, and the third to represent the one chosen to protect her. That simple bouquet was there at her funeral, and to that day, Afton never knew who had sent it. She had assumed it was from some long-lost relative in Ireland who had received word of her passing.

Now sitting before her were these three beautifully perfect flowers. One for Grandma Ruby, one for Afton, and the third for the one chosen to protect her. To protect her? She was gone. Why would she need protecting? Had the third been meant for her then and now?

Afton sat at the table for over an hour and savored every bite of the very special meal. Her eyes were constantly drawn to the Eyebrights. It was as though she was afraid to take her gaze away from them for fear they would disappear. She didn't even question whether or not she had gotten out of the tub, baked the bread, and set the table herself. It didn't matter. She knew one thing for sure; she hadn't put the flowers there.

It was a gift from Grandma Ruby. She was near her, even in death. Afton slept better that night than she had since before Grandma Ruby passed away. She didn't even remember dreaming. She felt ready for the new day and any challenges that might come. She told herself she wasn't really alone after all.

Chapter 3: Intake

From the moment she got to work, Afton could sense something was going on. There was a buzz in the air about a new inmate coming in. One would have thought a celebrity was arriving. There have been a few in the past, and they were just as foul as anyone—maybe even more so.

It was no big deal to her, though. She was only curious because she wondered if he could be any worse than the monsters she had already encountered. Just when she thought she had seen the worst, one always came along to prove her wrong. But the morning went without incident and still no new inmate.

Afton decided to heat up her leftovers from last night's dinner and take them out to the employee picnic shelter. She needed to breathe in some fresh air. The atmosphere of the ancient building could feel heavy and stale at times; as thick as the concrete and mortar of the structure itself. She sat quietly and ate her lunch, unaware of anyone or anything going on around her.

Eventually, she heard the commotion of gates opening and car doors shutting. She looked toward the noise. This has to be the new inmate arriving, she thought. There had been more talk of him than the new warden they were due to get at any time. All the fuss because he was supposedly from down in McDowell County. Some of the roughest inmates had come from that area. This one had been in the system for a mere six months, and he was already being transferred to them. It usually took years to transfer there.

You had to earn the right to come to the Duck penitentiary through good behavior at another facility.

The officers were blocking Afton's view and she couldn't get a glimpse of him. She could hear the clanking of the shackles as the inmate shuffled across the main courtyard, escorted away from the car by those around him.

It would be at least a couple of hours before he would be brought to Medical for his intake assessment. He would first have to make it through processing. Afton walked toward the gate, hoping to see him at least once before she had to come face to face with him in Medical. She needed some sort of idea who she would be dealing with, but she could only see the back of him. The weight of the shackles on their wrists and ankles tend to make them slouch. Even so, she could already tell that he was well over six feet tall. His head was down as they made their way to the entrance.

Their first encounter would have to wait. Afton hurried back to Medical and completed the afternoon sick calls. Nothing unusual that day, so it was a nice break for her. She got pill call set up and finished pill pass in record time. She was restocking the pharmacy when she heard a tap on the door frame. The medical staff keep the door open unless they were out of the unit. That allowed for the duty officer to have a view into Medical from his desk. The door locked automatically if it swung shut, and that could create a dangerous situation if an inmate were to slip in without being noticed. By the time the officer could get the door unlocked, the attending nurse could very well have met her death or any number of nightmares.

Afton's head shot up fast. There stood Sergeant Dawson, and next to him was the new inmate. He was no longer in shackles, and he had been assigned his new uniform—tan pants and a simple white T-shirt with his Department of Corrections number stenciled across the front and back. He still had his head down, though, eyes to the floor.

Dawson handed her his intake packet and said, "This is Offender Connor Whelan."

He looked at Whelan, who continued to look down, and directed a comment to him. "This is Nurse Sullivan. You are to address her as such. Do you understand?"

Whelan finally looked up and said, "Yes, sir."

For the first time, Afton fully laid eyes on the new inmate. She stared at him blankly, unable to find her voice. His eyes were unlike any she had ever seen in her life. They were a gray, much like smoke rising slowly from a midnight campfire on a cold winter night. The silence was deafening, and she sensed that both men were staring at her, awaiting her response. But there she stood, unable to speak. Her body felt rigid, as though she had suddenly turned into a statue.

Nurse Joetta suddenly walked through the medical unit door. "I'll take over from here, Nurse Sullivan," she said. "You're needed in the pharmacy. Some sort of mix-up with a shipment."

Afton looked at her with that same blank look on her face, and Joetta said, "You know—that shipment that was supposed to arrive yesterday? Well, it's finally here."

Somehow, Afton managed to say, "Uh … that's great. I've been waiting for it."

She escaped to the pharmacy and shut the door behind her. There was no shipment. Joetta had known that she needed to be bailed out of that new intake assessment and had made sure to get her out of there. But why? Whatever the reason, Afton was truly grateful.

She wiped off shelves and pulled out-of-date meds as she waited for Joetta to finish the admission. Time seemed to drag by. What would she say when she saw her? How could she possibly explain her unusual behavior?

Whelan. Inmate Whelan was his name. Afton tried to remember what he looked like, but all she could see were those strange gray eyes. He was tall. She thought his hair was black, maybe dark brown, maybe not, but he was definitely over six feet. As far as features or bone structure were concerned, it was all a blur.

Afton finally walked out of the pharmacy to face Joetta and maybe even Whelan. The medical unit was empty. She stepped over to the duty officer's desk, where George was leaning over talking to the officer. She could tell by the smirk on his face that he was telling another one of his inappropriate jokes. Afton interrupted without excusing herself first and asked where Joetta was. George looked offended that she had stopped him in mid punch line. He told her that she had completed the intake and headed home. The look on Afton's face told him she needed more of an explanation.

Reluctantly, George continued. "She'd been here for a class and came up to the medical unit, saw that you had your hands full with a new intake and a big order for the pharmacy. She asked if she could stay and help out until the intake was done, then she was on her way."

"I see. That was nice of her to help out like that."

Afton's relief came, so she gave her report and headed down the three flights of stairs to the main floor. She didn't notice anything around her. That was careless for someone working in a prison. The staff are supposed to be well aware of their surroundings at all times.

She looked up just in time to see Inmate Doyle coming straight at her. He was an offender that she'd had trouble with in the past, but not for several months. Why now? He looked like he had fire in his eyes, and he was on her side of the stairs, which was his first mistake. Offenders were to stay to one side and employees to the other. He was mere inches in front of her when she looked up into his angry eyes.

He's going to kill me, was the first thought that crossed Afton's mind.

Then, out of nowhere, a large hand appeared on Doyle's right shoulder. It clamped down firmly and Doyle flinched in pain, then quickly jerked to his side of the stairs. He looked behind him to see who dared to lay a hand on him. His shoulders suddenly dropped, and he relaxed his balled-up fists.

He looked up apologetically. "Sorry, Nurse Sullivan. I was in too big of a hurry and didn't notice I was on the wrong side."

He looked again over his shoulder and spoke to the man behind him. "Thanks for stopping the collision, Whelan."

Whelan? Is that what he said? Afton had yet to see the man attached to the large hand that had placed the death grip on Doyle's shoulder. Then Doyle was gone in a flash, leaving the two of them alone on the stairs. Afton was standing only a step or two away from Inmate Whelan. She looked directly at his face. The smoky gray color of his eyes seemed to be changing—dark slate that lightened to pearl gray in a second. Once again, she found herself at a loss for words. This time, he didn't lower his head. He continued to gaze directly at her, or, rather, into her. Afton opened her mouth to speak, but her voice caught in her throat. She tried desperately to clear it, and finally a weak sound crossed her lips.

"Thank you, Mr. Whelan." It was more of a whisper than anything.

"You're welcome," said a deep voice, almost like a low growl.

Whelan's voice startled her almost as much as his eyes had. He must have seen her tense up because he quickly lowered his head in a gesture that seemed to say, *I'm sorry*. What was this man hiding behind those gray eyes? For the first time ever, Afton wished she had a reason to touch an inmate. She needed to see what secrets his past held and what terrible things he had in mind for the future. Abruptly, his head shot back up as though he knew what she had been thinking. He looked at her as if she had slapped him hard across the face.

The flesh of her neck and face flushed hot with embarrassment and … fear? Had he actually read her thoughts?

They stood there for an awkward moment. Then both hurried away in opposite directions.

Afton couldn't get out of there fast enough. She pulled into her driveway without fully remembering the drive home. So many thoughts were swirling around in her head that she couldn't keep even one of them straight.

Clouds had been moving in fast and darkness came early. As she stood at her kitchen sink trying to replay what had taken place on the stairs, the first raindrops fell. Rain usually had a calming effect on her, but this storm seemed different. The wind picked up quickly and began to sound like a train plowing through the woods next to her house. She heard the first tree fall, then another. Afton had nowhere to run. She had no basement, and she didn't want to risk going to her car. She rushed to her bedroom and looked around the room, trying to figure out the safest place.

Then, just as quickly as the storm had started, it was over. The power had gone out, and it was pitch-black inside and out. She felt her way to her dresser and found her emergency flashlight. She lit a couple of candles and lay down across her bed. Afton felt completely drained. Surprisingly, she fell asleep without much trouble.

She could hear Grandma Ruby calling her name ever so quietly. "Afton, my dear, it's time to get up. We have much to accomplish today."

Her eyes felt so heavy. She wasn't sure if she was awake or asleep. As she drove down the winding road that led to her home, she struggled to see through a heavy fog. All of a sudden, the mist separated just enough for her to catch a glimpse of a figure; the figure of a man who seemed familiar to her. In an instant, she knew her world was about to change.

Afton swerved to avoid hitting the man and her jeep started fishtailing. It eventually spun completely around in the road. She braced herself for the impact she knew would follow. But it never came. Just as the tires on the passenger side dropped off the shoulder, the jeep came to a standstill. She loosened her grip on the steering wheel and tried to figure out if she was pointed in the right direction. Then she remembered why she had swerved. There had been a person in the road. It was Inmate Doyle.

She opened her door slowly and cautiously stepped out onto the road. The fog was so thick that she immediately felt droplets of moisture settling on her skin. The instant she turned to survey her surroundings, Doyle was upon her. She could feel his breath in her face. His arms rose overhead. She looked up, trying to figure out what was happening. A rock. No, not just a rock; it was more like a boulder towering above her. His massive hands were gripping the object like it was no heavier than a marble. Before she could make a move toward the open door of the jeep, the thing was descending toward her head. She flinched with what she knew would be a killing blow; crushing pain, followed by death.

Nothing. She felt nothing.

Her eyes opened, and she was in her bed at home. Tears coursed down her face; hot and burning.

"Don't cry, my dear child. You are fine. It was only a nightmare." It was her Grandma Ruby.

Afton was never so glad to see anyone in her entire life. She grasped Grandma's hands and pulled her closer. She needed to feel her and know that she was real. Her grandmother went on to assure her that what she had just experienced was more of a warning than a nightmare. Afton's stare must have seemed blank and unknowing. She tried to explain that Inmate Doyle wanted to destroy her because he somehow knew that she was a threat.

"You must stop him first," Grandma Ruby spoke softly. "Before it's too late."

Another dream, but not just any dream. It was a warning, a sign that Doyle would make his move soon. Grandma Ruby was letting her know that monster had every intention of causing her harm and possibly death. Her gaze was no longer fixed on Grandma Ruby as she looked down at her trembling hands. When she looked back up, she was gone.

So, today was the day. The day that inmate Doyle would have to die.

On the drive to work, Afton's thoughts raced. How was she going to do it? Doyle was one of the younger inmates with no apparent health problems. He was strong as an ox. A heart attack or stroke seemed out of the question. It would have to be some sort of accident. Then it came to her: the fourth floor. The inmates were not allowed up there, not even to clean. The entire floor was used for storage.

On her makeshift tour, she had been taken there. The one thing that had stood out most was the massive window facing the track and baseball field. It must have been at least eight feet tall and six feet wide. It was so old there were little bubbles running through the glass of the panes. It had to be the original window and well over a hundred years old. If she could just get him up there and close enough to the window, maybe, just maybe …

The drive to work flew by, and before she knew it, she was pulling into the parking lot. Afton intentionally parked where she could get a glimpse of that window. It took on a life of its own. It seemed to be looming there, calling to her.

Today was doctor call for the inmates. It was usually so busy, how would she ever get away? As she walked through the door into Medical, everyone had sullen looks on their faces. Afton didn't speak. She just walked over, clocked in, and picked up the doctor call list to see how many names were on it. At the bottom of the list was the name Darcy Doyle, and beside it were words written in red ink: Counsel/death in the family.

Dr. Gray informed her that she should call Doyle in first so that he and the counselor could inform him that his mother had passed away. The expression on Gray's face changed to a look of genuine concern. "Afton, we don't know how Doyle will respond to this news. His mom was the only person he had left. You need to wait until he is out of Medical before you start calling in the other inmates."

She assured him that she would do just that. Time seemed to stand still as she waited for the officer to bring Doyle in. Finally, about ten minutes later, they came through the door. Doyle looked more intimidating than ever.

Dr. Gray took Doyle into the exam room, where the counselor was waiting for them. Afton listened intently for any sign of how he was taking the news. The unit seemed eerily quiet. Then, without warning, the exam room door shot open and Doyle stormed out. Gray told the officer to keep a close eye on him.

Doctor call went on without any further events. Before stepping out for lunch, Dr. Gray told her that Doyle had taken the news of his mother's death as he had expected. The look on the physician's face told her that he knew Doyle was devastated, even though he had not shed a tear.

The bells sounded for the first group of inmates to go to lunch. She knew Doyle didn't go until the second group went, so she had twenty minutes to try and figure out what she was going to do. She had replaced some old chart holders with the new ones that had arrived the previous week. That would be a good time for her to take the box of old covers to the fourth floor for storage. It would also give her a chance to look around for possibilities. Afton locked the pharmacy and medical unit. There was no officer at the desk, so she ran up the steps and dropped the box in the corner.

She was turning to check things out when she came face to face with Inmate Doyle. He didn't appear to possess the usual grimace, but his eyes were red and swollen. Afton almost felt sorry for what he must be going through. His mother had been the last person he had who maintained contact with him and showed him some semblance of love.

And then, in an instant, there it was—the monster she knew from before was back. Doyle grabbed for her wrist and ended up with her hand in his. She immediately saw the depth of his grief. This made him angry. He tried to release his grip, but she wouldn't let him. She looked deep into his hate-filled eyes. Afton saw the image of a young boy being beaten because he had not folded his shirt exactly the way the man thought it should be. The man was his dad; she could tell by the horrified look in Doyle's eyes. The image then changed to a woman gently holding the boy and rocking him. She was telling him that she would take him away so he would be safe. That didn't happen soon enough, because the abuse continued and became more severe.

Next, she saw an image of Doyle years later. He was driving past a boy riding a bicycle. He pulled over, grabbed the boy, and threw him onto the floorboard of his truck. The child's head slammed against the gearshift and blood trickled down his forehead. Doyle drove to a lonesome stretch of woods. He picked the boy up and carried him bodily into the thicket. He started screaming at him for soiling his truck and said that he would have to teach him a lesson.

That's when it happened. He killed the innocent child by crushing his skull with a huge rock. That took Afton back to her nightmare on the foggy road. Her grip on his hand tightened. Tears flowed freely down the inmate's face. He finally felt remorse for what he had done.

Doyle looked at her once more, then turned to walk away. She let go of his hand and watched him move toward the huge window. Almost tranquilly, he stepped up onto the wide sill and looked out over the prison grounds. Then, with no hesitation at all, he leaned forward and easily broke through the brittle barrier of the ancient glass.

She made it to the window in time to see him falling. It seemed to be happening in slow motion. As Doyle fell, his body turned and faced upward. She could see the expression on his face. There was a calmness, a certain peacefulness, in that moment. Before he hit the courtyard below, she turned and walked away.

Afton was back in the unit before the calls started coming across the radio. She grabbed the emergency bag and started outside. She met Dr. Gray in the hallway leading to the outside door and they went out together. When they reached Doyle, he looked like he was merely sleeping. Dr. Gray assisted with CPR, but they both knew it was useless. He had no choice but to pronounce the inmate dead, even if it meant breaking the "no dying in prison" rule. Before long, the coroner came, loaded the body into his van, and took him away.

Back in Medical, the doctor sat quietly at his desk as he filled out the necessary paperwork. When he finished writing, he looked at her and softly said, "Afton, I should have put him on suicide watch."

She tried to sound as sympathetic as she could, assuring him that he had no way of knowing. "He gave us no reason to believe he would try anything."

Dr. Gray accepted her words as good logic and went about his duties. Afton went on with her day, but felt that her shift couldn't end soon enough. George came in to inform them that they would be having a mandatory meeting at eight a.m. the following day to discuss the apparent suicide. He went on to tell the staff that a new nurse would be starting tomorrow as well. She was to be the ADON—Assistant Director of Nursing.

CHAPTER 4: THREE GATES

Home felt so safe and inviting that night. Afton showered and put on her favorite gown and robe. She sat in the old wooden rocker that had long graced the corner of her little parlor. It had been Grandma Ruby's favorite place. She referred to it as her "thinkin' chair."

After the events of that day, she truly needed to think. Once again, she felt unsure about whether or not she had caused the death of someone. Yes, she had been there, and yes, she had seen his past. But had she actually made that monster jump to his death? She hadn't pushed him out the window … at least, not physically. No answers came to her, only more questions.

Thoughts from the thinkin' chair had completely deserted her that night, so she decided to go on to bed. It must have been well after midnight when she drifted off to sleep, hopeful that Grandma Ruby would visit her dreams. It seemed that she was the only one who came visiting anymore … other than the occasional monster from prison.

But that night's slumber was different. A stranger entered her dreams. She didn't recall having ever seen her before, though she had an eerie familiarity. The manner in which she carried herself spoke of confidence. Her long, dark locks fell loosely over her shoulders. Her eyes were dark and held an icy coldness, but when she turned to look at Afton, her features softened. Her lips curled upward in a timid smile. Afton felt weak because she was at a loss.

No matter how hard she tried, she could not judge her character or her intentions. The strange woman reached her hand slowly toward Afton's face, and she could feel her body tense. She very gently touched her cheek with the back of her hand, attempting to settle her apprehension.

This stranger spoke only four simple words: "Dark clouds are near."

Afton's alarm went off and the person who had visited her in her sleep was gone. She tried, but could not shake the dream or the touch of the stranger's hand on her face. Only a few times in her life had anyone reached out to her. Even less frequently, had anyone actually touched her in a way that did not cause her physical harm. It was her own doing; she wasn't one to trust easily. Grandma Ruby's touch was always so warm and full of love. The stranger's touch had been frigidly cold. It made her feel as though she was frozen in time, blocking any human connection whatsoever.

Afton rose, dressed, and ate a quick breakfast. She only had a short while to get to the eight o'clock meeting, and she was known for her promptness, among many other irritating qualities.

She walked into Medical expecting to be the first to arrive, as usual. That would not be the case that morning. George had his back to her and was in deep conversation with a woman; you could always tell by his posture and tone. The woman had her back to Afton as well, and they were looking out the window that faced the employee parking lot.

Perhaps they had seen her reflection in the window. Before the woman turned to face her, she was already speaking. "This must be the famous Nurse Afton I've heard so much about."

Afton's mouth dropped open, and she took a step back, startled.

George had a stranger-than-usual look on his face as he said, "Afton, you look like you've seen a ghost."

"No ghost. Just surprised."

"Well then, let me introduce the new Assistant Director of Nursing. This is Dechtire Massey."

All she could do was stare at the woman who had, only a few short hours ago, appeared in her dreams. Her hand was outstretched toward Afton's. She recalled the icy touch of her hand on her face, but slowly reached out in return. Not knowing what to expect, she braced herself. No icy touch this time, only flesh, bone, and warmth.

Afton's grip hesitated as she looked into her eyes. This time the woman was the one to flinch as she abruptly withdrew her hand. George didn't seem to notice. But Afton did, and Dechtire knew it. She had only ever been able to lay hands on someone and see their thoughts or past if they had done something horrible, and she hadn't seen anything at all when she shook Dechtire's hand, but she had pulled back too quickly. It was almost as if Afton's hand had scalded her.

Joetta was at the meeting that morning, as were all the other medical unit staffers. Afton made a point to sit next to the elderly nurse. She needed to see what she thought of their new ADON, Dechtire. The meeting went as she had expected. Handouts were distributed on how to deal with grief and spot a potentially suicidal offender. When the lecture was over, George asked Dechtire to come to the front. He introduced her to everyone and asked that she share a little about herself.

Dechtire seemed a bit hesitant as she came forward. All eyes were glued to her. Afton watched Joetta's reaction closely, but there was nothing unusual in her facial expression. It was when Dechtire began to talk that she noticed a change in the old woman. Her muscles seemed to tense, her jawline tightened as her teeth clenched, and her eyes narrowed in on Dechtire with immense concentration. What was it that Joetta saw or heard—or sensed—in their new assistant director? Dechtire was telling everyone about her education and that she had always wanted to be a nurse. For the past sixteen months, she had served as the nurse manager at a county jail, but the facility had closed due to budget cuts.

One of the other nurses asked where she was from. It seemed like a simple enough question, but Dechtire hesitated—only briefly, but enough for Afton to take note. She looked down at her shoes, a pair of black Dansko clogs that were polished to a mirror-like shine. Then she spoke softly as she said that she had grown up in War, West Virginia.

Afton was pretty sure that was in McDowell County. Was it a coincidence? She could feel Joetta next to her as she shifted uncomfortably in her seat. She turned in time to see her exhale in what seemed to be almost a sigh, but not one of relief. Joetta stared down at her lap, where her hands had been tightly folded, but now lay open and visibly shaking.

Inmate Whelan was first on the doctor call list that day. Afton hadn't seen him since that day on the stairs when he had kept Doyle at bay. Joetta was teaching a class on medication compliance to the offenders, so she wouldn't get to talk to her until the afternoon. Afton definitely wanted to ask her about her impression of Dechtire.

She hadn't realized it, but Whelan had been standing in the doorway. He looked at her as though waiting for permission to enter. She told him to come in and take a seat so she could check his vital signs—and it dawned on her that she had never laid hands on him before. All of a sudden, she was on edge.

Afton did all the simple things first. She took his temperature, checked his ears, and then prepared to check his blood pressure. She asked him to roll up his sleeve. As he did so, it revealed a mark on his deltoid. It wasn't a tattoo, though. It looked like a birthmark, but almost in the shape of a symbol of sorts.

He caught Afton staring. She fumbled with the blood pressure cuff, then reached toward his arm to feel for his pulse. Her hand found his wrist and her fingers hesitantly touched his skin. It was the first touch on a new monster. What would it reveal? His pulse was slow and steady, not fast like most inmates when she first touched them. His pulse was rhythmic like a drum.

Her eyes found his face. He was watching her intently. Whelan didn't look away as he had done in the past. Those smoky gray eyes looked into her so deeply that she could focus on nothing else. An officer walked past the door. It was just enough distraction to pry her stare from his. She managed to get the cuff on and check his blood pressure. It was common for people, especially inmates, to be a little uptight when they came into Medical, therefore elevating their blood pressure a bit. Not Whelan, though. His was actually a little on the low side. And Afton saw no visions. She wasn't sure if she was glad or disappointed.

Whelan spoke, and it made her jump. Did she see a half smile cross his face? She didn't recall what he said and had to ask, "What?"

"Doyle deserved it," he said.

Afton told him that she couldn't discuss other inmates, but then felt compelled to add, "No one deserves death."

Is he testing me? she wondered. To see how I would react to such a blunt statement?

"But don't they?" he continued. "Especially those who inflict only pain on others? Did he show any remorse?"

"What do you mean?" Her mind was racing now. "How would I know?"

"Forgive me, Nurse Sullivan. I thought maybe you were with him in his last moments."

"Of course I wasn't there," she said, almost too sharply. "How could I have been?" She jotted down a few things on a clipboard, attempting to avoid his eyes. "Mr. Whelan, I believe Dr. Gray is ready to see you now."

He stood up and towered over her. Afton felt small and helpless. Just then, Dr. Gray called Whelan to the exam room.

She quickly stepped into the pharmacy and closed the door behind her. The room felt as though it was spinning—or was she spinning? She laid her head on the cool countertop. Had Whelan seen her go upstairs? Now, what was she going to do? Before she had time to process any of it, Dechtire walked in.

"I don't care for that Offender Whelan," she blurted out.

Afton was curious. "What don't you like about him?"

"Well …" she started, "I just think he is up to no good, and I believe you should make a point to stay as far away from him as possible."

Afton gave her a blank look, then managed to say, "Okay." Without another word, she walked out of the pharmacy and away from Dechtire.

Home. Afton desperately needed the safety of her little home.

When she first started working at the prison, she had actually considered moving closer to it. But, looking back, she was thankful that she didn't. The hour and fifteen minute drive home allowed her time to think about and review what the day had brought.

Home sweet home at last … the one place where she truly belonged. Afton had barely gotten through the door and taken off her shoes when she heard footsteps moving across the porch. The steps were followed by a brief pause and then a light knock at the door. Company was the one thing she rarely, if ever, had. She glanced out through a crack in the curtain and saw Joetta standing at her door. The woman seemed to nervously glance around, as if checking to see if anyone had followed her.

Afton hurried to unlock the door and invited her inside. There they stood, face to face, just staring at one another. Now what? Neither of them knew exactly what to do next.

Joetta drew in a long breath and then began. "Afton, I really don't know how to tell you this, so I am just going to say it. I'm going to tell you exactly what I believe."

"Okay, Joetta, go ahead."

She felt the sudden need to sit down. Joetta followed her lead and sat in the chair that faced hers.

"Afton, don't be afraid of the old woman that I told you about from my childhood," she said. "You will need her soon. For now, though, you must know you are in danger."

As soon as she saw Afton's eyes widen, Joetta motioned for her not to interrupt and just listen. "Someone is going to do their best to hurt you, or maybe even worse. I can't say for sure yet, but I know one thing for certain. Under no circumstances should you trust Dechtire."

Then, without another word, she simply got up and left.

How many more things did Afton have to add to her weary mind? Was Joetta right in her prediction? Was Dechtire somehow evil, even murderous perhaps?

Dinner consisted of an apple and a cold glass of milk. As she sat at her modest kitchen table, she stared out the window. The curtains were open to allow Afton a view of the sun dipping behind the mountain. Her eyes caught a movement in the patch of woods that lay just beyond her garden. Was it a person? Had Joetta returned?

No, she didn't feel as though it was a person. She stopped by the sink and rinsed her milk glass before stepping out onto the back porch and making her way down the steps into the yard. Curiously, she walked past the garden and into the woods. The shadows of evening were beginning to thicken. The sun wouldn't be above the mountain much longer.

Afton quickened her pace. Before she realized it, she was a hundred or so yards into the forest. She didn't recall ever being in such quietness. She closed her eyes and took it all in. At that very moment, a grouse took flight, its fluttering wings resonating like thunder in her ears. Or was that the pounding of her heart?

She turned to head back to the house. A breeze swirled the leaves up off the ground and twirled them about. Someone called out her name. She looked all around, but saw nothing.

Again, her name. "Afton."

She heard it plain as day.

"Joetta?" she called out.

"Yes, Afton, it's me," the voice of Joetta confirmed. "I will do all I can to help you. You will soon be with people who are like you. Just remember what I said earlier."

The twirling leaves settled back to the forest floor and the whip-poor-wills started their nighttime calling. The quiet was gone, just as Joetta was.

When Afton returned to the house, she sensed that something was not as it should be. She went from room to room, not knowing quite what she was looking for. Eventually, she gave up and sat down in Grandma Ruby's little wooden rocker. She turned on the lamp and picked up the Bible; the much-worn book that Grandma Ruby had read to her each night for so many years. Some pages were torn and most were curled along the edges. The brown leather cover was so smooth. She ran her hand across the front as she remembered the smoothness of Grandma's hands.

Afton opened the book, and a picture fell into her lap. She picked it up and studied it. The black-and-white photo was of a young girl. She stood between a man and a woman, and both of her arms were wrapped around the woman's legs. She appeared to be leaning away from the man. His face was void of expression as he stared into the camera. The woman, however, had a look of tenderness as she gazed down at the girl, her right hand resting on the child's shoulder as if to provide comfort.

Afton began reading, but her mind kept drifting back to the picture that she had laid aside. She didn't recall having ever seen the picture or the people in it. After an hour of trying her best to read, she finally closed the book. She went to bed with that little girl still on her mind.

What had she heard and seen in the woods? Had Joetta really been able to warn her without actually being there? She could feel herself drifting into sleep. Soon, she was surrounded by darkness … the sort of darkness that always made her uneasy and unwilling to let go and give in to that unknown place of true sleep. As a child, the nighttime had been the hardest time for her. Her mind would conjure imaginary monsters and terrifying images. She sometimes wondered if they were actually memories.

Afton found herself walking along a dirt path. It was somewhere new. The trees were different and the dirt beneath her bare feet felt strange to her. Even the air had an odd aroma. She continued ahead. Something was pulling her forward. She should have felt fear of the unknown, but she didn't. She felt compelled to discover why she was in this new place and what was waiting ahead for her.

She came to a gate. It was to be the first of three, and all had old, rusty padlocks on them. She climbed over and kept walking. She could hear footsteps not far behind her. Afraid, she ducked behind a brush thicket, and two people appeared. One was a man—the man in the picture that had fallen out of Grandma's Bible. His clothes were tattered and his face looked tense. The other person was an old woman, dressed completely in black. She wore a long dress and a hooded cape, and she clutched a wicker basket with both hands. They were talking quietly, but became silent when they approached the thicket where Afton was hiding. The woman turned her head as if to look straight at her. She paused only momentarily, then continued down the pathway.

Afton waited until she no longer heard their footsteps. She left her hiding place and started along the path again. She could hear water trickling in a small stream nearby. After a few more steps, she saw it. Several hundred yards farther on was an opening in the trees, and just beyond that stood a cabin. It was a pitiful-looking structure that had long since seen better days. The old woman and the man were standing on the porch, deep in discussion. Afton got as close as she dared, trying to make out their words. Then the door to the cabin opened and a young girl stepped out. She looked up at the man and told him that her mama was getting worse. Her eyes went from the man to the woman's face. She stepped back so fast she almost fell off the tiny porch. Her eyes never left the woman. It was as though she couldn't look away. The young girl was visibly shaken.

The man took the girl by the arm, steadying her. "Joetta, go on now and check on the animals," he told her. "I'll let you know when you can come inside."

It hit Afton like a brick wall. Joetta had told her of the old woman who had come to their home when her mother fell ill. The picture that had fallen from Grandma Ruby's Bible was Joetta with her mom and dad. This was their cabin, and that was the old woman; the one person who reminded Joetta of Afton.

Was the old woman about to kill Joetta's mother? Joetta had described her as old, but she couldn't tell exactly what age she was. This was the woman who had made her feel as if she could peer into her soul and see anything bad Joetta had ever done. She had also told Afton that she would need her soon.

Joetta was out of sight, but Afton could hear her talking to what must be the animals in the run-down barn. She knew she had to get closer. Reaching the side of the shack, she peered through the cloudy glass of the old window. The shack had only one room, and there was a bed against the far wall. Afton could see that there was someone in it, even though their body barely caused a bump beneath the patchwork quilt. The man said something to the person in the bed—Joetta's mother—then leaned over and lifted her out of the bed and carried her to a chair that the old woman had placed in the middle of the room. Joetta's mom looked like a shell of the woman in the picture. She was so weak and frail, she could barely hold her head up. A second chair was set in front of her, and that's where the elderly visitor planted herself.

The old woman pulled her hooded cape off and laid it aside. Finally, Afton caught a clear glimpse of her. Her hair was as white as snow and her skin nearly as pale, but it wasn't weathered and wrinkled as she had expected. The woman looked around the room, and as she did, Afton saw her eyes. She gasped. Her eyes were an icy pale blue. They were like her eyes, but there was a harshness in them—or perhaps it was pain from a lifetime of seeing things that were difficult for one to see; things that perhaps one should never be allowed to see.

The old woman now directed her attention to the basket she had clasped as she walked to the shack. She removed the cloth that covered what lay inside. Afton couldn't make out what the basket contained. Joetta's dad fumbled around in the cabin, gathering items that the woman must have requested.

The door opened slightly and Joetta slipped in without either of them noticing. The one person in the cabin who did notice was her mother. She seemed to strain with all of her strength to see around her husband and make eye contact with her young daughter. Their eyes locked and they appeared to be talking to one another without speaking a word. Joetta didn't make a sound as tears flowed down her cheeks. Afton could tell she wanted to run to her mother, but the look on her mother's face seemed to be telling her no. It was as though she knew that Joetta was utterly powerless to prevent what was about to happen.

The strange woman lifted a handful of herbs out of the basket and told the man to sprinkle them into the fireplace. He did as he was told. The room filled with white smoke, but it lasted only seconds before clearing. The woman then took the lace from the table that Joetta's father had brought to her earlier. It looked like an old-time wedding veil, though its original color had faded to a dingy off-white. The woman carefully unfolded the veil and laid it across Joetta's mother's face. She placed her hands on either side of the sick woman's head and tilted it toward her until they were face to face. The woman mumbled something to Joetta's mom and then stared into her eyes. A palatable tension filled the room. You could have heard a pin drop.

The man shouted at the old woman, "Tell me, Maddie O'Sullican, what do you see!"

The woman released her grasp and solemnly turned to the man. "It's as you suspected. She will be leaving you today."

She watched the man's face carefully. He nodded his head and turned to leave. That's when he saw Joetta standing nearby, trembling in horror. He grabbed her roughly by the arm and pulled her toward the door. Joetta looked back at her mother as the old woman was lifting the veil from her face. Her mom's face appeared frozen, and her mouth was partially open as if trying to speak, but no words came out. Joetta and her dad were gone from the shack, and Afton could hear the girl's sobs coming from outside. She turned her attention back to the woman.

The woman in black pressed her face close to Joetta's mother's as she spoke three words. "Suffer no more."

Joetta's mother gasped once, then her body went limp as she slouched in the chair. It was over. She was dead.

The black-clad woman was a monster. Afton felt like she couldn't breathe. Is this what I am? she thought. Joetta's mother had been planning to leave that strange place, and she had died because of it. Joetta had told her not to fear the old woman, so she must be misinterpreting what she had just seen. Afton's head was spinning. She could feel herself starting to fall. Just before she hit the ground, her eyes flew open.

It was only a dream. Afton was home in bed with sweat pouring off of her. She threw back the heavy quilt and swung her legs over the side of the bed. She sat there for the longest time, trying to take in what she had just experienced. She reached for the phone to call Joetta, but quickly realized that she didn't have her number.

Afton called the prison medical unit. She could hear George's voice on the other end. After hesitating, she asked if Joetta was there. He paused for what seemed an eternity before answering.

"I really didn't want to tell you something like this over the phone," George said.

Before he could say anything else, she blurted out, "She's dead, isn't she?"

"Yes, she died last evening. Her neighbor found her just before sunset. She died from a massive heart attack, it appears."

"Okay, George, I'll be in later." Afton hung up before he had the chance to respond.

She thought back to the previous evening. Joetta had come to her home to warn her and tell her she would do all she could to help her. That was why she died. She was trying to help her. I'm no better than the old woman who had come and ended her mother's life, Afton thought.

Why would she want to help such a monster? It was something that she had to know.

CHAPTER 5: SPECIAL BREW

As soon as Afton got to work, George found her and took her to his office. "Afton, I cleaned out Joetta's locker this morning, and I found something for you."

He handed her an envelope. It had four words written on it: This is for Afton. She held the envelope in her hands and simply stared at it.

George broke the silence. "Are you okay? Do you need to take the day off?"

"No, I'm fine. We didn't know each other well at all. I can't imagine why she would leave something for me."

Afton folded the envelope, put it in her pocket, and turned to leave the office. George stopped her at the door. "If you ever need to talk, I'll be right here."

She left the office without replying. She had never been very good at saying thank you. Perhaps she had been wrong about George.

That day seemed to drag on and on for Afton. She had difficulty focusing on anything she tried to do. When she'd finally had enough, she walked down the three flights of stairs to the pop machine. Even deciding what to choose to drink was a task. She settled on ginger ale in hopes that it would calm her stomach. She leaned over to retrieve the can from the drop slot, and as she rose, she could sense someone close to her.

She turned to find Inmate Whelan standing about four feet away. He must have been aware of the three-foot personal space rule. Maybe it wasn't a real rule, but it was hers. Once again, she found herself unfocused, so when he spoke, it startled her.

"Nurse Afton, may I ask you a question?"

What is so different about this inmate that he makes the hair on my arms stand on end? she thought to herself. "Yes, Mr. Whelan," she answered, "you may ask me a question, as long as I don't feel it's inappropriate."

He looked slightly offended, but continued, "I was wondering if what I heard about Nurse Joetta was true."

"Yes, Mr. Whalen, it's true. Nurse Joetta passed away."

"Yes, ma'am, I know she passed, but I heard that she did so trying to protect you."

Afton was disturbed by the convict's statement. "Listen, Whelan, I don't know what you're playing at, but I don't take kindly to what you just said. Nurse Joetta and I barely knew one another, and she died of a heart attack at home … her own home. Where did you hear such a thing?"

"Nurse Afton, I meant no offense," Whelan assured her. "And as far as where I heard it, well, that part wasn't exactly true."

"What do you mean?"

He glanced down at the floor and went on. "Nurse Afton, you may not want to hear what I'm about to say."

"Mr. Whelan, my patience is growing short, so please just say it."

"Okay … I dreamed it last night. I dreamed Nurse Joetta knew you were in danger and tried to help you, but whoever she thought was going to hurt you, well, they got to her first." His smoky gray eyes were concerned as he stared at her. "Please, be careful when you travel to her funeral. That part of West Virginia can be an unforgiving place at times."

"Mr. Whelan, I don't even know that I will be going to her funeral. I think it's best that we leave this subject alone." Then, abruptly, she left him standing there, and hurried up the stairway.

Back in Medical, Afton thought about the conversation she'd just had with Inmate Whelan. She realized that she had lied when she told him she didn't know if she would be going to the funeral or not. The truth was, she had already made up my mind that she would. It was Friday, and it was her long weekend off coming up. She didn't know what day the funeral would be or where exactly it would be held. Then she remembered the envelope in her pocket. Afton pulled it out and held it in her hands for a full minute. Finally, she opened it. Inside was a piece of paper with a phone number and a name written underneath: Miss Betty.

Afton slipped into the pharmacy and dialed the number. A young man—more like a boy, really—answered. She asked if she could speak to Miss Betty.

"Yes'm," he said and laid down the phone.

A minute or so later, a woman said, "Hello?"

"Is this Miss Betty?"

Before she could get any further, the woman stopped her and said, "This must be Afton."

"How did you know?"

"Child, no one has called this number for a very long time," said Miss Betty. "That is, until Joetta called last week and told me about her concern for you. A cold, bone-chillin' wind blew through the Holler last night, and I knew that Joetta was no longer a part of this world. She told me last week that she would leave my number for you to find in case somethin' was to happen to her. Child, we have already sent someone for Joetta's body. Do you have somethin' to write with?"

"Yes." Afton stumbled over even that simple word.

Miss Betty gave her the directions, and she jotted them down and stuck them in the same envelope as the slip of paper, then shoved it back into her pocket.

"I will be there in the morning."

"Yes, child," Miss Betty declared. "I expect you will."

She hung up and Afton was left with only the humming of the dial tone in her ear.

She avoided everyone at work the best she could for the remainder of the day. Her shift ended and she headed to her car. She almost made it there unhindered, but not quite quickly enough.

Dechtire was crossing the parking lot toward her. "In a hurry, Afton?"

"Just to get my long break started."

"Oh yeah, this is your five-day break. Any big plans?"

Afton could tell she was fishing, but she simply said, "No. I'm just glad for the break. See ya next week."

She jumped in her car and was on her way. She knew she had to get home and pack, and perhaps map out those directions Miss Betty had given her. They seemed a bit confusing.

Home. She always seemed to sigh in relief when she pulled into the drive. It was her safe haven.

Afton hurriedly threw a few things into her suitcase. Before closing the lid, she got the black-and-white picture out of Grandma Ruby's Bible and placed it carefully inside the case.

She realized she had not eaten lunch, and now it was well past dinner. Her stomach rumbled in protest. She fixed herself a sandwich and a glass of lemonade and took it out on the porch. She sat on the swing and enjoyed her dinner as she listened to the whip-poor-wills talking to one another out in the woods.

It was almost dark. She felt an excitement inside of her that she couldn't quite understand. She was going to a funeral. That should be a somber occasion. Perhaps it was the trip to an unknown place that stirred her emotions.

Back inside, she straightened the kitchen and made sure that all the plants were watered. She wasn't exactly sure how long she would be gone. Would the funeral be tomorrow, Sunday, or even Monday? She had forgotten to ask Miss Betty. She had five days off, however, which would be more than enough time. It should only take two or three hours to get there—unless, of course, she got lost. The chances of GPS working in that neck of the woods were slim to none. Afton decided to set her clock for 4 a.m. and be on the road by 4:30.

She crawled into bed and stretched out. She felt tired but not sleepy. Lying there thinking about the old shack that Joetta had lived in, she wondered if it would still be standing. Eventually, she drifted off to sleep.

Rain was pelting noisily against the metal roof. Afton sleepily opened her eyes. Where was she? An oil lamp was burning a low flame on a table in the middle of the room. After a moment, she realized where she was. It was the cabin Joetta had lived in as a child. One thing that wasn't very clear was whether or not it was actually real or a dream.

She got up and walked toward the window on the other side of the room. Afton felt drawn to that window. Was it the same one she had peered into from the outside when she dreamed of Joetta, her parents, and the old woman? As she grew closer, she could hear something besides the rain. It sounded like mumbling, but from far away. She peered through the windowpanes and strained to see outside. It was night and pitch black. She could barely make out something glowing in the distance. Not just one glow, but several.

Afton stepped to the door and slowly opened it. The hair on the back of her neck stood on end as the cool night air rushed in. It took a moment for her eyes to adjust to the gloom. She could make out that the glowing objects were arranged in a pattern … the shape of a circle. The mumbling grew louder. It sounded more like chanting now.

Chill bumps prickled her arms. A shiver—partly from cold, partly from fear—seemed to overtake her entire body. The thought of what she might be seeing and hearing scared her. Could there be people out here in the middle of nowhere performing some sort of ritual? Did they know she was there?

Suddenly, she realized the chanting had stopped. Afton stared intently at the lights, but they too were fading, and seconds later, the night was completely black. It was a darkness that made you see spots if you stared into it long enough. A crack of thunder boomed and a streak of lightning lit the ebony sky. For a split second, she thought she saw shadowy figures moving across the field just past the lake. Afton swiftly stepped back into the cabin and closed the door.

Catching her breath, she turned around … and saw Joetta sitting at the little table.

Music, loud music. Afton's alarm was going off. Jolting, causing her heart to thunder in her chest.

She awoke to find herself still at home. Like before, she was drenched with sweat. It felt like something was weighing heavily upon her chest and she gasped for air. She sat in bed for a few minutes, trying to sort out her thoughts. What was she getting herself into? Despite her concern, Afton felt compelled to proceed as planned. She showered and dressed in record time, threw her things in the car, and was on the road by 4:25 a.m.

Her eyes began to water and she realized she was no longer driving. Afton had pulled over along the side of the road. The sun had just come up, and it was making her eyes burn. She rubbed them, which only made them hurt worse. She blinked a few times and looked around to see how far from McDowell County she was. Her mouth dropped open when she looked at the seat beside her. The handwritten directions were still neatly folded, just as she had placed them when she got in the car at home. The GPS hadn't been plugged in, either.

She looked ahead and saw a sign. Welcome to Robinson Holler. Not only was she already in McDowell County, but she had driven straight to Robinson Holler without looking at the directions or the GPS. Afton had no recollection of the drive from home to there. How could that possibly be?

There was a hard tap on her window, nearly causing her to jump out of her skin. There, beside her door, stood a boy that looked to be about ten years of age. His hair was sandy brown and hung loosely down in his eyes. He wore a dingy white T-shirt, cut-off jean shorts, and no shoes. Shaken, Afton stepped out of the car and said hello.

He looked up at her like he had never seen a stranger before in his life. "Miss Betty said for me to come down and meet you because it was time for you to get here."

"She did, did she? My name is Afton."

"I know who you are," he stated.

"Since you know who I am, it seems only fair that you tell me who you are."

The boy looked at her like she was dense for asking. "I'm Silas. We need to go now. Miss Betty is waiting."

She followed Silas as he walked away from her car. When he didn't take the path by the sign, she stopped.

He looked back at her and said, "No one goes that way anymore. Miss Betty's cabin is just over the hill yonder."

Miss Betty was waiting on the porch for them. She was a small woman with hair as white as untouched snow. She stood with one hand on her hip while the other hand gripped an odd-looking pipe. As Afton's eyes met hers, she exhaled a cloud of bluish smoke. The smoke was mesmerizing. It spun into gentle circles, then made a beeline straight to Afton's face. The sweet smell of the tobacco tickled her nose as she breathed it in. When she began to cough, Miss Betty chuckled and told her to follow.

Inside the cabin, there were herbs hanging everywhere. They were tied in small bundles with twine. The herbs filled the house with a mixture of aromas that seemed both fragrant and earthy. The smells were inviting and had a calming effect on Afton. She couldn't stop yawning. Miss Betty noticed her reaction. "Take a load off and I'll make you a cup of tea," she said.

Afton gladly accepted the offer. The trip had caught up with her, and she felt completely drained.

Miss Betty set her pipe down on a little wooden stand that appeared to have been made strictly for that purpose. The pipe was unique. The bowl was carved into the head of a wolf, and around its neck hung a strip of leather that appeared to have a shiny stone tied to it. The stem was long and thin, like a churchwarden's pipe. The grain of the bowl's wood held a variety of hues that ranged from yellow to brown to deep red.

Then Afton noticed something odd on the neck of the wolf. It was a mark—something she had seen before, but couldn't quite place. At first, it simply resembled various small circles, but as she examined it more closely, it was clearly the shape of a paw print. Then she remembered. Inmate Whelan had a strange mark on his arm that she'd noticed the day she checked his blood pressure. It was this same mark. Not a tattoo, but a natural blemish, though rendered in a pigment darker than that of his skin. What did it mean?

"Here, Afton, drink this," Miss Betty instructed.

She was still staring at the pipe, deep in thought.

"Afton," she began, "that pipe has been in my family for many years, centuries even."

She sipped the hot tea and listened intently, wanting to know more.

The elderly woman continued, "It has a little gem that's hangin' from it. Can you guess why?"

"No, I can't imagine why it's there. I figured it was only for decoration."

Miss Betty explained. "That's one thing you need to know about me—nothin' I do is solely for decoration. Everything has a purpose. The gem is an agate; it protects one from danger."

"What sort of danger?"

"It is believed that this stone protects against animal attack."

"Is that why there's a paw print on the pipe? Does it protect against a wolf?"

Miss Betty smiled an odd, crooked smile. "No, child. I've found that wolves are gen'rally good. It protects against the things that're usually chasin' after the wolves."

"Miss Betty, I've seen that marking before. There's an inmate who bears that paw-like mark on his arm. Most of the inmates have tattoos, but this wasn't one. It was more like a birthmark."

Miss Betty held up a narrow finger and said, "We'll talk more about that later. We need to discuss other things first. How's your tea?"

"It's different, but not in a bad way. Do you brew it yourself?"

"Yes, from herbs that grow around here. It tends to make some people sleepy or just relax them."

"I don't feel sleepy, which surprises me after the long drive here."

The old woman began talking. "Afton, I need to tell you a thing or two about me. You will lay witness to things while you're here that you won't likely understand. Some around here call me the Appalachian Granny. Folks come to me when they need help. Many times during the course of a week someone'll yell, 'Fetch Granny,' and I go where I'm needed. I take care of deliverin' the babies. Sometimes I look after the sick, both the young and old. Children have always been my favorite. That's why I took in Silas. He lost both his parents. There's a belief that there are Little People in these mountains, and it's up to us to take care of 'em. If we don't, they may turn bad. Each night, I leave fresh cream and a wedge of cornbread by the door.

"Speakin' of doors, that's why it's painted Haint Blue, which is the combination of shades of blue and green to resemble water. It's believed to keep out the bad spirits, because they're afraid to cross water.

"There are some places that believe the Appalachian Grannies are witches, but that's simply not true. What I practice comes from generations of studyin' herbs and remedies. They're tried and true. There are a few old wives' tales that have lingered, like openin' all the windows when it's time for a woman to give birth. It's supposed to open the birth canal for delivery. Some place an ax under the birthin' bed—supposed to help cut the pain. I choose not to do that because of what took place in the Garden of Eden. Pain is part of childbirth."

Afton's head was starting to feel fuzzy. She began to wonder if her conversation with the old woman was no more than a dream. It had to be the special tea that was making her feel that way. She needed to stay awake and find out what the arrangements were for Joetta. The quicker the funeral, the quicker she could get out of there. She cleared her throat and asked Miss Betty when the service would be.

She looked at Afton strangely. "You need to rest a bit before lunch," she said. "Then we will talk about the arrangements. After all is settled, I'll take you to Joetta's, where you will spend the night."

"I thought I would be staying here with you."

Miss Betty smiled her crooked smile and said, "No, child. There are things you need to do for Joetta, and it's best you stay at her home to do them."

Afton stretched out on a small bed. That's the last she remembered before drifting off to sleep. Finally, a sleep that was deep and untroubled. A sleep without dreams.

Afton heard whistling coming from another room. She opened her eyes to find that it had not been a dream after all. She was indeed in Miss Betty's house. The whistling had to be Miss Betty in the kitchen, fixing lunch. It felt so good to rest without strange dreams or worries. She stretched her arms above her head as far as they could reach. She was so comfortable that she practically had to force herself to stand.

She made her way to the little kitchen, where she found Miss Betty and Silas busily preparing their meal. It smelled delicious, like bread baking in the oven. They seemed so in sync, working side by side, not saying a word, but happy because they were together. Afton hated to interrupt them.

Silas looked up at Afton first, then Miss Betty.

"You look rested," the old woman observed.

"I feel great. Maybe I will have to take some of your special tea with me when I leave. It's been a long time since I've rested so completely."

"You're in for a treat, ma'am," Silas said with enthusiasm. "Miss Betty is makin' dumpling soup and drop rolls."

He was such a precious boy, so wide-eyed and eager to help. It made her think of what she'd missed out on by not having children.

As though reading her expression, Miss Betty said, "It's not too late, ya know."

"Oh, I think I've long since missed that boat, Miss Betty," she replied and left it at that. "Is there anything I can do to help?"

"No, all done. Let's have a seat and enjoy the meal."

She said the blessing over the food and they began to eat.

Chapter 6: Cunnin' Folk

After the lunch dishes were cleaned up, Miss Betty announced that it was time to head to Joetta's.

The feeling that came over Afton was much like the one she got on a hot summer day when a rare event happened—like unexpectedly encountering a deer in the woods, face to face, or a dragonfly landing on your arm as though to say a brief hello. If you hadn't experienced either thing, let's just say it left you breathless. That is how she felt at that moment: breathless. She found herself wondering what Miss Betty had meant by "things you need to do for Joetta".

Afton was careful to get up slowly for fear she would lose her balance. She stood for a moment before she headed out the door. Miss Betty stopped her when she started walking back the way Silas had brought her. She told her it would be best to take a shortcut through the woods, past the lake, and through the field. The hairs on the nape of Afton's neck stood at attention. Miss Betty's suggestion brought back visions of her dream about the people by a lake, chanting in a circle.

During the walk to Joetta's cabin, they talked.

"Afton, you are about to meet some people," Miss Betty told her. "I imagine they are unlike anyone you've ever met before. Here in these hills and hollers, they're known as 'Cunnin' Folk.' They tend to know things that most don't. These people protect the mountains roundabout and those who belong here. They go to great lengths to keep the secrets of the mountain people and their legends. Some people that they look after, well, they don't even realize they're bein' looked after. Joetta was very much part of the Cunnin' Folk. Now that she's passed, they need to prepare her for the journey, so no harm can come to her."

Afton listened in quiet bewilderment. Grandma Ruby had told her about the old ways people had taken care of the dead, but she had no idea that it still went on.

Miss Betty reached down into her apron pocket and pulled out an old iron ring. On it was a rather large key. As she passed it to Afton, she told her that it would open all three gates that led to the cabin. She informed her that they wouldn't need it since they were going in the back way, but to keep it safe, nonetheless. Once again, she found herself thinking about the dream and the three gates that she had come to along the pathway.

Miss Betty made small talk to help keep Afton calm. She told her about the wild roses they passed along the way, and how each year she gathered the petals for tincturing. To Afton, it seemed like they had been walking forever. Again, as if reading her mind, Miss Betty told her it wasn't much farther. They continued on.

Through the last thicket of woods stood Joetta's cabin. It looked as it had in Afton's dream, only much older. Something that stood out were the flowers. Lots of fresh flowers had been planted. A perfect row of sturdy marigolds stood at attention as though guarding the cabin. Two large pots sat on either side of the door. They contained an assortment of wildflowers. The door had a fresh coat of blue paint. Haint Blue.

The door opened, and they stepped inside. The strong smell of herbs hung heavy in the air, and Afton quickly identified the aromas of rosemary, sage, and mint, among many others. Were they there to transition the dead or perhaps, more likely, to help cover the odor of the recently departed?

The cabin had been cleaned out. Straight-backed chairs were lined along the walls. In the center of the room was a wooden table. Fresh flowers had been delicately woven together and draped over the edges. Mounds of sweet-smelling honeysuckle, mock orange, Sweet William, and Harrison's rose were arranged atop the table. In the center was Joetta, dressed in a long white dress with embroidered flowers on the bodice. Small wildflowers were woven through her hair, as well. She appeared much younger than her eighty-three years. The lines on her face had softened, and she had a look of complete peace about her.

There was movement in a dark corner of the room. A woman stood up from one of the chairs. Had she been there the whole time and Afton just hadn't noticed? She slowly moved across the room toward them. Miss Betty stepped forward and greeted the woman with a hug. The woman from the corner was a very tall and beautiful black woman. Her hair was peppered with gray. Her eyes were green like the underside of a mint leaf, with specks of brown radiating from the pupils outward. As for her age, that was difficult to say. Her skin was flawless.

Miss Betty said, "Dear child, you need to listen closely."

Afton replied in a murmur, "Yessum." But she was still mesmerized by the woman from the corner.

The old granny finally took her by the arm to get her attention. "Dear child, please snap out of this mind fog you've slipped into." She seemed to prefer calling her "dear child" instead of by her name. Afton couldn't complain; "dear child" sounded quite endearing.

"Dear child, where are your thoughts? This is Nola May. She's a good friend of mine. She is one of the three who've been caring for Joetta and takin' turns sittin' with her. That's somethin' that must continue till she's buried. Nola May gathered all these mountain flowers to surround our precious Joetta. She also sings the old folk songs so that Joetta can enjoy her journey home. The songs are just as important as anything that's done. It eases the departed into the other world, as if floatin' on the current of rhythmic mountain tunes. Remember that, dear child."

Nola May had yet to get a single word in edgewise. When she finally had the opportunity, she acted swiftly. Afton was surprised at how deep her voice was. Not like a man's, but like the soothing hum of honeybees when they get to carrying on around the hive. Every sentence she spoke sounded like the verse to a song. She was like a long-lost mountain poet. What a calming effect this woman from the corner and her deep poetic voice had on her. She felt as though she had been around her entire life, and she longed for her to tell her a story.

"Afton, I'm pleased that you are here with us," said Nola May. "Now our collection is just about complete."

Collection? Is that really what she had said? What did she mean by that?

Afton found herself still staring, enraptured, at Nola May. She was definitely a mountain woman, but there was a simple elegance about her. The dress she wore was long and white with tiny green flowers on it. That only made her unique green eyes stand out even more. One necklace hung loosely around her neck. It held a variety of shiny stones and beads with one silver leaf that was at least three inches longer than the rest.

She could hear music playing outside. Afton walked to the window that faced the lake. A bearded man stood on a large rock next to the water. He held an instrument that was unlike any she had ever seen before. It was at least two feet long and made of a wood that glistened when the sun shone upon it. There appeared to be something hanging down from it, perhaps a long piece of leather. The music he was playing sounded like that of a flute, but, then again, not really. It was more rustic, earthier, a sound so peaceful it carried a sadness with it that chilled her to her core. As though sensing that he was being watched, he turned toward the window and stared straight at her. Even at a distance, she recognized those smoke-gray eyes. Her heart skipped a beat, and she stepped quickly aside.

The door creaked and Afton spun around. She turned a little too fast, which caused her eyes to lose focus. The silhouette of a figure now stood in the doorway. It was a dark figure, and she strained to make out the person who stood there. Finally, the form stepped forward, and the door closed behind her.

Afton no longer heard the music being played by the man on the rock by the lake—the man with the familiar smoke-gray eyes that she had only seen once before—when she looked into Inmate Whelan's face.

Her attention was back on the woman who now stood before her, dressed in a long black cape with a hood that was pulled up over her head. The garment shaded her eyes as well as her face. The woman's hands gravitated slowly toward her head. She pulled back the hood, and what was revealed made Afton go weak in the knees.

It was her, the woman Joetta had told her about. The woman from Afton's dream. The woman who had killed Joetta's mother all those years ago.

How could that be? She looked the same as in her dream. Joetta was only twelve when her mother passed. That was over seven decades ago. That would make the woman standing before her a hundred years old, if not older. This woman appeared to be in her fifties at the very most.

Now what? Here she stood with a woman who might be like her … might possess the same gift. That, in itself, could be a good thing, or it could be bad. Come to think of it, Afton didn't know if she was actually good or bad. She simply continued to stare into her eyes, and she did the same to her. Eyes that were so like Afton's. The longer they stood there, the more questions came to her mind.

The first question was, how old are you? The number 103 came to her as if it had been whispered in her ear. Next was, are we alike? Again a whisper: In many ways, we are alike. Then, did you kill Joetta's mother? There was a pause, then the answer, No more than you have killed anyone. That didn't help much since Afton wasn't sure of the answer to that herself. Finally, why are our eyes the same? Another pause, even longer, then the whisper: I am your father's mother.

Then, without warning, the room went black.

When she opened her eyes, Afton was lying on a quilt beneath a huge sugar maple.

There was a slight breeze that made the leaves move in such a way that they appeared to be dancing above her head. She turned to find that young Silas was sitting on the quilt with his back against the tree. He sat quietly, whittling away at a small stick. A favorite pastime for boys his age, she imagined. He realized Afton was awake. She could tell by the expression on his face that he didn't have a clue as to what to say to her. She figured he had been told to sit with her, probably by Miss Betty. She couldn't help but smile. It was amusing to think that she was being babysat by a ten-year-old.

Gradually, it dawned on her why she had blacked out. She actually had a grandmother who was alive and 103 years old. Not only that, but she looked half her age. Afton felt like she was floating between reality and a feverish dream. But she knew she wouldn't be waking up from this one. Not this time. This time it was for real, and it was almost too much to take in. Her mind seemed to be spinning out of control.

Maybe I'll just close my eyes for a few more minutes, she thought.

Minutes turned into an hour.

She heard the calming wooden flute again. She strained to look for the rock by the lake and the gray-eyed man standing atop it. He wasn't there. Afton heard something in the woods behind her. She turned to look, and there he stood, only inches from the quilt. He continued playing until he had finished the song. Then he stared down at her. She felt so small lying there looking up at that tall, dark man. He spoke first. His words sounded like velvet as they crossed his lips.

"My name is Phillip Whelan," he told her. "I am Connor Whelan's uncle."

He had answered all her questions in one simple and to-the-point statement.

"I can see the resemblance." Afton was shocked that she had even been able to find words to reply. She stood up so she would not feel so vulnerable there on the quilt, but it only helped a little. The bearded man towered over her.

"I know you are bound to have many questions, Afton," he continued. "Miss Betty has tried to prepare you as much as she dared. I understand you have met Nola May. She is very in tune with nature and uses that ability to keep these mountains and her precious people safe. As for little Silas Wade, he would spend all his time amongst the animals if you let him. The animals wouldn't mind it, either, because they love Silas and would do anything he asked. Then, of course, you met Maddie, your grandmother. There is a good reason that your parents didn't tell you about your father's mother. I'm sure they would have if they had lived until you were older. You were so young when the fire happened. Your Grandma Ruby had to act quickly. You needed to be kept safe."

He paused to look at her for a minute. She guessed he needed to see how she was handling the story he had just dumped on her. And what a story it was. Her head started to swim again. Did he say she needed to be kept safe? She wondered from what or from whom.

Phillip Whelan seemed to take notice of her confused state. He began once again to talk, but more carefully and with a much calmer tone.

"Afton, I know this sounds crazy, but just take a deep breath and let me tell you some of what I know. There are but a handful of Cunnin' Folk left, and that includes Appalachian Grannies like Miss Betty. But you are rare and untainted. You are of the purest form of the special mountain people. You see into people and allow them to take into account the actions of their lives while they are still living. And if they choose to do so, they will be sorrowful. Sometimes people tend to block out the bad they have done. What you have is a gift … a gift that must be kept safe. There are those who would go to great lengths to stomp out what you possess.

"Miss Betty was there with your mother when you were born. From the moment you entered into this world, your mom, dad, and Miss Betty knew you were special. You had this glow around you that was like a happiness you could touch with your hands. You didn't cry like most babies did. You smiled, and your pale blue eyes melted the hearts of all who looked into them. The bells on the mountain tolled for twenty-four hours straight when you were born. We all knew that someone very special was amongst us. But ringing those bells proved to be a big mistake because it alerted the bad ones of your birth. Your parents tried to keep you safe, but the bad ones eventually found you. They burned down the cabin, believing you were inside. We had to make sure they thought that you perished with your parents. Ruby took you away from here and kept you safe. Maddie stayed behind to keep them off your trail."

Afton inhaled all the air she could fit into her lungs, and then slowly let it out.

"Phillip, you told me your name and that you are Connor's uncle, but exactly who are you?" The questions abruptly came like the rush of a flood and her tongue could not dam them or hold them back. "Do you have a special gift as well? The wooden flute that you make beautiful music with, is that your gift? Does it calm people's souls? Why is your nephew really in jail? He's not like any other inmate I've ever met. Is he one of the Cunnin' Folk? Is he good? Was he actually put there to watch over me?"

Part Two: Two Funerals

Chapter 7: Replica Home

Afton felt out of breath and somewhat lightheaded. She needed answers, but more than that, she needed to sit down. As it turned out, she didn't act quite quickly enough on that thought. She could feel herself falling or floating. She wasn't sure which until she felt Phillip's strong arms catch her and lift her up before her body could hit the ground.

An unfamiliar instinct took over, one that she wasn't aware she possessed. Her arms pushed against his chest in protest—but only for a moment. Then she found herself holding on. Her hands clasped his shoulders and her face pressed against his warmth. His earthy mountain smell caressed her nose. She closed her eyes and savored the wonderful feeling of being truly safe with someone. She didn't want the feeling to end, but it ended all too soon. Silas came to get them because it was time to dig the grave for Joetta.

Back in the cabin, Nola May told her they no longer rang the bell to signal someone's passing if that person was one of the Cunnin' Folk. "It is especially dangerous now with you being here," she said. "We don't want to draw in the bad ones. They could start nosing around and discover who you really are."

Afton took that opportunity to ask Nola May about Joetta. She had referred to her as one of the Cunnin' Folk, and she was curious to know what Joetta's gift had been. Nola May told her that Joetta had been able to see when one of their own was in danger. She was connected spiritually to each of the Cunnin' Folk and Appalachian Grannies.

"That's why she went to work at the prison," Nola May explained. Joetta had sensed that Afton was in grave danger, but she could not see who it was that wanted to cause her harm. She had gotten too close, and that was why she had ended up dead.

The grave was dug and the burial ceremony commenced. There was a beauty to the whole event. The mountain songs about death and passing over to the other side were breathtaking. Then there was the Native American flute that Phillip played with so much heart and soul. How could the music be so haunting yet so soothing at the same time?

At least a hundred people were present. Phillip seemed to be on edge. The later it got in the day, the more his tension escalated. Finally, Afton asked, "Phillip, what's wrong?"

He answered, "I caught wind of someone who shouldn't be here."

"You caught wind? Does that mean someone spoke to you about an outsider, or can you actually smell the person?

Phillip didn't respond.

Miss Betty was busy going from one person to the next. She must have wanted to make sure she didn't leave a single person out. At least, that was what Afton thought she was doing. But the longer she watched her, the more she thought differently. It appeared as if she was appraising each person as she shook their hands. She thanked them for paying their respects. Afton believed she was searching for the one Phillip Whelan was concerned about; someone among the gathering who seemed out of place or should not have been there at all.

Eventually, a man and woman made their way over to Miss Betty. As she greeted them, something changed in her body language. She did not readily let go of the man's hand, but instead hesitated and stared at the two of them. As she did let go, she looked around, and when her eyes met Afton's, she moved on quickly— almost too quickly.

Afton knew that she had to find Nola May and Phillip. She saw young Silas and told him to go fetch Phillip for her, but to do so quietly.

Nola May was standing with a group of women discussing herbs. Afton tried to make her way to her without drawing attention. Thus far, she had blended in with the crowd, and she didn't want to alert anyone of her identity. People had assumed she was one of the many children that Miss Betty had delivered over the years, and she needed them to continue believing that. She just had to get close enough to tell Nola May about the couple that was with Miss Betty and the uneasy feeling she got as she watched them. Nola May looked at her, and with a slight nod, prevented her from coming any closer. Leisurely, without drawing attention, she came to her. Before Afton could tell her about the couple, she motioned for her to keep quiet.

They were just turning the corner of the cabin when they ran into Silas and Phillip.

"Two of them are here and they're with Miss Betty," Nola May told Phillip. "She is trying to stall them, but it won't take them long to figure out what she's up to."

Phillip's gray eyes seemed to pierce Afton like daggers. Then he turned to the boy. "Silas, take Afton to the safe place."

"Wait a minute," she protested. "If Miss Betty is in danger, I want to help. I can't just slip away to someplace safe if she's in trouble."

She could see the frustration building in Phillip's face. "You are the one in danger. If you want to help, then do as I say and go with Silas. I believe the couple you saw with Miss Betty are Claire and Roy. If that's the case, there's going to be trouble, and I can't allow them to find out about you."

Silas beckoned silently and led her away from the cabin. Her heart felt heavy with guilt as they walked away from Joetta's funeral and the people so eager to protect her.

"We're doing the right thing, Miss Afton," Silas assured her. "Staying will only put more folks at risk."

Afton nodded and silently followed. She knew she had already caused too much hurt. It was because of her that Joetta was gone. She didn't want anyone else to be hurt or killed, so she continued walking with Silas.

Afton's young guardian had taken her hand and, after a while, brought her to a halt. When she finally realized they were no longer moving, she looked up and, right there before her eyes, stood her little house. The house that had been her Grandma Ruby's. The house where her maternal grandmother had taken her last breath. The only home Afton knew. The home where she still lived to that day. But they were several hours from Clay County. They had walked thirty minutes at the most. Why was there another house exactly like hers – board for board, shingle for shingle – there in Robinson Holler?

Silas shuffled from one foot to the other as he tried to find his words. "Miss Afton, all I can tell you is what I been told. And that's not a whole lot when it comes to this house. When your mom and pop died in the fire, the Cunnin' Folk had to make sure you were kept safe. You were only about six years old, so you must not remember it all. Ruby took you in to raise, but she knew the bad people would come. The bad ones would want to make sure you weren't here. Some of the mountain people went ahead to Clay County and bought a piece of land and built Ruby's house on it. They built it as close as they could to be just like this one, inside and out. Ruby didn't want you to be affected by the move because you were already in bad shape after losin' both parents. Honest to goodness … that's all I know about the houses and what happened to you."

She let go of Silas's hand and stepped onto the porch. It was the same as hers, right down to which boards creaked when stepped on. She touched the doorknob and gently turned it. The door swung open, and Afton stepped inside, letting the door close behind her. It was as if she had just gotten home from work. Grandma Ruby's thinkin' chair sat in the corner. In the center of the small kitchen was the hand-carved wooden table with a bench down each side and a chair at each end. Eight quilted placemats were on the table, and beside all but one there was a red gingham napkin. Afton had the eighth one at her home in Clay County. She thought it was the only one that remained, but knew differently now. In the center of the table was a blue Mason jar with three Irish Eyebrights in it. She felt like she was floating between two strange worlds, not knowing which, if either, was real.

She hadn't realized that Silas had entered the house until he gently placed his small hand in hers. He told her that she had been sitting there in her grandma's thinkin' chair for almost four hours. It was dark outside and Silas had lit several candles. Apparently, the electricity had been turned off long ago.

Silas had brought a couple of his animal friends in with him. There were two tiny field mice. One had white on top of its head, and the other had a white streak down its back. Strange little critters, but Silas treated them like little people. They crawled in and out of his pockets and up and down his arms as if he was their personal playground. He said their names were Graham and Dalton.

Afton was about to ask about Miss Betty when Silas mentioned her himself. "I think we'll be able to go back in the mornin' to check on Miss Betty. Phillip is powerful strong. He'll protect her. You had to come here to the safe place while the bad ones were so close. And another thing … you can't be around when Phillip turns strong. He told me so."

It took a minute to untangle what he had just said. But then she looked him in the eye and said, "Silas, what do you mean, when Phillip turns strong? You make it sound like Phillip changes or something."

Silas's face turned red. He knew he had revealed something that was not to be shared with just anybody. She was about to question him when they were interrupted by footsteps on the porch.

"Hello in the house!" called a melodic voice. "It's me, Nola May. I'm comin' inside. Silas, don't you go and sic one of your critters on me."

Afton knew the last part had been added to lighten the tension that hung thick in the air. "Nola May, every time you speak, I long to hear more. Especially at a time like this. Could you tell us what happened after we left the funeral? What of Roy and Claire? What about Miss Betty?"

Nola May didn't answer those questions. Instead, she said, "It's been such a long time since I've been in this little house. Nothing has changed, other than Ruby not being here. I miss her so much. She was more than even a sister to me."

Afton thought her head would explode with questions. Her impatience got the better of her. She couldn't wait another second. "What about Phillip?" she exclaimed, then quickly added, "And Miss Betty?"

Silence fell on the tiny house. Then, as quickly as the silence fell, it was lifted and replaced by Nola May's unique way of talking.

It was always smooth and controlled, no matter the circumstances. It seemed that Roy and Claire had not been looking for Afton, after all.

"They were lookin' for Miss Betty," Nola May told us. "Years ago. Miss Betty took care of Claire durin' her pregnancy. Miss Betty would never turn away anyone who was pregnant, even those who were known to be bad. She always said that a woman with child had the opportunity to turn her life aroun' for that child's sake. Roy and Claire were more than bad; they were very dark people. There was no chance of turnin' them aroun'. Miss Betty said she knew for a fact that the babe would not have a fighting chance with Roy and Claire for parents. They were like a wormy apple ... rotten to the core.

"Well," she continued, "Roy was away when Claire went into labor. Miss Betty brought Claire to her cabin to deliver the baby. There was another lady already at the cabin who'd been there for a day and a half. Miss Betty knew she would be deliverin' anytime as well. She kept the ladies apart because she didn't want anyone aroun' Claire and her evil ways. As fate would have it, the women delivered only minutes apart, an' both of 'em delivered girls. Miss Betty made a hard decision that day. Who's to say if it was the right one? She thought she was doin' what was best for the baby. You see, Claire's baby was born and didn't make a sound. Then Bernice, the other lady who was in labor, delivered and her baby didn't make a sound, either—but it was because the child was stillborn. Miss Betty switched the babies. As soon as Bernice's husban', Big John, arrived, Miss Betty hurried him, Bernice, and the baby girl away."

Nola May paused and sighed. "After they were out of sight, Miss Betty told Claire that her baby girl had been stillborn. She brought the baby in and left her and Claire alone to say their goodbyes. Before long, Roy showed up. He blamed Miss Betty for the baby bein' born lifeless. Roy claimed she hadn't tried hard enough to save their baby girl because she didn't care for their kind. Before he left, he warned Miss Betty that if the day ever came that he found out she'd done somethin' to harm their baby, he would give her cause to regret it."

Afton couldn't believe Miss Betty had taken it upon herself to make such a life-altering decision. In the short while that she had known her, she had seemed so honest and caring. For Miss Betty to change the outcome for two families the way she did seemed totally unfair. What could Miss Betty possibly have known about Roy and Claire to justify telling them their baby was dead and believing that it was the right thing to do?

Amid her troubled thoughts, the conversation between the three of them continued. Little Silas also wanted to know about Miss Betty and Phillip.

"Phillip is fine," Nola May told him. "He and Maddie sent everyone on their way so they could keep an eye on Roy and Claire. Miss Betty didn't fare as well. In the midst of the commotion, harsh words were exchanged. They claimed that they knew their daughter had not died, and they intended to find out what Miss Betty had done with her. Miss Betty flatly refused to tell 'em anything. After that, somethin' happened and Miss Betty was wounded."

Afton gasped. "Wounded? How? Did they shoot her, stab her, beat her? Tell me what happened!"

Nola May tried to explain. "Afton, there's so much about the mountain people and their ways that you just don't know about. I'm not sure how to tell you to make you understand. I can start by tellin' you that Roy and Claire are descendants of the Mingo. They were formed by those who broke away from the Iroquois. The Mingo are part of the original people who settled here in West Virginia a very long time ago, and they were a great people. Phillip and his family were also part of the Mingo."

"So they're descendants of Native Americans. What does that have to do with anything?"

She could tell that Nola May's patience with her was wearing thin. She took a deep breath, trying her best to settle her frustration. Then she sat down in Grandma Ruby's thinkin' chair and waited for her to answer.

"The Mingo descendants had and still have certain traditions and beliefs," she continued. "The majority of all people are good, like Phillip and Connor. But with any groups there are generally a few who are not so good. Those few had beliefs the rest turned away from. Some members of the tribe believed that, through ceremony, a person could change into an animal. They called it skinwalking, and people who did it were known as skinwalkers. Roy and Claire are two who genuinely believe they possess such an ability. They drape themselves with the hide of the animal they wish to change into and perform a ritual around a fire, and then they believe it happens."

Afton felt her mind drifting back to the dream she'd had. She was in Joetta's cabin when she heard strange noises. When she looked outside, she thought she saw chanting figures around a fire. Then they seemed to disappear toward the lake. Had she witnessed one of the skinwalker ceremonies? Afton recalled what Silas had slipped up and said about Phillip—that Phillip turned strong. Could Phillip and his nephew Connor be part of this tradition? She had come there for Joetta's funeral but had fallen into something much more. The ways of these mountains and their people were more than she could comprehend.

There was the faintest sound of footsteps approaching. The sound got louder, and without warning, Phillip walked into the house. His eyes found Afton's. It only took him a second to figure out that she knew something about him. She was still not sure what it was that she actually knew or thought she knew, but the expression on his face said it all. He regarded her as though she had already judged and convicted him. He looked hurt. Afton had thought that the life she knew was difficult because she could see into the very being of the monsters she provided care for. But that seemed easy compared to what she was now trying to wrap her head around.

Phillip cleared his throat, which made her jump because it sounded more like a growl. "We need to go back to Miss Betty's now and take care of her," he said. "Afton, she asked to see you first."

Phillip Whelan was out the door without a second glance at her. What would she find when they went back? Why would Miss Betty want to see her before her lifelong friends? Afton could offer her nothing, but perhaps she believed differently.

As they walked back to Miss Betty's cabin, Nola May told her more about the descendants of the Mingo people who had settled in that area. Their original chief had been friendly to the white people until his family was massacred, and legends of a curse had been passed down for generations. The "mixed-races" were part Mingo and part white, usually of Irish descent. Roy and Claire definitely fell into that category. Afton got the impression that Nola May wasn't certain if she believed that people could skinwalk. But one thing did seem sure: Nola May knew that the people from these mountains were different from those in the outside world. They could see things that others couldn't. They could heal the sick, and sometimes they could cause harm to those who betrayed or threatened them. Nola May knew this to be true because she was one of them, and according to her, so was Afton.

As for her, Afton knew that she was experiencing something that would forever change her, and the way she looked at the world, and she was full of questions. She thought the replica of Grandma Ruby's home was strange. But how much stranger was it that Miss Betty had swapped babies between two families years ago? Or the idea that descendants of the Mingo people believed they could skinwalk? How much more could she possibly be expected to accept?

CHAPTER 8: ONE OF FIVE

Afton didn't recall much of the walk to Miss Betty's cabin. Her thoughts were a mishmash of bewildered revelations and nagging unanswered questions. But suddenly she was crossing her porch and walking into her house alone, while the others waited outside. Miss Betty had, after all, asked to see her first. She wasn't sure how she would react when she saw her. Afton was disappointed and more than a little disillusioned by what Nola May had told her. She believed what Miss Betty had done concerning the babies was wrong, and she was doubtful that her opinion could be easily swayed.

"Afton, my dear sweet child," Miss Betty said softly. "Thank you for coming."

She was taken aback by her appearance. She was lying in bed and looked so pale and feeble.

Miss Betty was weak, and it was such a struggle for her to muster the strength to talk, but she did. "I imagine Nola May told you what I did," she went on to say. "This took place twenty-three years ago. I had and still do have a duty to protect. I thought and hoped that if I could get that baby girl away from Roy and Claire, she might have half a chance at a normal life, one without hate and wickedness." Miss Betty paused to catch her breath before continuing. "Afton, I was wrong. Not for the reason you think, but for another. I was wrong, because it didn't work. That baby girl grew up to be just as wicked as her birth parents. The evil is in her blood and bein' raised by other people didn't change a thing."

"Miss Betty, what are you saying?" Afton interrupted. "It was wrong for you to switch the babies at all. You didn't have that right. How can you say different? No matter what you thought of Roy and Claire, they still had a right to their daughter. Shouldn't they have been given a chance? Maybe if they had raised her, things could have turned out differently."

Near tears, Miss Betty replied, "You'll just have to trust me, child. Soon enough, you will know the truth about Roy and Claire. Only then will you fully understand why I did what I did."

Suddenly Afton's anger faded, and all she felt was concern for Miss Betty's wellbeing. The old woman looked as though she was growing weaker by the minute. She knew she shouldn't have berated her the way that she had.

"Miss Betty, what happened at the funeral? What did Roy and Claire do to you? I keep hearing about people changing. It's difficult for me to understand."

Miss Betty struggled with her answer. "None of us really know all the secrets of the 'Mingo-Irish.' One thing for certain is that some, like the Whelans, are good. They would go to great lengths to protect the Cunnin' Folk. Afton, my dear child, you are one of us. Connor Whelan was placed in your prison to watch after you. Joetta saw in a dream that you were in danger, so arrangements had to be made to protect you. She sensed the danger but could not see who it was that would try to hurt you. And don't condemn Maddie for what you think she did to Joetta's mom. It wasn't like that, and when the time is right, Maddie will tell you the complete story."

"Was it Darcy Doyle, the inmate? Was he the one who was going to hurt me? For some reason, he seemed to hate me. When he grabbed my wrist, I could see his past. Miss Betty, he died that day. I watched him jump to his death."

"No," said Miss Betty. "Darcy feared you only because, through you, he'd be forced to come face to face with his past and all those he had hurt. Afton, you know who wants to hurt you. You dreamed of her. You work with her. Dechtire Massey. She is the daughter of Roy and Claire. She found you once and she will find her way here. She has already killed Joetta. Dechtire won't stop until she gets what she wants."

Afton had sensed something about Dechtire. And she was right … she had dreamt of her before ever meeting her. The day they met, she had felt uneasy. Did she imagine for one second that she was out to hurt her? No, she told herself.

She felt left out somehow, left out of this life of hers. It wasn't about her—none of it was about her. It never had been. There had been something greater all along. Afton only played a small role. She would not ask, "Why me, God?" She had never understood why people felt the need to ask that. She knew everything happened for a reason, but sometimes that reason remained out of reach of human understanding.

Nola May and Maddie entered the cabin. Afton could tell by their faces that they knew Miss Betty was fighting for her life. When she looked again at the frail little lady in the bed, she feared that this would be a fight she would not win. Afton realized that her long weekend would soon be over. What then? Could she leave this place? She didn't feel that she could. Not yet, not the way things were now.

She heard noises coming from the kitchen and knew right away that the two women were doing their best to come up with a mountain remedy that might help Miss Betty. Afton stepped outside for some fresh air ... or maybe it was simply to get away. She wasn't sure which.

She found Silas under the big shade tree. Graham and Dalton, his pet mice, were chasing one another on the boy's shoulders. Afton asked, "Silas, do you mind if I sit with you for a spell?"

He shrugged his shoulders. "I reckon it's okay with me. Is Miss Betty going to die?" The boy's eyes were tearing up. He blinked, and the moisture spilled. He wiped his cheeks roughly with the back of his hand.

"Silas, I'm not going to lie to you or give you false hope. I can't say for sure one way or another, but it doesn't look good."

"Miss Betty took me in when no one else was willing. She's all I have. I can't lose her. What will happen to me, Afton?"

Afton held Silas close to her and tried to give what comfort she could. She never wanted to let go. He'd been through so much in his young life.

Haunting sounds from the wooden flute murmured gently in her ears. Phillip stood by the lake as he played his songs. Did he believe that Miss Betty was going to die soon? Was he playing the death songs that he had so recently played for Joetta?

It was nearing dusk. Afton had always considered those hours to be a mysterious time of day. The mixture of light and darkness caused shadows to race across Silas's face as he lay with his head in her lap. He was such a special boy. Her heart ached for him. She knew he belonged there in the mountains with all his animal friends. She could not imagine him anywhere else. Afton wondered which of the Cunnin' Folk would take him in. Surely one of them would, wouldn't they?

A crack of thunder brought her back to reality. She flinched as the dark sky brightened with lightning. Afton was yanked up from under the tree with Silas still in her arms. He wrapped his arms around her neck and held on. Phillip tightened his grip on her arm and quickly led her back to Miss Betty's cabin. She opened her mouth to protest, but decided otherwise. The intense look on Phillip's face told her she needed to follow without question. Afton could think of no other man she would have followed without resistance. Phillip was not like other men, and it both scared and excited her.

Once they were inside the cabin, she laid Silas down and covered him with a heavy quilt.

Graham and Dalton scurried out of his shirt and burrowed beneath the cover. Even the mice seemed to be aware of something that she wasn't.

"Afton." She could tell by the tone that it was Nola May who had spoken.

She looked up to find Phillip, Nola May, and Maddie sitting around the kitchen table. An extra chair had been pulled out for her. She felt more and more that she was becoming a part of this unusual collection of people. Afton really didn't know how to feel about that. She sat down and scooted her chair in. She was immediately absorbed by Nola May and the words she shared.

"Afton, there are many things that we can't tell you right now, even though you are one of us. You have to allow the answers to come to you. You must be open to receive what's unknown. The old ways go back for generations. They were brought across the ocean for some of us, and for others, the traditions were born here in the mountains."

Afton stared at Nola May with all her beauty and grace. She wondered if some of the Cunnin' Folk were excluded from the aging process and if that was one of the forbidden questions. Maddie was another who appeared to have stopped aging. Miss Betty, on the other hand, looked every bit of her age—or did she? Her thoughts turned to Phillip, and she found herself wondering how old he was. He looked to be in his mid-forties. His black hair and beard was streaked with silver and there was the hint of fine lines below his eyes.

Maddie spoke up. "Afton will soon return to Clay County and her job. She will inevitably be confronted by Dechtire. We need to decide here and now what we should do. Connor is there at the prison, but he can only do so much to help her. Once she is at home and on her own, she will be vulnerable. When Roy and Claire eventually meet up with Dechtire, it will be a trio that the wise would not want to reckon with."

Afton stared intently at each of the three unique people sitting at that little wooden table as they discussed her future and how to protect her.

"I can't understand why Roy, Claire, and Dechtire would be interested in me," she told them. "Miss Betty switched the babies at birth, and that was twenty-three years ago. Yes, she delivered me, but that has nothing to do with Dechtire. The only people I ever loved were my parents and Grandma Ruby. And they are all gone."

Phillip stood up and walked over to her. "Afton, forty-seven years ago, in 1966, Miss Betty only delivered five babies. Three of those babies turned out to be gifted with goodness. One of the babies was a dowser, but he was far from being your typical dowser. One of the girls was Cunnin' Folk. The other girl born was you and you were different. Yes, you were Cunnin', but you also had a very old Appalachian soul, like Miss Betty. The last two were a boy and a girl. They turned out to be Roy and Claire. A handful of the tribe's elders hated Miss Betty, but they knew of her gift. They believed if Miss Betty were to bring the two babies into this world, that they, too, would possess great power. They were wrong. The boy was nothing but pure evil, and the girl struggled somewhere in between.

"The elders blamed Miss Betty. They held onto the belief that, at puberty, the children would become powerful and possess the skinwalker gene. Those same elders wanted to get rid of you because you were the most special of them all. You were meant to die in the house fire, but you didn't. The only reason you are alive is because Ruby took you away from here. The 'mixed' were jealous of the Cunnin' Folk, and the gifts they possessed. What they had were their beliefs about the skinwalkers. Afton, I think it's superstition. Your abilities are real, and that poses a threat to them. If all the mountain people knew the truth, fear of the 'mixed' would be lost."

Afton's mind tried not to devour the story but instead savor each word that had been spoken to her and about her. One thing that stood out was the word abilities, not ability. The only so-called gift she knew she possessed was seeing the darkness in a person. Was there more to her than she was aware of? Once again, her mind started to curl and turn in on itself as if going up a never-ending spiral staircase. Would she reach the top in time to see things straighten out? She wanted to be able to reach out and grab the answers she so desperately needed.

Nola May touched Afton's forearm. "Are you awake?"

Before answering, Afton thought for a moment. "Surely, I'm awake, even this was too much for a mere dream. I'm fine, but maybe it's best if I at least try to get some sleep."

"Of course it is," Nola May agreed. "We should all turn in for the night."

"I'll take the first watch," said Maddie.

Afton heard this, and it replayed in her mind. First watch? Did they think Miss Betty would pass before the sun rises?

Afton lie down on the spare bed beside Silas. He was sound asleep, and so were Dalton and Graham. Her head spun each time she tried closing her eyes. It must have been well after midnight before sleep allowed her entrance into the unknown. The "unknown" darkness of sleep is how she had referred to it for as far back as she could remember. She believed people took sleep for granted. She did not. For her, sleep represented the chance to rest or the chance to explore the unknown. What would it bring for her that night in this strange place that became more familiar to her with each passing hour?

In the darkness, she could sense someone's presence in the bedroom. Could Silas feel that they were not alone? If so, he did not let on. He lay perfectly still.

It crept closer and closer to the bed. A putrid odor like rotting eggs attacked her sinuses and made her gag. Beams of moonlight shone through the cabin window. Whatever this creature was, it was now only inches from the nocturnal glow. Afton strained her eyes through the darkness, trying her best to get a glimpse of what was coming toward her. Her heart raced, and she resisted the urge to cry out. One more step and she would be able to see the invader. Her eyes were fixed and her body frozen.

It took one more step. Were her eyes playing tricks on her? It was a man. No, not a man. It was a beast! The odor was overwhelming. The thing was barefoot and had talons for toes that glistened an oily, wet black. It was clothed in deerskin britches but no shirt. Its chest gleamed with sable streaks, and she knew they were streaks of blood only appearing to be black in the moonlit dark of night. The creature's head was not the head of a man. It had ink-like feathers reaching outward on either side, a razor-sharp beak in the center, and sooty, coal-like eyes. What looked like yellow pus dripped from the corners of those horrid eyes and slid slowly down the thing's face. Shortened arms with curled black talons on the ends reached out for her.

Afton opened her mouth to scream, but only silence came. She could feel one lone tear as it made its way free from her eye and glided down her cheek. Death hovered close, and she could do nothing to prevent it. She could only watch as it came for her.

"Wake up, Afton!" called Silas, shaking her and wrenching her from the grasp of that terrible nightmare. "Wake up! What were you dreaming about? You were crying out for help. Was someone trying to get you?"

His eyes were huge and frightened as he looked around the room, half expecting to see a monster hiding in a corner. Afton wanted to take him in her arms and hug him tight and thank him for saving her from certain death. Instead, she simply smiled and told him she wasn't sure what she had been dreaming about, but was glad to be awake. That part was true. She was definitely glad to be free from the awful creature in her dream.

The pale light of dawn pressed against the panes of the windows. Suddenly, the walls of Miss Betty's cabin seemed to be closing in around her. She told Silas she would return shortly. His big blue eyes looked up at her in protest, so she assured him it would be okay. "I just need a little fresh air and some time to think on my own." Then she slipped out before anyone else noticed.

She stood on the boards of the porch for a long moment, feeling disoriented and out of sorts. Afton needed to feel like she was at home. She needed Grandma Ruby's thinkin' chair. And, most of all, she needed Grandma Ruby.

She left the porch and worked her way through the woods, determined to find the duplicate house. When Silas took her there it had been from Joetta's cabin. The woods all looked the same. Abruptly, she thought she heard someone call out her name. Without hesitation, she hurried in that direction. Silas must have told Maddie or Nola May that she had gone out. There was no mistaking that it was a woman's voice, so it had to be one of them. She made her way through a thicket of mountain laurel and there was her home—or, rather, Grandma Ruby's original home.

The hairs on her arms prickled, and she shivered.

"Afton, dear," someone called softly.

Grandma Ruby, she thought. Could it possibly be?

She opened the door and rushed inside. She called out for Grandma Ruby, but got no reply. Her heart sank. It must have been the wind or her desperate need for comfort.

Afton walked to the old wooden rocker. A crocheted shawl of ivory yarn was draped over one corner. She picked it up and held it to her face, breathing in her grandmother's memory. She wrapped it around her shoulders and a portion of her anxiety drifted away. It felt like a loving hug from her dear Ruby.

As she sat in the chair, slowly rocking, she tried piecing together her entire life. There was so little that she remembered of her time with her mother and father. Her whole life seemed to revolve around her and Grandma Ruby. All the stories she used to tell her. All the advice, like what herb to use for what ailment or what gemstone to put under your pillow to get a good night's sleep. What Afton had thought were old wives' tales were actually lessons. She had instilled values in her about how all people should be treated with respect. There was no color or racism in their little Village of McKinley. They were all the same; just different shades of tan … some lighter, some darker. That's what she had taught her. She was thankful for her wisdom.

When Afton started her nursing career, Grandma Ruby told her she would meet all kinds of people. She warned that she should try her best not to judge, because it was neither her job nor her place to do so. Afton found the not judging part to be difficult, especially in a prison environment. She recognized that there were those who made bad choices from time to time, but she also came into contact with what she felt to be true, unrepentant evil. She struggled with what she saw when she laid her hands upon them. She also struggled with whatever it was that she possessed. Was it a gift or a curse? She didn't have the answer.

Again, she heard my name being called. She halted her rocking and listened. The boards creaked on the porch. All she could think of was Silas's big blue eyes looking up at her as if to say, No, don't go … not alone!

What if Roy and Claire had found her? The skinwalker legend might not be true, but they could still kill her. It wasn't as if she had a weapon to defend herself. Then again, what if the legend was true? The horrifying dream she'd had last night was enough to cause doubt.

The jiggling of the doorknob brought her back to the here and now. She lunged out of the rocker and was at the door in three steps. Now what? She placed her right hand on the doorknob and her left on the lock. She held her breath as she prepared to turn the latch.

A deep voice growled, "Afton."

She jumped back. Stumbling, she fell against one of the kitchen chairs and went crashing to the floor. As she dropped, her forehead clipped the edge of the seat. A feeble cry escaped her lips, and she hit the floorboards hard.

She felt herself sinking toward unconsciousness. Then someone had their hands firmly on her shoulders, shaking her. She cracked open her eyes, but blinding pain shot through her skull. Afton's hand flew to her forehead, and when she pulled it away, there was blood dripping from her fingers and down the palm of her hand. She could feel the warm liquid oozing down her temple. With a low moan, she closed her eyes.

"Afton, are you okay?" It was Phillip's voice. Deep and clear, but no longer sounding like a growl.

When she opened her eyes again, she found that she was lying in bed. Phillip was sitting on the edge, holding her hand in his. "Phillip, what happened?" she asked quietly. "Someone was on the porch and I heard someone calling my name. It sounded like Grandma Ruby."

Phillip looked disturbed by her questions. "Afton," he started, "I told you it was all just made up and the legends about the skinwalkers aren't true."

"I didn't say anything about the legends. I told you I thought I heard Grandma Ruby calling for me."

He stood and paced back and forth across the room before answering her. "There is more to the legend than skinwalking. Supposedly, those with the ability can also disguise their voices to sound like the loved ones of their victims. I assumed Nola May or Maddie had told you this."

Afton took that opportunity to try and find out as much as possible. "Phillip, what else is there to know about this legend? After all, these people may be out to harm me. I should be privy to all there is to know."

"Many of the half-bloods believe that when the bloodlines were crossed, it increased the strengths on both sides," Phillip explained. "If you were a 'changer,' you could change faster and at will, and you didn't have need to perform a ceremony beforehand. Those who possessed the power to cause harm could now cause fatal harm. Some were able to read minds and influence folks' thoughts. Afton, there are times that I feel stronger, but I don't believe it's a gift. I think it's the emotions and adrenaline that get stirred up in the situation."

"Thank you, Phillip. I appreciate your honesty. I know it's difficult to confide in anyone; I feel the same way. I believe that if I were to tell someone all that I've been through, they would think

I was crazy. The longer I'm here, the more I recollect about my childhood. I can remember listening to Grandma Ruby for hours. At the time, I thought she was just spinning stories and tall tales, but now I know she was telling me the history of where we came from and about the special people here."

"Do you truly believe someone was calling your name?" Phillip asked.

"I tried to tell myself that it was just the wind, but I'm certain I heard something. You may find it hard to believe, but I often have experiences where I see Grandma Ruby and talk to her. Sometimes I convince myself it was only a dream, but at other times, there's overwhelming evidence that I wasn't alone."

Afton went on to tell Phillip about how the Irish Eyebright flowers had appeared on her kitchen table, just like the ones that were on this table. Phillip focused all his attention on the flowers. She explained that, as far as she knew, they only grew in Ireland. They were Ruby's favorite, and the first time she ever saw them was at her grandmother's funeral.

Now Phillip was being the sensible one. "Couldn't someone grow them around here?"

"I'm only telling you what Grandma Ruby told me as a child, and that was that the flowers grow in Ireland. She had requested a bouquet of only three of them at her funeral—one for herself, one for me, and one for the protector. I hadn't thought the protector was for someone looking out for me until just recently."

She studied Phillip's face, searching for any sign of belief or disbelief. Instead, he wore an expression of worry and apprehension.

"Phillip, I have to leave tomorrow. I need to go back to work. I feel guilty leaving here with Miss Betty in the condition she's in, and I'm also worried about Silas. What will happen to him should Miss Betty pass?"

His answer was short and to the point. "Do what you must, Afton. Silas will be looked after. Right now, we should get back to Miss Betty."

Chapter 9: Hazel

Phillip led the way back to Miss Betty's house. They walked in silence, but Afton's thoughts were unbearably loud. Her head was throbbing; she probably needed stitches on her forehead from her embarrassing fall, but she didn't dare bring it up.

When they got there, Silas came barreling out of the cabin. There was a look of horror on his young face.

"Afton!" he shouted, although he hadn't seen them yet.

She called out to him and he ran straight into her arms and buried his head on her shoulder.

"What is it Silas? Is it Miss Betty?"

He was inconsolable.

They walked into the cabin to find Maddie and Nola May standing by Miss Betty's bed. Their faces were sad and dejected. "Is she gone?" asked Afton. She knew the answer before the question had even crossed her lips.

"I'll take Silas," said Phillip as he reached for the boy from her arms. Arms that suddenly felt so heavy to Afton, she almost lost her grip on Silas before he was safely in the strong arms of Phillip.

"Yes, Miss Betty passed." Maddie answered the question anyway.

Phillip said, "Let's go outside, Silas." The boy buried his face against Phillip's shoulder.

Afton went to the window to watch Phillip and Silas. They went to the big rock by the lake, and within a few minutes, the three women heard the haunting sound of the wooden flute.

Maddie stated the obvious. "It was only recently that we listened to the death songs for dear Joetta. This is another loss for these mountains. Joetta and Miss Betty will be sorely missed by many."

Nola May only nodded her head in agreement. She, too, was grief-stricken as she told them of the moment Miss Betty had taken her last breath. Nola May had felt the flutter of wings against her skin as her dear old friend had passed from this world. They stood in silence for several moments, remembering the Appalachian Granny.

Afton worked alongside those two strong women and helped to bathe and dress Miss Betty in one of her two dresses. The old woman had lived simply, and she knew she'd had no need for a closet full of clothing. The small cabin held a different kind of riches. It held decades of bringing hundreds of babies into the world, and looking after them had been priceless.

They placed a sheet of plywood under her bed sheets to keep her body straight, knowing rigor mortis would soon set in. They worked for hours in silence, carefully placing herbs and flowers around Miss Betty. It was just about dark when Phillip and Silas came back inside. The boy placed a bouquet of wildflowers in Miss Betty's hands.

They went to the kitchen and prepared their meal, then sat down together around the table and ate.

Afton was the first to speak. "Please forgive me. I know this is hardly the time, but I must leave tomorrow."

"We will have the funeral midmorning tomorrow," Maddie told her. "Afterwards, you can leave."

Phillip looked disagreeable. "What of Miss Betty's friends? Should we not notify them so they can pay their respects?"

"Maddie is right," stated Nola May. "If we send out word of her death, Roy and Claire will have the satisfaction of knowin' they killed her, and possibly return to do more harm."

Phillip nodded silently, grudgingly accepting the decision.

Afton couldn't help but wonder about what Nola May had just said—that Roy and Claire could do more harm.

Nola May knew what she was thinking. "Afton, when we bathed Miss Betty, I noticed a rash on her right palm. This could explain her fallin' ill and ultimately her dyin'. When those two devils shook hands with Miss Betty, they could've taken that opportunity to poison her."

Afton lie awake in bed that night, going over everything that had happened in this strange but unique place since her arrival.

The existence of Cunnin' Folk, Appalachian Grannies, and Skinwalkers seemed far-fetched. Could any of it actually be true? Could people really have the gift of healing powers or harming powers? Perhaps instead it was the passed-down knowledge of how to use the vast variety of herbs and plants that grew so abundantly in those wild and beautiful mountains. Mountains that seemed scarcely touched by the outside world, and somehow remained unchanged for many generations. The battles in the modern world hadn't tainted or influenced this place. There was right and wrong. There was only good versus bad. And the people there knew the difference.

She slept, but for how long, she was unsure.

Afton sat straight up in bed and listened. A strange noise had severed her ties from sleep. A crack in the silence that generally embraced night had been disrupted. The sound was so eerily close to the cries of a woman, it caused goose-flesh to rise on Afton's arms.

"What's happening?" Afton screamed.

Phillip's answer was muffled by all the commotion. Dishes were crashing to the floor. Guttural murmurs echoed throughout the house. Afton opened her bedroom door and looked out. Blackness darted about in the air with such speed, it was hard to be sure what she was seeing. A whirlwind of feathers began to descend onto the furniture and floor.

She ran from the tiny bedroom to find Phillip opening the windows and door. He was trying to rid the cabin of two large ravens. They had been circling above Miss Betty in the bed, swooping down and clawing at the flowers that surrounded her body. Nola May had been sitting in the room with Miss Betty and had managed to swat the birds through the bedroom door and slam it shut behind them.

The frenzied ravens flew about the kitchen, knocking down anything in their path. Bundles of herbs that hung from the rafters to dry were scattered about. Jars of tinctures were broken, and the liquid poured out like open veins. The birds cawed as though speaking to one another. Then they focused in on something—and that something was Afton. Wings were flapping so loudly she couldn't make out what Maddie and Phillip were yelling until it was too late. The ravens were on her, tearing at her gown with their long black beaks. She held her hands up in defense as they tried to sink their razor-sharp talons into her flesh.

Suddenly, the cabin filled with gray smoke. When the smoke cleared, the ravens were gone.

Phillip and Maddie were quickly at Afton's side, inspecting for injuries. They pulled on her arms, raising them this way and that, and lifted her hair to check her face and neck. Nothing, not one single scratch. What if I had been injured? she wondered. Would I have fallen ill and died like Joetta and Miss Betty? For people who insisted such things were merely legends, Phillip and Maddie sure went into a frenzy at the thought of me being wounded.

Nola May opened Miss Betty's door and stepped into the main room. The three of them looked at Afton. They knew exactly what she was thinking. They looked at one another as if to silently ask, Well, who's going to say something?

Finally, Phillip spoke up. "Afton, I have to be honest with you."

"I had hoped you were honest all along. But I see that wasn't the case."

Phillip continued without missing a beat, "Afton, there's always been doubt about the legends, and letting them go to chance is not something we are willing to do. We must protect you at all costs, even if that means chasing ravens around as if they possess evil powers. They probably do."

So now she knew. There were doubts among even the strongest of the Cunnin' Folk when it came to folklore and legends. That left much for her to try and comprehend. No one could do that for her.

'Silas," she said, concerned. "Where is Silas?"

At the expression of alarm on her face, Nola May quickly stepped back inside the bedroom. When she returned, she was hand in hand with Silas. Afton felt such relief that she wanted to cry, but she didn't. She held Silas close to her, which brought her as much comfort as it did him, maybe more.

Miss Betty's funeral went forward as planned.

Just the five of them were there—Nola May Waters, Maddie O'Sullican, Phillip Whelan, Silas Wade, and Afton. It was a far cry from the celebration her life deserved. Heavy rain clouds hung threateningly low and darkness filled the sky as the hand-carved pine casket was lowered into the ground. The gates of heaven seemed to open and a torrent of rain began to fall. The drops were so large they stung Afton's cheeks as they pummeled her face. It was as though angels were shedding tears from heaven, as mournful for their loss as they were.

Nola May put her arm around Afton's shoulder and told her that Miss Betty was in a far greater place. She had no doubt that was true, but she grieved her death, nonetheless. They were left behind to struggle with the madness that had taken root in this place. She felt a part of it now, but in another sense, still like an outsider looking in through shattered glass. It all seemed distorted, and she wasn't certain if the picture ahead of her was real. One thing for sure was the fact that she needed to get on the road and back to the Village of McKinley.

Her car was parked near the cabin. How lonely it appeared, there by the big oak tree. Afton hadn't been in it since arriving five days before. She remembered the day Grandma Ruby had bought it for her. It was 1984, and she had just graduated from high school. She had never expected a car because she couldn't afford one. But Grandma Ruby said she needed a way to get back and forth to nursing school, and, bless her heart, she had found a way and was so pleased with her purchase. It was a 1966 Dodge Dart coupe with a six-cylinder engine, and it was painted Haze Green. So, naturally, Afton named the car Hazel. It didn't bother her a bit that the car was eighteen years old. Perhaps that was why Grandma had chosen that one: it was the same age as Afton was. She no longer drove it every day, but instead drove Hazel just on special occasions—and this certainly seemed fitting.

It didn't take Afton long to pack because she hadn't brought much with her. Silas helped load her belongings into Hazel's trunk. His freckled face was full of sadness.

"I'm going to miss you, Afton."

"Silas, we'll see each other again."

She tried to comfort him, but didn't want to make any promises that she wouldn't be able to keep. He had already been through enough. Maddie came out first to say her goodbye. She still felt somewhat awkward when they talked. Their conversations did not come with the ease that had flowed so freely with Grandma Ruby.

"Afton, I would have liked things to have been different between us," Maddie told her. "I longed to watch you grow up and to be there to help teach you the things you needed to know. It wasn't to be, though. Your safety came first and foremost. I hope someday you'll understand. I do love you."

Afton was deeply touched by Maddie's words. She too hoped that, with time, they could become closer and told her so. Her paternal grandmother handed her a box wrapped in plain brown paper and told her to wait until she was home to open it. Afton promised her that she would, then hugged her goodbye.

Nola May was next to appear. As she approached, Afton noticed her eyes looked glassy. She knew she would be hard-pressed not to cry. The black woman had a gentleness about her that made Afton want to run and embrace her. If she did, she knew it would make her feel like everything would be okay; she just had that way about her.

Nola May reached out and cupped her hands around her cheeks. "Afton, my sweet and special one, what shall I do without you? In the short time you have been here, I have grown to love you, just as I always knew I would. These mountains have suffered the loss of two great women. They now call out to me with the night wind for new hope and for new life. When the time is right, you will hear the voices as they come to you on the night air. It will be then that you return to us."

"I love you, Nola May." Afton wasn't sure of the true meaning of what she had just told her, but she felt comforted by the words she spoke.

Phillip must not have felt the need to see her off. Afton supposed there was no reason for him to. It was silly for her to feel a sudden pang of disappointment in the pit of her stomach, but she did. She opened the car door, slid behind the Dart's steering wheel, and started the motor. It purred like a kitten, just as it had for the past twenty-nine years.

Afton drove away, and as she glanced in the rearview mirror, she saw Maddie, Nola May, and Silas standing by Miss Betty's cabin, waving goodbye. She hung her arm out the window and waved back.

Just as she turned the bend and lost sight of the cabin, Phillip stepped out of the woods and onto the dirt road. Afton stopped and shifted the gear into Park. She wasn't sure whether to roll down the window or get out. Phillip made the decision for her by opening the passenger door and climbing in beside her. They sat there in silence for a long, awkward moment. Phillip stared down at his hands as though he was searching for an answer to a question that had not yet been asked.

"Phillip, I want you to know how very sorry I am for everything," she told him. "I feel like I'm the cause for all the havoc that has gone on here. And I feel responsible for the deaths of Joetta and Miss Betty. I should have been able to do something."

Afton wasn't known as the crying sort, but she could feel the tears welling up. She didn't want Phillip to think of her as weak, so she turned to look out her window and tried to control her emotions.

Phillip's hand cupped her elbow ever so gently. She turned and found his face close to hers. She couldn't find words. Afton simply stared into the smoky grayness of his eyes. A single tear made its way from her eye and slowly down her cheek. Before she could wipe it away, Phillip placed his index finger on her face and traced the path of the teardrop. Chills ran down her spine and she shivered.

Phillip took his hand away. "I didn't mean to make you uncomfortable. I need to talk to you. There's so much I want you to know. I had meant to tell you during your stay, but the time was never right. Roy and Claire didn't make things any easier by showing up. I've heard from my nephew, Connor. He told me that the new warden has arrived and is a good man. You can trust him, Afton. He is an ally. Someone who is on our side."

"What does that mean exactly … someone on our side?"

"His name is Clayton Tolley," Phillip explained. "He comes from a small place called Monkey's Eyebrow, Kentucky. He is gifted like the Cunnin' Folk. I believe he will be an asset to your well-being at the prison. Connor can only do so much to watch over you. Clayton is the warden, so no one will question his comings and goings."

Phillip's words frightened her. "What are you saying? Do you actually think someone will follow me to Clay County, to my home, or to the prison? I don't see why anyone would feel the need to come near me, let alone threaten me. You're overreacting. From what I was told, Roy and Claire don't even know that Dechtire is their daughter, nor does she know who they are."

"I know all of this is hard for you to take in. Afton, you're going to have to finally trust someone. You need to realize that what you possess is a gift. For goodness' sake, you can touch someone and see all the bad things they've done in their lifetime. And it's so much more than that. What you do allows the person to come face to face with their past, no matter how deeply they've buried it. In turn, they have a choice as to whether or not they are remorseful of their crimes. No, you are not their judge, nor can you save their souls, but you do unlock their past before it's too late. This is the only gift you've tapped into, but I know there's more."

"I don't understand. How you can be so sure?" Once again, her head was swirling, and she wasn't quite sure which way was up. How could she possess more of this "gift" and not be aware of it?"

Afton closed her eyes and took a deep breath, attempting to settle her nerves. "Phillip." she said, "I feel like I need to sit here for a few minutes and pull myself together before tackling the drive home. I really think it'd be best if I did that alone."

Phillip didn't seem offended by her request. "I understand," he said. "Then I'll take my leave and respect your wishes." He got out of her car and walked away.

When she opened her eyes again, she looked around, but saw no sign of him.

Phillip had vanished into the woods. He was gone.

Chapter 10: The Dowser

Afton closed her eyes again, feeling a little guilty. She hoped that she hadn't offended him.

"Hazel, I wish we were home already," she whispered softly. A long drive in her old faithful boat of a ride was something she usually looked forward to, but not that day.

She had put off the inevitable long enough. Afton opened her eyes and reached for the gearshift. She blinked several times and was certain that her eyes were playing tricks on her. They weren't. She was sitting in front of her little house in Clay County.

"Well, Hazel, you must have been on autopilot," she told her old friend, "because I surely don't remember a moment of that drive."

Afton felt numb as she walked through the door with her luggage in tow. It had only been five days, but it felt like a lifetime. Robinson Holler in War, West Virginia, would forever be embedded in her brain, not unlike a tick's head buried beneath the hide of an old hound dog.

She put her belongings on her bed and flopped down next to them. She noticed the box that Maddie had given her, set it aside, and opened her suitcase. As she sorted through her clothing to prepare a load for the wash, she discovered another package wrapped in plain brown paper among her belongings. She placed it next to the first one and unzipped the side pouch in her suitcase to make sure nothing was left. To her surprise, there was yet another package. This one was small but also wrapped in the same brown paper. Perplexed, she sat on the side of her bed and stared at the three packages.

The phone rang and snapped her back to the present. Afton hesitated for a moment before answering, because she wasn't quite sure she was ready to be disturbed. She thought of Silas and decided it was best to answer the phone in case he or one of the others needed her. Possibly, being needed was a good thing.

"Afton, this is Dechtire Massey from work."

This was followed by silence. Afton guessed she was waiting for some kind of response from her.

"Dechtire," she said, "is there something you need to tell me?"

She hadn't meant for her reply to sound so matter-of-fact, but she did feel disappointed that it wasn't one of her new friends from Robinson Holler.

"Well, yes," she said. "I was wondering if I could come over and talk to you."

Now her disappointment was coupled with dread. This was the person that Phillip, Miss Betty, Joetta, and Maddie believed to be a threat to her. Not to mention, possibly the one responsible for Joetta's death. How dare she call and ask to come to her home? What was she supposed to say?

"Dechtire, it really isn't a good time. I just got in the door and haven't finished unpacking."

This was all true, but would it be enough to put her off?

Dechtire released an audible sigh, then said, "I guess it'll have to wait, then. You do come back to work tomorrow, don't you?"

"Yes, today is the last day of my break. I'll be back tomorrow morning for the day shift. We can talk then, okay?"

She accepted that answer and they both hung up.

Afton started her laundry and put the rest of her things away. Her focus now returned to the three packages. She knew one was from Maddie because she had given it to her herself. She gathered up all three and went to sit in Grandma's thinkin' chair.

Maddie's was the largest of the three, so she started with that one. She unwrapped the box slowly, and as she did so, she noticed that her hands were trembling. It had been a while since she had received a gift of any kind. Afton lifted the lid to find a photo album. She set the box and brown paper on the floor and held the album on her lap. She ran her hands across the smooth cover of burgundy leather.

She hesitated, then opened the album. On the first page was a photo of a woman holding a newborn baby. The year 1966 was written below the picture. That was the year Afton was born. She looked closely at the black-and-white image. The woman was Maddie O'Sullican, and she didn't appear much younger than when Afton had left her earlier today. The baby she was holding must have been her. Her heart ached as she looked into Maddie's eyes. She looked so proud of the granddaughter lying in her lap.

The next page was a picture of Afton at age one. She was sitting beneath a tree and both hands were squeezing fistfuls of grass. A big smile was on her face as if to say, Hey, look what I'm doing! As she turned the pages, each one held a picture of her, one year older than the one before. The picture of her at age five was in color, and her pale blue eyes stood out more than all the other colors in the photo. She looked so happy, sitting on the steps of a small cabin. It looked familiar. She wondered if that was her home, the one she had lived in with her parents until her sixth birthday.

Afton turned the page to a picture of her at age six. She was sitting on a log beside a creek. Maddie was sitting next to her, holding her hand. They were looking up at the camera and their eyes glowed with the same icy blueness. Below the picture was an inscription. I didn't realize this would be goodbye to my sweet Afton. This must have been the morning of her sixth birthday, before Grandma Ruby had taken her to her house and before the fire had started.

To Afton's surprise, there continued to be a picture for each year until 2013. They were all on special occasions—the first time she rode a bike without training wheels, graduating from high school, and graduating from nursing school as well. Had Maddie been there to take the pictures, and she hadn't even known it? The photos weren't like the ones from Ruby's camera or any that Afton had ever owned. Maddie must have been there at least once a year as she grew up, even as an adult.

On the last page was a note from Maddie that read:

My dearest Afton,

I never wanted us to be separated, but I knew you would be safer away from here and with Ruby. I hope the day will come when we can spend enough time together, truly know one another. I want to share my life with you. There is so much more that I need you to know.

Love, Grandma Maddie O'Sullican

The album and note melted away any doubts Afton had had about her paternal grandmother.

The next box held an envelope and a book. She opened the envelope and discovered there was a letter from Nola May that read like poetry:

I counted down the days, months, and years, until you would return to us, without fears.

That day has yet to be revealed, so I shall patiently wait for you, my dear.

The time draws near for you to learn the remaining ways of the mountains.

Listen closely for the call; it will come quietly and ever so small.

This book is what you will need, so study it all and keep it close.

Miss Betty has kept it just for you, the sweet child with eyes so blue.

Love, Nola May

Afton read and reread the poem, hoping to discover the meaning in each word that Nola May had written. She closed her eyes and concentrated on her unique voice and manner of speaking. She could hear her reciting the poem, and only then did it make sense to her. She would indeed return to her people, the Cunnin' Folks, someday.

She started reading Miss Betty's book and found it nearly impossible to put down. Miss Betty's life's work was on every page. Afton devoured each remedy, each recipe, and each handwritten word, then locked them away in her mind. It must have been rare for the healing methods and beliefs of those people to be written down. She would guard and treasure Miss Betty's book with her life. She knew precisely where to hide it.

Afton had forgotten about the last little package until it fell out of her lap onto the floor. She picked it up and unwrapped it. She knew at once that it was from dear little Silas. It was a necklace with a small round piece of wood with a wolf carved on one side and a raven carved on the other. The circular medallion was set inside another thin strip of wood. The center piece turned freely, and when you spun it around, it appeared that the raven was chasing the wolf. The pendant hung on a long leather cord. Afton immediately tied it around her neck. It made her feel close to her new family.

After opening the three gifts, she had an urgent desire to talk to them. She dug through her purse and found the piece of paper with Miss Betty's number on it. She hadn't thought of asking where Silas would be staying, but Miss Betty's number was the only one she had. Afton quickly dialed the number and waited for an answer. Finally, on the seventh ring, someone picked up.

"Hello?" rumbled a gruff voice. It was Phillip.

Suddenly, she felt silly for calling and fumbled for words.

"Afton, is that you?" Phillip asked. Was that concern in his voice? "Are you okay?"

"Yes, Phillip, I'm okay. I just, well, I needed … I mean, I was wondering how Silas was, so I thought I would try this number in case he was there. I hope I'm not bothering you. I must admit that I'm missing you—I mean, Silas."

"You're not bothering me," he said, "and I kept Silas here tonight because I didn't want it to be so hard on him. I knew you had this number, and I hoped you would call. You left so quickly today. I walked away to give you a few minutes like you asked, but when I came back, you were gone."

"About that … it was so strange. I put my head down on the steering wheel for what felt like a minute, but when I looked up, I was home. Please, don't think I'm crazy."

"Afton, I know you're not crazy. I was just worried that I'd said too much and upset you. I'm glad you called. As for Silas, he's asleep. I could wake him, though. He may get mad if I don't."

"No, just tell him I told you to let him sleep and I'll call tomorrow after work. Now that I'm talking to you, there's something that I should tell you. Dechtire has already called and asked if she could come over. I told her it wasn't a good time and she seemed okay with that."

Phillip was furious. "I knew this was a bad idea! Going home before we could get things straightened out could put you in harm's way … or even get you killed. Something has to be done to clear this up with Roy, Claire, and Dechtire. It's like a ticking bomb ready to explode, and I don't want you there when it goes off."

"I'll be okay," she assured him. "You said that the new warden was a good guy, and there's always your nephew, Connor. Between the two of them and me being careful, things will work out."

"I need for you to be safe, Afton."

Afton pretended not to notice. "Phillip, I promise to take every precaution. I'll see you again."

"I hope so," Phillip said.

Afton told Phillip those things to settle his nerves, but it did nothing to settle hers. She knew the prison she was about to step into would not be the same one she had left only a few short days ago. Phillip and Afton said their goodbyes. The exchange was pleasant and respectful, but nothing more than that.

The next morning, Afton arrived at work a bit early.

She sat in her car and watched the sun rise over the massive structure of the prison. A haze hung heavy in the air and she wondered if anyone else had noticed it. She felt an uncomfortable sensation of foreboding and knew that she had put off going inside long enough. She walked across the parking lot to the gate, taking in everything and everyone around her as she went.

George was the first person she ran into in Medical. His greeting seemed cordial, but exaggerated. "Afton, I'm so glad you're back! I hope the funeral went as well as one could be expected to go. Oh, I need to talk to you about a couple of things."

"Okay, George. Just let me know when."

George's eyes drifted to the door and tension instantly crept across his face. Afton searched for the cause of his anxiety. Dechtire stood in the doorway. She looked different from the last time she had seen her. She no longer seemed to be trying to make a good impression for the people at her new job. That demeanor had been replaced by an air of darkness and a glare so intense it seemed to cut right through you.

Dechtire started toward them and Afton felt George cringe beside her. He told her that he would catch up with her later and quickly headed toward his office, neglecting to look directly at Dechtire as he walked past. Exactly what had happened there while she was gone? George had been so on board with the new assistant director of nursing five days ago, but now he almost seemed afraid of her.

"Afton," Dechtire called out, "just the person I was looking for."

She couldn't muster the same level of enthusiasm. In fact, her tone was a little cool. "Hello, Dechtire."

Her eyes widened as Dechtire reached out and placed her hand on her shoulder. The vision came unexpectedly, like a punch to the gut. Afton saw Dechtire standing in an inmate's cell. Her hands were waving back and forth over a sleeping man as she quietly said several words that she couldn't make out. Afton couldn't see the inmate's face, but she could clearly see Dechtire's. Her eyes were blacker than usual and filled with so much hatred that she could almost feel the heat radiating from them.

"Afton," Dechtire said, "are you still with me?"

The vision quickly faded, and she found herself back in Medical. Dechtire's hand was no longer on Afton's shoulder. She just stood there staring at her, waiting for an answer.

"I'm right here. What can I do for you?"

Dechtire had a look of adulation on her face as she said, "Afton, I have a very special job for you today."

Afton had worked there long enough to know what needed to be done, so she was a little curious as to what that "special job" might be.

"I need you to teach a class on appropriate behavior while in the medication line," Dechtire continued. "I have already sent out notices to the inmates who are to attend. You will teach the class in the third-floor common room. There will be an officer present, of course."

You've got to be joking, Afton thought to herself. All inmates get that lecture during their entry orientation upon arrival. Maybe this had something to do with why George wanted to talk to her. She had planned on giving the pharmacy a thorough check that day, as well as prepping the charts for labs that should be due. She guessed those things would have to wait, because they certainly wouldn't be happening during her shift.

As agreeably as possible, she replied, "Okay. What time is the class?"

Dechtire couldn't hide the gleam in her eyes as she said, "The class will start in approximately five minutes. You're probably an old pro at this, though. I hope you don't feel rushed."

"No. Not at all." Afton felt the need to be away from her before she had a chance to see the heat rise to her face.

She didn't bother waiting for any further comments from her. Afton headed out of Medical and up to the common room. There were ten inmates in the class, and officer Byler was the one assigned to the room. The inmates were all new admissions since her break except for one, and that was Connor Whelan. Her attention paused on Whelan for a moment, because his appearance was disturbingly haggard. He looked like he hadn't had a good night's sleep in days. She knew she couldn't allow his beaten-down appearance distract her. She walked to the front of the room and began the class.

About ten minutes into her lecture on how they were expected to conduct themselves, they heard a commotion in the hallway.

Officer Byler stepped out to see what was happening. That proved to be a dangerous mistake. The medical staff was never to be left alone with inmates. It was a rule that an officer had to be present in the room at all times. In a split second, things went from Officer Byler's simple mistake to the room erupting into a violent battle. The ten inmates engaged in a free-for-all, although Afton had no idea what had triggered it. Tables and chairs toppled, and punches were being thrown left and right. Before she could reach the door, something crashed forcefully into the back of her head.

Afton felt herself falling and struggled to remain standing. Before she could gain her bearings, unseen hands gripped her ankles and jerked her feet out from beneath her. She knew her impact on the floor would be fierce, and she wasn't wrong. Her skull collided with the common room floor, sending painful starbursts coursing through her head like fireworks. She could feel herself being dragged, but did not know by whom or where she was being taken.

She found herself drifting in and out of consciousness. For the most part, she was unaware what was happening and had no idea what was being done to her. When she had felt the wallop to the back of her head, Afton realized that things had gone south in a hurry. Her last thoughts were that the inmates were killing each other, and they were taking her with them. The idea that she would never see her newfound family again hurt more than any physical pain she experienced. Just before the blackness swallowed her completely, she thought she saw Silas's sweet face, and her heart felt like it was breaking in two.

Afton's eyelids fluttered as she started coming to. She tried raising her head, but to no avail. Once she was able to keep her eyes open, she asked, "What happened? Where am I? Someone was dragging me. Who was it?"

Hours later, she would learn from Officer Byler that Inmate Whelan had dragged her out of the room to safety. She had a huge knot on her head, and her back ached terribly, but she was alive. Afton shuddered at the thought of what could have happened.

Byler hadn't fared much better than she had. He required stitches to his lip, and he had a broken nose. He received a two-week suspension for leaving Afton in the room with the inmates.

"Byler made a mistake, but suspending him when he is most needed here isn't the answer."

The decision was final. Dechtire took pleasure in telling her that all ten inmates would be shipped out to other prisons within twenty-four hours.

"Why is Inmate Whelan being moved?" she asked, trying not to sound troubled by the news. "He's the one who came to my rescue."

"I don't see it that way," Dechtire said with a scowl. "He put his hands on you, and that is definitely prohibited. Who's to say he wasn't dragging you off to rape you? All ten of the inmates were involved in this fight, so all ten of them will be transferred from this facility."

"But Officer Byler clarified in his formal statement that Whelan helped me."

Dechtire's gaze was unyielding as she continued with her explanation. "Byler is only trying to cover his ass. He's lucky he only received suspension. If it had been up to me, he would have been fired on the spot."

Afton couldn't believe what was happening. After her meeting with Dechtire, she set off to find George. He was sitting at his desk in his office. He physically flinched when she walked in, but relaxed when he discovered it was her and not Dechtire.

"George, I need to talk to Inmate Whelan. I want to thank him for what he did."

"I'm sorry, Afton," he said. "I would have liked to have talked to him myself, but he was the first inmate to be taken out. I've heard some very disturbing talk among the other officers. They seem to think it was some sort of set-up; a twisted plan to attack you and get rid of Whelan in the process. Someone has it out for you, and I have a pretty good idea who it is, although I don't have any proof."

"It's Dechtire, isn't it?"

The look of regret on George's face told her she was right.

"This morning you wanted to talk to me, but when Dechtire came in, you left. What did you want to tell me?"

His eyes shifted to the pencil in his hand. It looked like a rat had been gnawing on it. "Afton," he began, "you've worked here a long time and you truly are the best nurse I've ever known. I regret playing any part in hiring Dechtire, as well as everything that took place with your attack and what happened while you were away for Joetta's funeral."

"What do you mean? What happened while I was on break?"

George glanced toward his office door and lowered his voice. "I walked in and found Dechtire going through your personnel file. I questioned her about it and she just blew it off. She told me that she liked to review the files for all the nurses under her charge so she would know more about them. I didn't fall for it, though. She's up to no good and I can't do anything about it. My hands are tied. I just want you to know how sorry I am about all of this."

Afton was moved by the man's troubled confession, as well as his apology. "George, I truly appreciate your concern. I agree that Dechtire is up to something. I believe it may be more sinister than you or I could ever imagine. That's all I'm going to say on the subject, because I don't want to put you in harm's way."

George seemed to be puzzled by what she had said, but before he could respond, there was a knock on the door. Without hesitation, a tall black man stepped inside the cramped office. He was a stranger; not anyone she had ever met before.

But George knew who he was and made the introductions. "Afton, I'd like you to meet our new warden, Clayton Tolley. Warden Tolley, this is Nurse Afton Sullivan."

Warden Tolley stepped toward her and stretched out his massive hand. She shook it and, as she did, she could hear him say, *You will be okay, Afton. I am here to look after you.* The strange thing was, he had not even opened his mouth. It was as though his thoughts had whispered into her ear, rather than his physical voice.

George was watching her closely. Maybe he could tell that something odd had just occurred between them. Afton had become somewhat accustomed to seeing people's thoughts or actions as pictures, but never had she heard words without the pictures … unless you counted Maddie feeding her answers to the questions that she had about her. Was this big mountain of a man from Monkey's Eyebrow, Kentucky, blessed with the ability to communicate without speaking?

Afton could only hope there wasn't a look of astonishment on her face as she said, "It's good to meet you, Warden Tolley."

She glanced over at George, then politely excused herself.

Her shift ended and she had to force herself not to sprint to the parking lot. She expected to find her jeep there, but instead was pleasantly surprised when she saw Hazel parked on the far side of the lot. During the hectic events of that day's shift, she had forgotten that she had driven her to work that morning. She missed her Robinson Holler friends and found some comfort when she drove her. Afton felt closer to them as she seemed to float peacefully along in the sturdy old car. The hour and fifteen minute drive home allowed her time to reflect on the day.

When she arrived home, she parked Hazel near the big sugar maple. Afton took a long, hard look at the house. It was the only home she ever really remembered living in. She sometimes had short glimpses or dreams about her parents' home, but she was never quite sure which were memories and which were only dreams. She finally got out, and as she closed the door, she gave Hazel a gentle pat on the roof.

"Thanks for bringing me home safely, ol' girl."

It was probably a silly thing to do, but that car had reliably gotten her back and forth for twenty-nine years. That had to be worth at least a pat on the roof.

Afton heard the house phone ringing as she unlocked the door. She hoped it wasn't Dechtire. She simply couldn't deal with her at that moment. Today had been rough, and the drive home had given her muscles ample time to stiffen up, not to mention the knot on the back of her head that felt like it had a pulse of its own.

She knew she would sound out of breath when she answered. "Hello?"

"Afton?" a small voice asked.

"Silas!" she said, happy to hear from him. "Yes, it's me. I just got home from work."

"Are you okay, Afton? I had a bad feeling that you were hurt. Phillip told me not to worry, but I couldn't help it."

She didn't want to lie to Silas, but she also didn't want to upset him. The boy had been through enough already. "It was a trying day, Silas. And, yes, there was some trouble at work, but I'm okay, really."

She heard Silas lay the phone down, as well as some mumbling in the background. Then someone else picked up.

"Afton, this is Phillip. Is something wrong? Silas said you weren't telling him the whole truth. You know he's developed a connection with you in much the same way he's able to communicate with his animal friends. He's never felt this way about a human, though. He paced the floors all day until it was time to call you."

"Oh, Phillip, it was an awful day, but I didn't want to upset Silas. Dechtire set me up to teach this bogus class with ten inmates. One of them was your nephew. Nine of them turned on him and me. I got banged up, but I'll be okay. Connor saved me from what was probably supposed to be my death. A guard was suspended and all the inmates involved are being transferred out. Dechtire made certain that Connor was the first one out of the gate."

She could hear the emotion in Phillip's voice. "Connor can take care of himself. It's you that I'm worried about. Dechtire obviously has connected you with Miss Betty, and she will stop at nothing to get what she wants. It makes no sense for her to want you dead, though, unless she already knows about Roy and Claire."

"My supervisor told me that he caught her going through my personnel file while I was gone. It makes no reference to McDowell County or Robinson Holler, though."

Phillip continued as if she hadn't spoken. "We have no idea whether Dechtire is gifted or not. We only know she comes from darkness, and being raised by people other than her own parents didn't save her from that darkness. Who knows? It may have made her even more evil. Now, tell me exactly what happened to you."

Afton tried her best to hold it together while she told Phillip what had taken place at work.

"It all happened so quickly. One minute I was teaching and the next, there was an altercation in the hallway that drew the guard away. I started for the door, but before I could get there, someone walloped me on the back of the head and I blacked out. Later, I found out that Connor had dragged me out into the hall where I would be safe and in view of the security camera. I tried to see him to thank him, but he was taken out too quickly. I'm sorry I've caused all this pain to fall upon your family."

Phillip's voice was reassuring, even gentle. "Afton, when are you going to get it through that thick skull of yours that you're part of the strange collection of people who make up this family too? You are a very important part of it—more than you know. Have you met Clayton Tolley yet?"

"That's another strange thing, Phillip. All my life, I've been able to see what's in a person's past or what they have planned for the future, like a movie. When I met Clayton and shook his hand, he talked to me. He talked to me without saying a word out loud and with no pictures. I could hear him, though, just like I can hear you."

Phillip didn't sound surprised. "Clayton Tolley has a reputation for being a particular sort of man. He comes from a long line of dowsers. But his dowsing abilities reach far beyond just finding good water sources for wells, like most modern dowsers. He can find things that are missing, like, for instance, answers or sometimes even people. Apparently, he's also a 'silent talker' as well. I'm glad he's at the prison with you, but I still think you need to get away from there."

"A 'silent talker.' I've seen so much at this point, I won't even bother to question such a thing. There's nothing I can do about the situation at work right now. If it comes down to it, I have four weeks of vacation that I can use before the end of December, or I'll just lose them. So, if need be, I could take off until the end of the year—but only if there's no other way. I would need to give some notice before taking that many weeks of vacation in a row so they could arrange for backup." She paused, feeling utterly exhausted. "Phillip, I'm so very tired. I feel like I need to go to bed and get some rest."

He didn't argue. He simply said, "Goodnight, Afton."

Then, with a click, the call ended between them.

Chapter 11: Raven

Afton couldn't let Phillip know how badly her head hurt—or the rest of her body, for that matter. She needed rest and plenty of it. The alarm clock would be blaring in her ears all too soon. She took one last sip of the apple cider she had been drinking and returned it to her nightstand. As she stretched out in bed, she winced at the pains that shot through her body. She closed her eyes and hoped that sleep would take her quickly. It did.

Unfortunately, sleep would not hold her in its arms for very long. Afton was startled awake by a noise and movement … movement that was coming from within her room.

She felt like she was in a nightmare and her body was weighted down. Her brain told her to slide to the edge of the bed, but her arms and legs were heavy and sluggish. Finally, inch by inch, she worked her way to the side. Her left leg teetered on the edge before it fell and her foot touched the floor. She pulled on her other leg, but getting her body to cooperate seemed nearly impossible. She struggled to keep her balance as she sat up on the side of the bed. She couldn't focus in the darkness, but she could sense the presence of another person.

A voice came from across the room. "Just stay where you are, Afton. You are much too unsteady to get up."

"Who are you?" she managed to say. "What do you want?"

Afton had tried to sound clear and alert, but what came from her mouth was thick and garbled. The sounds she made reminded her of a person drifting under anesthesia or a dying person whispering their final words. She suddenly realized just how dire her situation could be. She made a last-ditch effort to stand, and as she did, her arm flailed wildly and hit the juice glass. The glass seemed to float to the floor like a feather before crashing. The remaining juice splashed against her legs. Immediately, she wondered about the juice itself. Had it tasted different? Had there been an aftertaste that made her think it was rather bitter?

The voice came again. "I can see you're trying to piece things together. You're wondering how someone could have put something in your cider without your knowledge. It was easy enough, Afton. Now, what you are going to do for me is easy. You simply need to listen."

The room seemed to slosh about like a waterbed. Afton was too weak to stand. Did the voice belong to Dechtire? It sounded much deeper and filled with venom. There wasn't another choice for her, not yet. She did as instructed and listened.

The voice started again. "I am going to tell you a story about a girl who, for many years, asked herself a question: Why do some people choose not to tell?"

Without thinking, she interrupted the speaker, who she was now pretty certain was Dechtire Massey. "Why are you telling me this?"

"Shut up and listen!" she responded. "No more interruptions." The intruder paused for a moment, then continued. "After a couple of decades, I figured out the answer to that burning question. People don't tell because they are weaklings and they don't have what it takes to do what's necessary. If you never tell, you're doomed to spend the rest of your life getting screwed in one form or another. That is, unless you decide to take things into your own hands. That's what I did, Afton. I took care of every person who ever hurt me. It was quite a long process.

"I was raised in a family where I did not belong. I knew this from as far back as I can remember. I was nothing like them. Thoughts of them still make me quiver. Quiver? You may ask. Not with fear, but with sheer hatred. Have you ever hated so fully that the mere thought of someone makes you quiver? I doubt if you have. You seem to have it all together. Everyone says so. They all say Afton is the most skilled nurse they've ever worked with." Dechtire grew quiet, as though making sure that Afton was listening to every word. Then she resumed with her story. "From the outside, my so-called family appeared to have it all together too. There was the hardworking dad, devoted mom, three girls, and one precious boy. However, inside the walls of that home, it was a totally different story. The devoted mom resented keeping me. She wanted to give me up because she finally had the golden son that the dad desired. The dad, well, he molested me when I was eight years old. The two sisters used to beat on me and the brother tried to rape me when I was twelve.

"I remember that day like it was yesterday. It was a warm summer day and I was alone in the barn with my fourteen-year-old brother. That was the day I took control. He had lured me to the barn by telling me he had something he wanted to show me. It was something special he had been working on. Once he got me into his workshop, he locked the door and proceeded to try and rape me. A brother trying to rape his little sister. Can you imagine? No, I doubt you could. I saw it as an opportunity and I seized it. I grabbed a ball-peen hammer off a workbench, and with all my strength, slammed it down on his left temple."

"I don't want to hear any more." Afton's mouth was dry as cotton.

Dechtire went on with her story despite her protests. "You might wonder how I got away with it. Well, I'll tell you. I placed his body right below the five-hundred-pound anvil and smeared his blood on the edge of it. I cleaned the hammer, then went to the house to wash and dry my clothes. I cleaned myself up and put my outfit back on. Then I waited for the rest of the family to return. It was easy-peasy. They came home to find their pride and joy dead in the barn. It was ruled an accident. They assumed he had tripped over one of his tools and landed on the anvil. It was just a case of bad luck. Poor Mom and Dad would never get over it. As for the sisters, I had plans for them, too, but that would come later. You see, Afton, once I killed my so-called brother, I learned about who I really was. I had to kill someone before it was revealed to me. I had heard the stories of the half-bloods in the Appalachian Mountains of West Virginia. That's why I didn't resemble the rest of the family.

I wasn't even related to them. All the stories said that a female couldn't be a skinwalker … that is, unless she had taken a life."

"What does any of this mean? Dechtire, exactly what do you want from me?"

Dechtire was fuming. "Who do I belong to, Afton? Is that a secret you carry? Did you learn anything about me when you traveled to Robinson Holler? I know one thing for sure, there's a midwife there who knows all the secrets. Before the woman who raised me died, she told me that the only reason she didn't give me up was because a mountain midwife had told her I was going to be special and she needed to keep me. McDowell County, West Virginia. Bit of a coincidence that Joetta was from there, too, don't you agree? I went through your personnel file trying to find out all I could about you. It seems you've always lived in Clay County. There are not very many people who only have one address all their life. I just couldn't figure out why you felt the need to go clear to McDowell County. It's over a three-hour drive from here. And for what? To attend a funeral for an old nurse that you hardly knew? According to everyone you work with, you keep your distance and never get close to anyone. So, why now?"

Was Dechtire finished talking? The room filled with a very loud silence. Silence that made Afton's head hurt worse. Everything she had told her was swishing around inside her head like the old wringer washer Grandma Ruby had used for decades. Dear Lord, how she longed for Grandma Ruby to talk to her right at that moment. She would tell her what to do or what to say. Afton closed her eyes and pictured herself rocking slowly in Grandma's thinkin' chair. She thought of the meeting with the new warden, Clayton Tolley from Monkey's Eyebrow, Kentucky, and remembered the conversation he'd had with her without speaking a word. Phillip had referred to him as a "silent talker." Strangely, she could see his face in that instant. His eyes seemed to plead with her, as though telling her that help was on the way.

Dechtire broke through her thoughts. "Afton, are you still among the living?"

So, she was still there, just sitting and waiting. Was she waiting for Afton to come out from under whatever she had spiked her cider with? She found herself wondering exactly how long this had been going on? Had she been in and out of consciousness for hours, or had it been days?

In Robinson Holler, Silas was up and dressed and frantically shaking Phillip awake. Phillip's feet had yet to hit the floor when the phone started ringing. He tried hushing Silas so he could answer the phone.

Silas kept repeating, "Afton. We have to go help Afton."

Phillip reached the phone and pressed the receiver to his ear. "Afton, are you okay?"

"Phillip, this is Clayton Tolley. I believe Afton is in some trouble. I can hear her in my head. She's calling for help."

"We're on our way, Clayton!" Phillip shouted. "Thanks for the warning."

"No, Phillip, wait," Clayton told him. "I'm on my way to her house now. Let me go and check things out. I could be wrong. Give me two hours and I'll call you back."

"Perhaps I overdid it with the valerian root in your cider, Afton," mused Dechtire. "Try to focus and listen. I'm not through with the story of my young life."

Afton could only sit, stone still, on the edge of her bed. She had no choice but to listen to the woman's sordid tale.

"Let's see … I told you how I killed big brother when I was twelve. I'll move on now to dear old Dad. He never was quite right after brother John's terrible accident. I thought it best to put him out of his misery. I was fourteen by this time, and I was feeling my oats—being in the midst of puberty and all. It didn't take much, with Dad being so depressed. I just gave him the look one day, and he followed me around like a puppy. He followed me straight into his bedroom. I really gave him the look then. Thought my eyes were going to burn a hole right through him, but instead he had a massive heart attack and keeled over right in front of me. I guess he wouldn't be molesting another child, would he?"

There was a pause in Dechtire's monologue, and Afton could sense that she was irritated with her drifting in and out. "Perhaps I need to speed things up a bit for you, Afton. You look a little bored. I suppose if I inflicted a little pain, that would bring you back to reality. Let's see, I think this will do nicely. I'll just heat up my raven pendant and let it leave its mark on you."

Afton heard her striking a match, then sensed the room getting lighter. She had lit a candle. Was she now heating the pendant as she had threatened? She would get her answer to that soon enough.

"Okay, my dear, this is going to smart just a bit," Dechtire explained. There was an edge of cruelty to her voice. "Well, who am I kidding? It's going to hurt like hell."

She laughed like a lunatic and placed the red-hot raven pendant on the inner part of Afton's left forearm, weighing it down with something heavy so it would sink deeply into her skin. The pain that followed felt like molten lava eating through her flesh. Her own screams cleared the cobwebs in her head and brought her back to horrible reality. Those same screams then took her back to when she was only six years old.

Afton was walking along the path from Grandma Ruby's to her house. She was hand in hand with Grandma, without a care in the world. It was her sixth birthday, and the day was so bright and beautiful. She knew Mom was going to surprise her with a birthday cake and a new dress she had made especially for her. They saw the smoke just before they topped the ridge. The smoke rolled in billowing clouds of blackness like nothing she had ever seen before, and, in a strange way, those dark clouds would continue to loom over her throughout her entire life.

Her heart sank. Grandma Ruby squeezed Afton's hand tight, and they ran together toward the cabin. They got no closer than fifteen feet from her home before the heat beat against their faces and pushed them back. Afton broke free from Grandma's grip and sprinted toward the cabin door. She had to try to save Mama and Daddy! The door gave way without much resistance from her tiny body. She was engulfed by a cloud of ash so thick it was difficult to move forward. She screamed for her parents, but no one answered. She lost her sense of direction and could not find her way back to the door. Nearly overcome by smoke, she dropped to the cabin floor on all fours and tried to feel her way out. A beam from the low ceiling gave way, swung down against her side, and flipped her over on her back—then the beam landed on her chest and trapped her. That molten hot lava feeling burnt across her upper torso. Next thing she knew, she had been dragged outside and was gasping for air. That's how her chest had been so severely scarred. She had lived with those scars for four decades before finally having surgery.

Afton remembered how the inmates had glared at her when she returned to work. They had the look of predators leering at their next child victim. She had stopped a couple of them already. No, that was something Dechtire would do. Afton was there when they were dying, and she allowed them to see the pain they had caused. That was her only part in their deaths. She was not like Dechtire. The dark-haired woman was evil and out for vengeance. Now her sights were set on her.

Abruptly, Dechtire was shaking her. "Finally! Really, Afton, you were beginning to worry me." She laughed wickedly. "I hope you like ravens because that's going to leave a nasty mark. Maybe you're more into wolves. Take Inmate Whelan, for example. He smells like a stinking animal. He was determined to keep you out of harm's way. Whelan's out of the picture now, though, isn't he?"

Afton moaned. The flesh of her forearm stung where Dechtire had branded her.

"Enough small talk," said Dechtire. "Tell me about your trip to McDowell County. Did anything interesting happen? Perhaps you met some interesting people? I'm really anxious to learn about a particular mountain midwife. Tell me the truth, Afton. Was there an old midwife there?"

Although the pain in her arm was intense, Afton's senses had finally cleared enough that she could answer without slurring her words. "Dechtire, there were many people there, all of them strangers. I barely knew Joetta. I've lived in Clay County for as long as I can remember. I simply went to pay my respects to a co-worker who happened to be an excellent nurse. This old midwife you're looking for has probably long since passed away. That's it. That's the whole story of my trip to McDowell County. So, could you please stop this torture and leave me alone?"

Someone else was now in her small home, someone good. Afton closed her eyes and tried to focus through the burning pain. She could hear a voice—so faint it sounded miles away, but she knew he was close. She knew it was a male. It had to be Warden Tolley.

He was there to help her. He was talking to her, but not out loud. *Afton, did Ruby make you a special quilt? It would be a large one, and each square would be different.*

She tried her best to form the answer in her head. *Yes, Clayton, it's in the cedar trunk in the living room.*

Clayton's voice told her what she must do. *Afton, do your best to keep Dechtire talking so I can get closer.*

Her arm throbbed from the burn and her head was still full of fuzz. Was she really hearing Clayton Tolley's voice in her mind? She could only hope so as she asked Dechtire if she could tell her more about the midwife.

The woman seemed eager to oblige. "One thing is for sure. If she did take me from my true parents, she'll have hell to pay. I grew up in the little-known town called War. Do you know how close that is to Robinson Holler? It's only an hour away. It sickens me to think that I could have seen my real mother and father in the grocery store or at a gas station and never had a clue. The midwife had no right. She must be punished."

Once again, she heard Clayton Tolley's voice. She closed her eyes tightly, focusing on the words that echoed in her head. *Afton, I'm here now, and I need you to do as I tell you. I need you to be quiet and still, no matter what you hear. I'll let you know when it's safe.*

Afton heard a scream, followed by the sound of a body falling to the floor. A shrill cry rang out, like an injured animal … an unnerving cross between a wildcat and a rabbit being skinned alive. Her tiny bedroom was full of chaos; a chaos that seemed to go on forever but probably lasted only a few seconds.

Daylight was now peeking through the shade and curtains. She could make out Clayton's face. He was standing near the foot of her bed, looking down at the floor. Afton's eyes followed his. She saw Grandma Ruby's quilt in a heap on the floor and there was someone or something writhing beneath it.

Without speaking a word, Clayton told her to go into another room. She did as she was told, sliding out of bed and carefully walking across the room. Her body was still unsteady from the effects of the tainted juice. Once she reached the doorway, she glanced back just in time to see Clayton lift the heavy quilt. She couldn't believe her eyes. There was a large, black raven flapping around on the floor. It staggered and its wings were crumpled a bit, but it managed to take flight. The bird circled the bedroom twice, picked up speed, and crashed through her bedroom window like it wasn't even there.

There was no sign of Dechtire. Could the raven and Dechtire be one and the same?

Clayton took Afton's arm to steady her and led her to the kitchen. He sat her down at the table and poured her a glass of water from the tap. Afton's hands shook uncontrollably as she brought the glass to her lips. It was the best drink of water she had ever tasted. She didn't stop until the glass was bone dry.

When he knew she was steady, Clayton spoke again, but in his physical voice. "Afton, I need to call Phillip to let him know that you're going to be okay."

She pointed toward the phone and he quickly dialed the number. Phillip must have been waiting for the call, because he answered before the first ring could finish. Their conversation went back and forth for several minutes about what had taken place and how she was holding up. She heard Clayton tell Phillip that "she will be on her way soon." Then they said their goodbyes.

On her way soon, she thought. That was easy enough to figure out. She was being sent back to Robinson Holler for safekeeping. Afton guessed that would be for the best, since she wasn't doing so well on her own.

"Clayton, exactly how long did this ordeal go on?" she said, feeling her strength beginning to return. "I was so drugged up, I couldn't grasp how much time had gone by."

"Well, Afton, as far as I can tell, it's been about eight hours."

"Also, how did you know about the quilt that Grandma Ruby made for me?"

"My grandmother and I knew Ruby for many years," Clayton told her. "Most people like your grandmother kept a special quilt that showed the family history. Her quilt holds one extra quality. Legend has it that the quilt blankets the family with protection for generations to help keep them safe. This was accomplished through the prayers that were said as the quilt was sewn."

"I know I should be surprised, but I think I'm beyond that now. Exactly how did you and your grandmother know Ruby?"

Clayton patiently continued to answer her questions. "Actually, Ruby was in need of a dependable car for a very special young lady. That's what brought us together. I held the title to such a car."

Afton was surprised. "Clayton, are you telling me that my car, Hazel, used to belong to you?"

Clayton smiled and his entire face beamed. "Hazel, huh? When she was mine, I called her Haze. That's the name of the paint, but I guess you already knew that."

"Yes, I knew about the paint color. Please, tell me the rest of the story."

"Twenty-nine years ago, I came to the Village of McKinley with my grandmother," he went on. "She had business with your Grandma Ruby. You see, Ruby was looking to buy a car for you to get back and forth to nursing school. My grandmother was in need of a special quilt to send with her grandson while he was away at college. My grandmother brought the quilt pieces and our two grandmas sewed them together and prayed over each square for my safety while away from home. I couldn't take my car to college, so you got it in return. That car received many special prayers as well. This may surprise you, but Nola May is my cousin. She's the one who originally brought the two families together."

"Nola May is your kin? Did she tell you about the warden position that was open?"

"Joetta told Nola May, then she sent word to me about the job and about the situation."

Clayton tried his best to make her understand. In turn, Afton tried her best to absorb it all. Together, they prepared breakfast and sat in silence as they ate. She kept her mind as quiet as possible, wondering if Clayton was listening to her thoughts. Breakfast fueled her weakened body and restored some of her energy. She knew she had the long drive back to Robinson Holler ahead of her, but she didn't know when Clayton and Phillip planned on her leaving. She hoped for a little rest before that took place.

Clayton had stopped eating and was staring at her.

"I'm afraid you won't have much time to rest, Afton," he said.

He had been listening in that special way, after all.

"What about work? I have four weeks of vacation I can use, but I would have to give George some notice so he can get coverage for my shifts."

"Don't worry about George or your coverage. You went through a traumatic experience at the prison yesterday, not to mention what you went through all night with Dechtire."

She didn't have the heart to argue with him. "Clayton, do you believe that Dechtire is a skinwalker? Did she actually change into a raven under that quilt?"

"I don't know exactly what to make of it all," he admitted, "but I do know you need to go back to Robinson Holler for a while until this is over. Dechtire may have the ability to change … but then again, she may just be good at trickery."

Thoughts of the raven gave Afton chills as she began to gather a few of her things—just as she had done several days before. She showered and dressed. She applied aloe to her forearm, covered it with sterile gauze, and taped it into place. She was certain that Nola May and Maddie would have their own way of doctoring the wound when she returned to Robinson Holler.

When she walked into the kitchen with her bag, as ready as she was going to be, she found Clayton hanging up the phone. He assured her that everything had been taken care of with George and her long vacation. They closed up the house, and he walked her to her car. It seemed strange that the car had once belonged to him, so far away in Monkey's Eyebrow. Afton asked what he was going to do about Dechtire, when and if she came to work. He told her he would deal with her and left it at that.

As she drove off toward Robinson Holler, she had a familiar sense of excitement in the pit of her stomach. She couldn't wait to get "back home."

The drive seemed different from the time before, and she continually saw flashes of Clayton in her mind. She couldn't help but worry about him. What wrath would Dechtire unleash on him for coming to her rescue? She told herself it wasn't possible that she was a skinwalker. Surely it had been just a smoke screen of tricks to make the raven appear under Grandma Ruby's quilt.

A shiver ran down her spine that told her otherwise.

CHAPTER 12: GRAVEYARD DUST

Back at the prison, George and Clayton finished up the paperwork for Afton's four weeks off. They were unaware that Dechtire had shown up for work.

She had her own agenda, and it didn't include doing her job. She was busy in the pharmacy searching for the foot powder that the inmates were prescribed for athlete's foot. Once she found what she was looking for, she pulled an envelope out of her pocket. It contained a white powder. She added it to the almost empty container of foot powder, then placed it where she needed it to be.

George and Clayton left the office and headed toward Medical. They stopped by the officer's desk to check the transfer report and to see if the last of the ten inmates had been shipped out. Dechtire heard their voices. She knew she would need luck on her side if she expected to get Clayton alone. The two men entered the medical unit and immediately noticed Dechtire in the pharmacy. She waited until they were close, then announced that she thought Dr. Gray needed to speak to George. George excused himself and was on his way. Now she had her chance.

Clayton stood in the pharmacy doorway. Dechtire acted as if nothing unusual was going on.

"Oh, Warden Tolley," she said absently, "would you mind handing me that foot powder? Someone stuck it way up there on that shelf and it's out of my reach."

Clayton studied her for a moment, then finally nodded. "Certainly, Miss Massey."

Dechtire smiled inwardly as the big man made his way across the room. She had secretly loosened the lid to the point that it barely sat on the bottle.

Clayton Tolley easily reached the container, and as he started to pull it down, Dechtire bumped his elbow, causing the powder inside to spill. It created a dust cloud that filled the tiny pharmacy. Dechtire was already holding her breath as she stepped past the warden and out of the room.

Clayton gasped, causing a hefty dose to be inhaled into his lungs. Dechtire just stood by and watched as he collapsed and passed out.

"Strange," muttered George as he walked back into the pharmacy. "Dr. Gray didn't need me after all." Suddenly, he saw the warden on the floor, and also saw Dechtire standing there with her hands on her hips. "What happened?"

Dechtire smiled thinly. "Oh, I think he breathed in a little foot powder."

"And you're just standing here, doing nothing. It had to have been a massive amount to knock him unconscious," George scolded.

Dechtire simply watched as he started working on the warden. Smelling salts finally brought him back around. George and a guard helped him walk out of the prison to breathe in some fresh air. Once outside, George told Clayton that he just couldn't understand Dechtire's behavior.

"What are you talking about? How does Dechtire play into what just happened?"

George explained, "Dechtire was just standing there. I got the strangest feeling; she had no intentions of helping you. I'm going to have to write her up, or maybe fire her."

Clayton continued to cough. He couldn't remember anything which led to his collapse. Even in the fresh air, he could hardly breathe. But he already suspected that what he had inhaled had not been foot powder. He had heard stories of skinwalkers using graveyard dust to harm their enemies, and the effect depended on how much of the dust was inhaled. If one's lungs took in enough, the result could be fatal.

Afton was more than halfway back to Robinson Holler when the overwhelming feeling that something bad was about to happen came over her. She pulled Hazel over to the side of the road. Suddenly, her chest felt heavy. It was an effort to even breathe. She looked through the windshield and saw dark rain clouds passing over. It felt as if one of those heavy clouds was pushing in on her, causing their darkness to fill the car.

Darkness. It was one of those things she'd had a love/hate relationship with for a very long time. Dusk often brought with it intense anxiety that increased as the sun slipped behind the mountains. Shadows would dance through the backwoods, across the yard, and into the house. Afton would fight sleep until it almost had her in its arms, and then and only then would she let go. She would surrender herself to the darkness only at that point in hopes that dreams would soon follow. If she was lucky, there would be dreams of Grandma Ruby and the way things used to be. Sometimes there would be dreams of what was to come, and those were not always so pleasant. Now she found herself somewhere in between. She sat alone in the darkness of the car, waiting for the clouds to pass.

Then the unspoken voice came—Clayton's voice.

Afton, I believe I have got myself into a bit of a situation. Dechtire did come to work today. I'm pretty sure she let loose some graveyard dust on me. I don't know how much I inhaled, but it was enough to put a hurtin' on me. Maddie and Nola May should know what can be done for me, if anything.

The cloud lifted and Clayton's voice faded away. She checked her phone, but she had no cell service. Soon, she was back on the road, in a hurry and with a renewed focus.

George had returned to the medical unit, but Clayton remained outside a bit longer. He needed the fresh air, and he had a decision to make as well. Should he send Dechtire on her way before she could finish him off or anyone else that she felt threatened by? He knew for sure that George suspected she was a bad nurse, but he didn't realize she was rotten to the core.

Clayton noticed three inmates on cleanup detail just beyond the fence surrounding the visitation building and the outdoor employee break area. A big wind had come through the previous week, and limbs were still being cleared from it. Clayton sometimes overheard the thoughts of others even when he wasn't trying, and he knew for a fact that one of the three inmates had a joint in his pocket. Now he needed to focus and figure out which inmate was holding.

One inmate stopped and wiped his brow with the back of his hand. Clayton heard his thoughts as the inmate sighed and looked at the big pile of brush ahead of him. *I can't wait to get on the other side of this brush pile so I can fire up this weed.*

Clayton stared at the inmate and focused his silent-talking on him. He told the inmate to tell the guard he needed a bathroom break. The inmate immediately called out to the guard and told him that he couldn't hold it any longer and had to go to the bathroom. The guard radioed ahead and informed Control that Inmate Brown was en route for a bathroom break. As the inmate walked toward the building, Clayton silently told him what to do next. The inmate would blindly follow the phantom instructions without knowing why.

Dechtire was in Medical. She knew it wouldn't be long before the inmates were lining up for pill call. She checked the pharmacy one last time to make sure everything was ready. When she looked up, there stood Inmate Brown.

"What do you want, Brown?" she asked, a little annoyed.

"I feel like my blood sugar's getting too low," the man told her.

Dechtire glanced out the door to make sure there was an officer at the desk. She told Brown to sit down so she could check his sugar. He staggered a bit. She reached out to steady him into the chair. Brown's blood sugar was fine. He must be trying to get out of work detail, Dechtire thought.

She walked over and took a small carton of orange juice from a refrigerator in the corner. "Here, drink this."

Brown drank the juice and then quickly stood up and said, "I feel fine now. Can I go back to work?"

Dechtire looked at him. She didn't know what to make of his sudden interest in returning to his job. She was aggravated about the interruption, but glad he was so eager to leave the medical unit.

"Sure, go ahead," she said.

It was time to start pill call. Dechtire looked at the clock on the wall and wondered why the officer hadn't called for the inmates to line up yet. She grew impatient. She was about to call Control to ask what the hold-up was when George, Clayton, and the female shift lieutenant, Jones, entered Medical and closed the door behind them.

"Dechtire, we have to search you," the warden told her sternly. "As you know, we have every right to do so if we suspect any person may be in possession of contraband while on prison grounds. You should know this because you signed that agreement when you were hired."

Dechtire glared at Warden Tolley with disgust. "I don't have a thing to hide, so go right ahead and search away."

Lieutenant Jones began by having Dechtire step out of her obsessively polished Dansko clogs. The next step was to search the many pockets of Dechtire's sharply creased scrubs. Jones pulled a rolled cigarette out of Dechtire's right front pocket. She held it below her nose and sniffed. It definitely smelled like cannabis.

Dechtire's mouth dropped open in astonishment. "What the hell is this?" she snapped. "One of the inmates must have planted this on me!" She looked at the warden, then at George. "Or maybe it was it one of you!"

George answered, "You know the rules, Dechtire. If you have a drug problem and come to us, we're happy to get you the help you need, but if we find drugs on you, that's it. We have to let you go. Lieutenant Jones will stay while you gather your belongings and bring you down to Control. You will then be escorted from the premises, and you will not be allowed to return."

Dechtire glared at Clayton with sheer hatred, and he heard her thoughts loud and clear. *You son of a bitch! You're going to suffer a very painful death once that dust takes hold of you.*

George and Warden Tolley left Medical and went to George's office to do the paperwork. George told Clayton that he'd known something was going on with Dechtire, but he was surprised that it had been drugs. Clayton agreed with George, but his mind was already questioning if he had done the right thing.

What if Dechtire ran straight to Robinson Holler? He would head that way after work if he could keep himself together that long. He was feeling worse by the hour and knew he needed Nola May and Maddie's help.

Hazel glided along the crooked mountain roads with ease as Afton drew nearer to her Robinson Holler family. The radio was playing "Bad Moon Rising" by Creedence Clearwater Revival. It was one of Afton's favorite songs, but that afternoon it blared through the car's speakers like a dark omen.

"It seems to be taking longer to get back home this time, Hazel," she said out loud. "Maybe it's my desperation to see everyone. Since Grandma Ruby went to heaven, I never thought I would be part of a family again. I found out that my dad's mom is alive and well, but I can't seem to fully embrace Maddie O'Sullican yet. Maybe I'm not over the fact that I've been so alone and she knew it. She could have reached out to me. I feel more at ease with Nola May than my own grandmother." A moment later, she saw her destination in sight. "Finally. We're here, Hazel. You got us here safely once again."

Silas stood on the porch of Miss Betty's home and could feel that Afton was near.

He couldn't wait to see her again. Maddie, Nola May, and Phillip had all received Clayton's silent message, and they worked quickly to gather the things that would be needed to cleanse him of the graveyard dust that was coursing through his veins like snake venom. At the sight of the haze green car, Silas leapt off the porch and ran down the dirt drive.

Afton couldn't get Hazel parked fast enough. She jumped out and ran to her precious Silas. She gathered him into her arms and held him close so she could breathe him in. He smelled of the outdoors, like pine needles, smoke from the cedar logs in the wood-burning cookstove, and the homemade goat's milk soap that Miss Betty had made. Apparently, Phillip had made him take a bath before her arrival.

"Afton, I was so worried about you," Silas said.

Suddenly, she was aware of how concerned he had been. He was trembling in her arms, and she knew it wasn't from the chill in the air that surrounded them.

"Silas, I'm here now. That's what matters. Promise you'll try not to worry so much."

The boy looked into her eyes for a few seconds before answering. "I'll do my best, Afton, but sometimes I know before trouble is coming, and I just can't stop the worries."

Afton took him by the hand and, together, they walked to the cabin to greet the others.

Clayton grabbed his chest. The pains were getting much worse. He had only been on the road a short time, but the sun had slipped behind dark clouds and nighttime seemed to be coming earlier than usual. He had hoped to be able to drive straight to Robinson Holler, but if he got any weaker, he would have to stop for a while. Such a break could possibly cost him his life, but he knew he couldn't risk wrecking his truck and causing injury to anyone else.

Maddie and Nola May worked diligently at the cookstove, adding this herb and that to the concoction that simmered in the pot. Phillip was unloading an armload of kindling when they walked in. The three of them stopped what they were doing to welcome Afton back. Their attention was drawn to the bandage on her forearm. Flames from the stove flickered in Phillip's eyes, making them appear to be on fire. She knew he would be angry that Dechtire had hurt her.

Maddie spoke first. "Afton, we best take a look at your arm so we know what we're dealing with."

Silas took her bags to the room she had stayed in only a day or so ago. Before she could sit down at the table, Nola May gave her a big hug and told her she was relieved that she was back. Phillip remained silent, which was best because she knew if he had talked just then, he would only have ranted about how she shouldn't have gone back in the first place. And Afton didn't need to hear what she already knew to be true.

Maddie started removing the dressing from her arm while she told how she had cleaned the burn and put gel from the aloe plant on it. She pulled back the last bit of gauze and gasped at the sight. Nola May dropped the glass of water she had just poured for me.

Phillip suddenly found his voice. "What the hell did she do to you, Afton?"

She tried to hush him so Silas wouldn't hear the commotion. Afton looked down at her arm and her mouth dropped open. What had once been red, swollen, and blistered was now black, charred skin in the perfect shape of a raven in flight. Concerned, she looked up at Maddie and Nola May. "Can you do anything for it?"

"That mark will be permanent if Dechtire is a true skinwalker," Phillip said bluntly. Then he turned away sullenly and said no more.

Clayton was only twenty miles from Robinson Holler when he could drive no farther. He pulled over and managed to put the truck in Park. He collapsed on the truck's bench seat, then drifted in and out of a feverish sleep. Thoughts of his grandmother came to him in waves. His grandmother's name was Cordelia Rose Tolley, and Clayton had always called her Mommy Bud.

Mommy Bud called out to Clayton now, and he called back, "Mommy Bud, I can't go on this way. Help me."

"My gentle Clayton," she murmured, "you are stronger than you think. You will get through this and live a long life that is full of purpose. Remember all that you have overcome."

Then her voice faded like a puff of smoke in the wind. Clayton's mind drifted, and he felt he needed to tell his story, despite the fact that he was alone. He wasn't sure why. Perhaps he hoped Afton would somehow hear him.

Although weak, he spoke out loud. "Mommy Bud raised me from birth because my parents wanted nothing to do with me. When Cordelia Rose was a very young woman, she didn't live in Monkey's Eyebrow, Kentucky. She lived near Louisville. She was a stunning young woman with long blond hair, ivory skin, and beautiful hazel eyes. Her family had a mountain farm of about two hundred acres. One day, a fire broke out on the top of the mountain. Men were brought in by the truckload to fight the fire, and they had to pass through the family's farm to get to the logging roads that would allow access to the fire. One of the trucks brought a load of men, both black and white. After the men worked for twelve to sixteen hours fighting the fire, Cordelia Rose's family would provide a meal for them. A black man by the name of Webb Moseby struck up a friendship with my white grandmother, and they soon fell in love. Slavery had ended, but there were no interracial marriages in that community. Webb deserted Cordelia Rose when he found out she was with child. He knew he would be strung up if anyone discovered that he was the father."

Clayton paused and coughed fitfully before continuing. "Cordelia Rose was devastated by Webb's departure, but she knew his concerns were a real possibility. She went on with life and had the baby. It was a boy, but he looked nothing like Webb. The baby boy looked white. She had never told her parents who the father was, so when the baby arrived with a fair complexion, she kept the father's identity a secret. Cordelia felt the boy's life would be easier as a white child. She named him Ben, and he had a happy childhood on the farm. He grew up as a white man and married a white woman from the city. Her name was Patsy.

"Ben and Patsy were delighted when they discovered they were expecting a baby. When it was near the time for Patsy to give birth, Cordelia took the young couple to Miss Betty in West Virginia. Miss Betty delivered a healthy baby boy. That baby boy was me. Ben and Patsy were in shock when they saw that the baby was black. Ben accused Patsy of having an affair, but she denied it vehemently. Ben asked his mom, Cordelia Rose, what she thought of their situation, and she told him the truth. Patsy was horrified at the thought of her wealthy family finding out that Ben had a black father, so they told them the baby had died at birth.

"Cordelia Rose—Mommy Bud—took me and moved to Monkey's Eyebrow. We were welcomed into the small community, and she raised me as she would her own. She was honest with me from the beginning. She said that the minute she laid eyes on me, she knew I was special—that she knew it even before I was born, and that was why she wanted Miss Betty to help with the delivery. My grandfather, Webb Moseby, had been a dowser, and Miss Betty knew early on that I held that gift and more. Mommy Bud kept in touch with Webb's cousin, Nola May, hoping to learn what had become of Webb. He seemed to have vanished without a trace. She remained pen pals with Nola May and the people of Robinson Holler, and we visited them a few times. As for Ben and Patsy, we never saw them again after my birth. It broke Mommy Bud's heart that her own son could be so cruel, but she focused her energy on raising me."

Chapter 13: Locomotive

"Phillip, do you actually believe there's a chance that Dechtire could be a skinwalker?"

Afton's question came out a little louder than she had intended. Before Phillip could reply, Silas came running into the room. Maddie didn't have her arm completely covered, and Silas saw what Dechtire had done to her. Tears poured from his big blue eyes as he hugged her tight, as if he was never going to let go.

"Okay, we have to focus on what needs to be done," said Nola May. "Maddie, you tend to Afton's arm. Phillip, you can help me finish with the bear gallbladder, and Silas, you had better hold Afton's hand. She needs you to be strong for her right now. Can you do that for her?"

"Yes, ma'am," answered Silas.

Afton was puzzled. "Nola May, did I hear you correctly? Did you say a gallbladder?"

"Yes, you heard right. The gallbladder of a bear is the only thing that might save Clayton. I've had it dryin' for some time now. Must've known this day would come, eventually. Now we're soakin' it in our mountain herbs to prepare it for consumption. It will pull the toxins from Clayton's bloodstream and hopefully ease the awful pain that's bound to be deep in his muscles by now."

Afton couldn't believe her ears, but then why should anything surprise her at this point? "Have you done this before?" she asked.

Nola May's face was grim. "No."

Maddie gathered what she needed to prepare a poultice for Afton's arm. She sat quietly with Silas holding her right hand as her grandmother applied the poultice to the charred skin. Eventually, the raven was completely covered by the thick mixture. She could only hope that it would help. Afton was more worried about what Clayton was going through and if he would make it there in time. Maddie was just wrapping her arm when she noticed the cooling effect that the poultice had on her skin. It was such a relief.

"Thank you, Maddie."

Maddie looked into her eyes, which mirrored her own. "You are so welcome, my child. I'm glad you're here. I do wish it was under better circumstances."

Graham and Dalton, Silas's pet mice, scurried across the floor and up his body onto his shoulder. They stood on their tiny hind legs and started squeaking. It was as though they were telling Silas something urgent. He gently removed them from his shoulder and placed them into the chest pocket of his bib overalls.

Silas turned to the rest of them. "I believe Warden Tolley is close," he said. "I'm going to go and check."

"Stay close," Phillip told him.

Silas threw up a hand and gave a quick wave goodbye as he slipped out the door.

The cabin was filled with the aromas of different herbs and an undeniable smell of what had to be the bear organ. It was enough to make her a bit nauseous.

"Here, Afton, sit back down and drink this black tea," said Maddie, slipping a china cup into her hand. "It will ease your stomach."

Afton apparently looked as green as she felt. She started sipping the strong tea and felt thankful to have that time with her grandmother Maddie, even under such strained circumstances.

"Maddie, why was my last name changed to Sullivan?"

"Sullivan is a version of O'Sullican. When Ora and Ida died in the fire, we thought it best to change your name for your move with Ruby."

A horn started blaring outside. They all ran to see what was going on. Silas let off the horn and frantically waved them to the truck now parked at the end of the lane. Warden Clayton Tolley was slumped over in the middle of the seat. Phillip got in and drove the truck up to the cabin. They all but carried Clayton inside and laid him across the bed.

"Help me!" Clayton cried out feebly. "I have to get to Robinson Holler!"

Nola May tried to comfort her cousin. She told him that he was already there and she would take good care of him. Clayton's lips were swollen and cracked, and his breathing was extremely shallow. Afton could hear the death rattle in his lungs with each breath he managed to take. She knew from experience that congestive heart failure was taking hold. Would the bear bladder be able to pull the toxins out of his bloodstream and away from his heart?

Maddie had her mix up some Epsom salts, baking soda, and lemongrass, along with other herbs she didn't recognize. She told Afton to put them in a warm bath. Nola May had undressed Clayton down to his skivvies. Somehow, Phillip was able to pick the big man up, carry him to the tub, and gently lay him down in the water. They left Nola May to bathe him, and as she did, they heard her begin to pray.

Afton sat at the kitchen table with Phillip and Silas while Maddie put the finishing touches on the bear bladder. The organ was now rehydrated from the oils and herbs. It was ready for consumption. She asked Maddie about the ingredients that she had put in the bath water, and she told her that they would begin the detoxifying process and prepare Clayton's body for the next step.

Once Clayton had soaked for a good hour, Phillip helped Nola May dry him off and get him back to the bed. Mounds of goose down pillows were stacked at the head of the bed, as his head and chest needed to be elevated so that he could be fed some of the gallbladder. Maddie had prepared a few strips of bladder into slices as thin as prosciutto. Nola May explained that it would be a process of feeding him small amounts every three hours for the next several days.

Lying there on the bed, Clayton looked inflated like a carnival balloon. He was terribly swollen from his face down to his ankles. Afton used a stethoscope from a medical bag she always kept in Hazel and carefully listened to his heart and lungs. The crackles were nearly audible without even using the stethoscope. It sounded like someone walking on bubble wrap. His heart was pounding rapidly as it worked overtime to rid his body of the excess fluid.

Clayton moaned. "Mommy Bud, is that you I hear?"

Nola May was quick to his side. "Clayton, dear, it's me, your cousin Nola May. I'm gonna take care of you. Maddie and I have what you need to get through this. You just need to listen to us and do what we ask."

Clayton managed to give a slight nod of understanding. Maddie brought in the first dish of gallbladder. Nola May took the dish from her and started to feed Clayton. It was a slow process, but Clayton took it in and, most importantly, kept it down. Now all they could do was wait.

Dechtire's apartment was on a horse farm about a fifteen-minute drive from the prison. She occupied the space above the barn, which at one time had been used as an office. The farm had long since seen its heyday, so she had the barn to herself except for two thoroughbreds the owner could not allow himself to part with. The horses had belonged to his wife and daughter. The wife had died from cancer several years before, and the daughter was away at college and rarely came home to visit. Dechtire knew very well why the daughter hardly ever came around. She could see it in the horse farmer's eyes.

Dechtire had arrived home after being fired, but had not gone upstairs yet. She sat on a straw bale, staring at the two horses as they ate their hay. The owner always fed them after Dechtire left for work in the morning and before she came home in the evening. She knew he did it that way to avoid contact with her. She made him edgy, but he had not yet figured out why, so he simply did his best to steer clear of her. She knew what the horse farmer's dark secrets were.

Dechtire maintained her intense gaze with the horses. The two massive and beautiful creatures had sweat beads popping up on their backs and necks. The perspiration made their black coats glisten like silk. Dechtire felt a burning in the pit of her stomach. It reminded her of the times she had helped to make jams and jellies. She pictured the boiling strawberries and how you could not let the rolling boil stop until the allotted time had elapsed. That boiling was now in her stomach and she wanted it to stop, but she knew the only thing that could ease the boil was revenge.

The horses sensed Dechtire's nefarious thoughts and began to panic. They swung their heads up and down and stomped their hooves against the wooden barn floor. Dechtire continued to stare until the horses started their neighing screams. She stood up and tried to calm them, but her efforts were futile. She did not want the horse farmer coming down to see if a snake or some other critter had gotten into the stalls with his precious horses.

Dechtire's head ached, and the boil in the pit of her gut was about to overflow. There was no turning back now. She unleashed her fury of hate on the two animals.

Later, when the farmer walked into the dimly lit barn, he opened his mouth to scream, but no noise came forth. All he could do was stand there wide-eyed with his mouth hanging open as if it had come unhinged. He was overcome with a wave of nausea. His morning meal burned his throat as he heaved it up. He leaned forward with his hands on his knees and closed his eyes, trying to regain his composure.

Dechtire, standing just out of the farmer's sight, quickly looked around to calculate the damage she had inflicted. The two once-beautiful horses lay lifeless in a giant pool of blood that now looked more maroon than red. Their throats looked as though they had been cracked open like watermelons. Dechtire herself was covered in blood that was almost black in the dim light of the bulb swinging back and forth above her.

She turned her attention on the stupefied farmer, still frozen in shock. She reached down and picked up a scythe. As she raised it up, a large globule of blood dripped from its sharp point and splashed onto the barn floor. The farmer stared into Dechtire's eyes with disbelief as she swung the curved blade. With that one sure swipe, off came the head of the horse farmer. It bounced a time or two, then rolled lopsidedly across the floor, leaving a splattered trail of crimson as it went. The head came to its final resting place against the freshly shod hoof of one of the horses. The eyes remained open, and those eyes were still staring into

Dechtire. Turning away, she flung open the barn doors to allow easy access for the hungry coyotes that lurked near the farm. She knew when the stench was strong enough, they would come and eat their fill.

Dechtire did not rush to leave the scene. She knew it could be a long time before anyone found the lonely horse farmer.

As his tenant, she had taken advantage of his perverse desires. She knew that he would try to spy on her. She could feel his eyes on her at night, and she had found the peepholes in the bathroom and near her bed. Dechtire let him watch because she needed a place to live.

He had not advertised the apartment, so no one knew that she had been living there. She simply had had a feeling that day in the mini-mart down the road when she saw him buying a six-pack of beer. Dechtire had followed him home and fed him a sob story about having nowhere to live. It was a story he had longed to hear. She had moved in that day—the same day she had gotten the job at the prison.

Dechtire took a long hot shower. She found enjoyment in watching the blood swirl in the bottom of the tub before making its final circle into the drain. It was like seeing red streamers spinning in the wind as you ran across a field on a spring day. She dressed, but not in her typical scrubs. She chose a tea-length black velveteen dress. It was fitted at the waist, which emphasized her full breasts. Tiny green beads ran down the length of the neckline. Her raven pendant hung just above her cleavage. A pair of black leather boots completed the look. She gathered her belongings, then wiped down the apartment.

It was time to get on the road ... the road to revenge. Dechtire slipped into her car, started the engine, and turned on the radio—which happened to be playing "Locomotive Breath." She felt as if she held the strength of a locomotive and could not wait to release its great power and wrath onto the people who had betrayed her and her real parents.

Part Three: Givers and Takers

Chapter 14: Silas

Clayton had been able to keep that first helping of gallbladder down, and for a little while, it seemed to be helping. It was almost time for plate number two when the sweats broke out and the feverish talking began. Nola May knew he wouldn't be able to keep another helping down until the fever broke. It was back to the tub for Clayton. As his skin touched the tepid water, he screamed in agony as though it was burning his flesh.

Silas squeezed his eyes shut and covered his ears. Phillip looked at Afton and she knew what he wanted. She took Silas by the hand and led him outside into the cool night air. He sighed in relief to be away from Clayton's torment. He was a sensitive young man. You didn't have to look into his thoughts to know how much it hurt him to see the people he cared about in harm's way. He was a gentle soul, but not one to cross.

"Silas, would you like to walk to Grandma Ruby's house and stay for a while?"

"Yes, please," he sighed, anxious to be away.

An almost full moon shone brightly on the path, so finding their way was not difficult. The farther they got from Miss Betty's cabin, the quieter the woods became. It wasn't just the absence of Clayton's fevered hollering, but more the absence of all noise. The back of Afton's neck prickled with chills. Was it the crisp night air? Her senses said no. A light glowed up ahead on the path. It was Grandma Ruby's cabin and there appeared to be a candle flickering in the kitchen window. Silas's grip on her hand tightened, and he glanced up at her. She needed to keep going and opened her mouth to tell him so, but he already understood. He felt it too, so they continued on the path.

They stepped onto the porch, and the boards creaked beneath their feet. A few eerie night sounds, compounded with the creaking boards, made the prickling sensation spread down Afton's arms. Silas looked up into her face. Moonbeams glistened in his eyes, making them look like fragile glass. It was a scary sight, but she knew it was just the reflection. Silas could never be frightening to her.

Afton turned the doorknob, and together, hand in hand, the two stepped across the threshold into Grandma Ruby's original cabin. There wasn't just one candle burning; it was more like one hundred. The kitchen was illuminated with flickering flames as each candle took a turn, lighting their way out of the darkness. The door closed and there in front of them stood Grandma Ruby, Miss Betty, and Joetta. The grip Silas had on her hand was gone in an instant as he ran and wrapped his arms around Miss Betty. If Afton was imagining all this, so was Silas. Her eyes began to water at the vision of those three loving women. She dared not even blink for fear they would fade away.

She walked forward to the outstretched arms of Grandma Ruby and Joetta and welcomed their arms around her. It wasn't long before the three of them were gathered around her and Silas in a circle, all of them hugging and laughing. Afton wanted that moment of bliss to last forever, and she knew Silas felt the same. But she also sensed they were there with a purpose.

Miss Betty spoke softly. "Afton, do you have the book that I left you? Have you kept it safe?"

"Yes."

"You will need to know everything inside," she continued. "That book holds your future, as well as the others."

Joetta spoke next. "In the darkness of clouds, anxiety rises in your core. Remember that every dark cloud is followed by something miraculous. It is followed by light, precious light. With the light comes renewal and hope that darkness will not keep you in its grip forever."

Afton wanted to somehow record each word they spoke. She wanted to hold on to this reunion and never let go.

Grandma Ruby placed her hands squarely on her shoulders and looked deep within her being. "My dear sweet Afton, the battle is about to begin. You must dig deep for strength that you don't realize is there. There are those born in the same year as you that did not fare so well. You are special. For more than four and a half decades, you have lived in safety. But now it is time for you to live freely and embrace your gifts. You are with your true family."

The candles flickered simultaneously, and abruptly, they were gone. It was only her and Silas in the kitchen. And there they stood silently for several minutes. Neither one even tried to talk. They were both attempting to hold onto the moment for as long as they could.

Afton had read Miss Betty's book. It held every possible situation that could arise during the birth of a child and what to do for each circumstance. Herb after herb was listed along with all their uses. The stories she had heard from Grandma Ruby were also in the book, but as a child, Afton had thought they were only old wives' tales. She needed to reread the book because she must have missed something important.

She and Silas quietly left the cabin and headed back to Miss Betty's.

It took them longer on the way back. The moon now hid behind the night clouds, only coming out long enough to give the illusion that the trees were moving along with those clouds. As they neared the cabin, they heard fast-approaching footsteps. Silas told her not to be afraid, that he could tell it was Phillip. He was right.

"Clayton's fever has broken, and he's taking in more of the bear's gallbladder," he told them. "It seems to be working. He's asking for you, Afton."

Phillip took her hand as well as Silas's and led them quickly along the path. It was as though Phillip did not require any light to find his way through the darkness. The strength of his large hand gripping Afton's made her feel safe, and the warmth of his hand made her feel something more. No one spoke as they hurried back.

Once inside Miss Betty's cabin, Afton found that Clayton was indeed in better condition. The swelling in his face had decreased, as had his struggle to breathe. He opened his bloodshot eyes as she stood staring at him from the doorway of his room.

His voice was weak. "Come in, Afton."

"Don't try and talk, Clayton. Just save your strength."

He reached for her hand as she sat down on the bed next to him. They sat together quietly for a short while. Afton jumped when she heard his voice again—it sounded much stronger than before. She looked at his face, but it was motionless. He was silent-talking again. *Afton, remember when I told you that the last time I saw Ruby was twenty-nine years ago? Well, that's true. But I have been here in Robinson Holler on several occasions with Mommy Bud. Will you get my wallet?*

She did as he asked. It was in the drawer of the bedside table. In Clayton's special way, he told her to open it. She did, and inside she found an old picture of a little boy sitting in the lap of a beautiful woman.

Clayton spoke aloud. "That's Mommy Bud holding me. I was six years old. The picture was taken on my birthday. As you can see, my grandmother was a white woman. My parents could not accept the fact that I was black, so my grandmother raised me. She was the most special person in the world to me. You understand that, don't you?"

"Yes, I do, because Grandma Ruby was the most special person in the world to me. What about your birth parents? Have you seen them throughout the years?"

"No," answered Clayton. "Not since the day I was born."

Silence filled the little bedroom as they reflected on their upbringings. She studied Clayton's face and wondered about his exact age. There were no fine lines around his eyes, and she could not see a single gray hair. He had told her that they had traded his car when he went away to college. That was when she needed a car to drive back and forth to nursing school. It seemed a strange coincidence that they could both be the same age and both raised by their very unique grandmothers.

Clayton broke the silence. "Afton, there are no coincidences. Everything happens as it is supposed to for a particular purpose. Sometimes it may take us years to discover that purpose, and maybe we will never discover it. The answer to your question is forty-seven. I'm forty-seven years old, the same as you. I imagine you, too, are often mistaken for being far younger. Many of the Cunnin' Folk do not look their age. Mommy Bud told me she knew I was special even before I was born. I guess that's why she wanted Miss Betty to help bring me into this world. You are another of those special babies who were born here. You were born October 11th, 1966, and I was born one day before you. Mommy Bud told me about the baby girl that was born while I was here. She said everyone was in awe of your eyes, even as a newborn."

Afton was amazed. "Then you're one of the five that Miss Betty delivered in 1966. The two boys and three girls were the only babies she delivered that year. That was an extremely slow year as far as births for Miss Betty went, from what I've heard. Why so few, I wonder? Are you curious? No, of course you're not. Everything happens with a purpose and all. But I'm curious, Clayton. I know you and who two of the others are—Roy and Claire. I'd like to know about the other female."

She sensed that Clayton was starting to weaken. The latest dose of the bear bladder was wearing off.

His voice was barely a whisper as he said, "Afton, I can feel my heart grow weak in between doses. It feels like someone wrapped it in baling twine and submerged it in a dark sea so deep that the pressure is almost too much. My heart constricts under that pressure. My breaths grow short and quick, and it hurts to even breathe. I will tell you more of what you want to know, but later. Nourishment and medicine are what I need now. As it happens, both come in the same form."

Afton was a nurse, so Clayton's symptoms were nothing new to her. With congestive heart failure, there would always be fluid buildup because the heart couldn't pump efficiently enough to rid the body of the excess. Shortness of breath would follow, as would bouts of confusion. It pained her to see him struggle so. The remedy was helping him. She just hoped it had been started early enough.

She left Clayton in Nola May's hands. She and Clayton had talked much of the night, and morning came quickly. She found Silas playing with Graham and Dalton on the hand-stitched quilt under the shade tree. Afton thought playing, but sometimes they seemed so deep into what they were doing that seemed more like planning.

Silas looked up at her and smiled. "Come sit with us, Afton. You look tired. Do you want to lie down on the quilt?"

It was early December. The air surely had a bite to it, but the sun was shining so brightly that she said, "Why yes, Silas, I would love to."

So there they lay on that hand-stitched, much-worn quilt, staring up at the beautiful blue sky beyond the tree branches. They started a game and called out what each cloud looked like. Some were horses or dragons or mushrooms, and there was even one that looked like a bird in flight. A raven, Afton thought to herself as she reached down and touched the bandage that covered the blackened raven scar. She wondered if it would ever fade.

Maddie hollered for them to come in for breakfast, and with renewed energy, they raced to the cabin. Silas won, of course. Phillip had just helped Nola May get Clayton out of the tub and back to bed again for another feeding. Nola May stayed with Clayton while Phillip joined Maddie, Silas, and Afton at the kitchen table. She couldn't help but wonder if Phillip resented her for all the troubling events that had taken place. She stared down at her food as she pushed it around on the plate with her fork.

It startled her when Maddie said, "Afton, are you going to play with it, or are you going to eat? I can fix you something else if this isn't to your liking."

Afton blushed in embarrassment. She certainly hadn't meant to offend Maddie. "No, I was just worried about Clayton. The meal is delicious."

Her eyes met Phillip's, and she quickly looked back at her plate. She didn't want him to read her thoughts, but throughout the rest of the day, she caught him staring at her.

Finally, he asked, "Afton, would you walk down to the lake with me?"

She looked around for Silas so she could get him to come along as well, but he was nowhere in sight. Her words were all jumbled in her mind, so she simply nodded yes.

As she and Phillip stepped out into the early-winter air, she shivered as a blast of the crisp cold air brushed against her face. The sun that had shone so brightly just a few hours before had since dipped behind the mountains. Phillip lit the oil lantern, and they started down the path toward the lake. It was much darker that night. The wind had brought clouds that made the waning moon play peek-a-boo. They found their way to the big rock where she had seen Phillip several times before, playing his flute. She shivered hard against the memory of the haunting music the instrument made.

Phillip put the lantern down on the rock and they sat on either side. She was glad for the warmth that the old lantern emitted. They sat quietly and listened to the night sounds. An owl was close by in the woods, calling out with hoots and murmurs. Tree branches creaked under the weight of a small critter jumping from one branch to another.

Afton found herself thinking about young Silas, as she so often did. There were no other children around for him to play with, but he didn't seem to suffer from it. He was different; he embraced the solace there in the mountains. He had his animals and the small eclectic group of people who, for all intents and purposes, were his family. Afton's own childhood was comparable. She had grown up among adults and adult conversations. She was wiser than her years, just as Silas was. The similarities were strange, and she could see them plainly now.

When she was very young, Afton remembered riding the school bus to the edge of the Village of McKinley. The bus driver had refused her grandmother's request to pick her up and drop her off inside the village. He told her it was because Afton was the only child who lived there, and there wasn't a suitable place to turn around. Grandma Ruby thought he had other reasons, but she did not complain and Afton didn't mind the walk. The small village was very much a safe haven.

Unlike Silas—who was homeschooled by Miss Betty—Afton attended public school. She would walk into the village and head to the house that had been chosen that day as a meeting place for the women to gather and work on their quilting. There would always be a snack waiting for her. More often than not, it would be homemade grape juice and white mulberry cookies. It was a rare occasion for it not to be healthy food that had been locally grown. She did remember one time when she found black cherry Kool-Aid and boxed vanilla wafers waiting for her. That day, the women had been in a frenzy on a special project. She remembered that she did not pass up the store-bought treats.

Afton would have her snack, do her homework, and then lie in the shade below the quilt that was being worked on. It was like her own colorful retreat. Each of the women would tell a story of what the design meant as she sewed her quilt square into the pattern. It did not matter a bit to her that she was unpopular in school because there, beneath the beauty of those quilts, she was in the center of something more magical than any of the other girls in her class could imagine.

Later, in high school, Afton noticed the current trends: gold add-a-bead necklaces, blazers with suede patches on the elbows, and Gloria Vanderbilt jeans. She knew Grandma Ruby couldn't afford those things for her. Even then, she was above the latest trends and fads. Her focus was on learning—not just what the teachers taught, but the far greater lessons she learned from listening to Grandma Ruby. She knew there was a wealth of value in what she was trying to instill in her. Afton used to tell herself they were just stories, but deep down she knew they were much more.

"Afton, did you hear me?" Phillip asked.

She looked into his illuminated face, searching for an answer; a clue as to how long he had been talking and about what, but she found no answer.

She was honest. "No, Phillip. I was actually thinking back to my childhood. What did you say?"

"Clayton has been silent-talking to me. He told me that you had questions about the baby girl that Miss Betty delivered the same year you, Clayton, Roy, and Claire were born."

"Yes. Do you know who she is? Does she live around here? What is her gift?"

"Slow down, Afton," Phillip said. "You're getting way ahead of yourself. There is much to this story that you have yet to learn. I'm not sure if I should be the one to tell you, but I feel that you deserve some sort of answer."

Phillip sat silently for a moment, but it felt like forever. She could tell he was trying to arrange his thoughts into some kind of order. He was trying to decide what was safe to tell me and what was not.

Before he could speak, she heard herself blurt, "Talk!"

The flame in the lantern flickered once and went out as though someone had flipped a switch. The black of night swallowed them completely. Her heart skipped a beat or two. Had she made the lantern go out when she became so impatient? It certainly seemed so.

Afton could hear Phillip's breathing, so she knew he was still there with her. That was a comfort, because she surely had no desire to be alone on that rock in the dark of night. Nevertheless, she could feel her body start to tremble. It was one of the effects night had had on her since childhood. Afton focused her thoughts on light and warmth. She cleared her mind of everything else, and within seconds, the lantern was aglow again. There was more to her than looking into the dark thoughts of others, after all.

Phillip's eyes glowed against the tall flame that danced within the lantern's glass chimney.

He cleared his throat and began talking. "Afton, we've told you why Ruby took you from here. It was to protect you. No one here, other than Nola May and Miss Betty, knew about Clayton. Cordelia Rose had brought Ben and Patsy here to Miss Betty when it was time for him to be born, and they returned to Kentucky soon thereafter. Clayton has told you why his parents did not want to raise him and that Cordelia Rose took him to the small community of Monkey's Eyebrow to live. The two of you were kept safe all these years because of what your grandmothers did to protect you both."

He glanced at her briefly, then continued. "Roy and Claire were different. They were bad people, and their families felt entitled when it came to the legends of skinwalking. These particular people lusted for power, and they instilled that desire in Roy and Claire. Power would be gained—whatever the cost. Once they reached puberty, it was discovered that neither of them possessed any special gifts at all. But their marriage had been prearranged when they were children, and since Roy and Claire relied on the beliefs of the elders, they married as planned. The elders convinced them that if they had a baby, they could consume the life-force of that baby and it would give them the power they craved. This was Miss Betty's true reason for switching the babies. She was trying to save Dechtire's life."

Phillip paused long enough to let things sink in a bit, then went on. "As you know, the fifth baby Miss Betty delivered in 1966 was a baby girl. What you are not aware of is that the baby she delivered was her very own daughter. Miss Betty's husband was a good and gentle man. There wasn't a person or animal on this mountain that didn't feel his goodness. The mixed-race resented him for his gift, so they killed him. They tried to make it look like an animal attack, but everyone knew better. Miss Betty had told no one of the baby she was carrying. She knew the danger the child would be in if she did. Joetta instinctively knew Miss Betty was with child. She was always in tune with her fellow Cunnin' Folk.

"When the time grew near, Joetta, Maddie, and Nola May were all with Miss Betty when the child was born. They instantly felt the baby was special. Miss Betty had longed for a child of her own for many years, but she knew that in order to protect her daughter, she would not be able to raise her. Miss Betty gave the baby girl to Nola May and told her to bring her to my mother. You see, I had been born just prior to the baby girl and my mother was nursing me, so Miss Betty knew that she would be able to provide for her daughter. People assumed my mother had given birth to twins, a boy and a girl. Miss Betty wanted the baby to be named Lilly Dale, and my mother abided by her wishes."

"But Phillip, Miss Betty only delivered five babies that year," she said. "You would have made six."

"Afton, not all the women went to midwives. My mother was a strong woman, and her Mingo blood ran deep. She gave birth to me at home with the help of my grandmother. Lilly Dale was raised as my sister. Miss Betty visited on a regular basis and was very much a part of her daughter's life, just as she was mine. Great sacrifice was made for Lilly Dale, for Clayton, and for you, as well."

"Phillip, why haven't I met Lilly Dale yet? I want to get to know her."

Phillip shook his head. "That won't be possible. You see, when Lilly Dale was thirty-seven years old, she became pregnant. Her husband had died in a logging accident and never even knew she was carrying his child. She went to Miss Betty for help. It was a difficult pregnancy. Miss Betty wanted to take her to the hospital, but Lilly Dale refused. Miss Betty did all she could, but Lilly Dale lost too much blood when she gave birth. I was there when it happened, and it all but killed Miss Betty. Before Lilly Dale passed away, she reached up and put her hand on the side of Miss Betty's face and said, 'Thank you, Mama, for keeping me safe for so many years. I know you will do the same for your grandson, Silas.'"

CHAPTER 15: GRANNY BOTTLES

Clayton started to grow stronger by the day—by the hour, it seemed. He was sitting up in bed when Afton walked in.

He smiled. "I have a sense that a lot of your questions have been answered."

"You have your voice back loud and clear," she said. "Yes, Clayton, I have a lot of my answers. There are still a couple, but for now they can wait. Nola May says you're about finished with the treatments."

"Yes!" Clayton replied robustly. "And I hope I never have the need of bear again—gallbladder or any other part."

They laughed, and it felt good to do so. It had been a while.

"Maybe by tomorrow you will be up for some fresh air and sunshine."

"Sounds good to me, Afton."

Dechtire was in town snooping around for information. She had a way of making even the most resistant person talk. Most people fell into the resistant category or the "best mind your own business" category. Nevertheless, it wasn't long before she found out about the recent death of Miss Betty, the local Appalachian Granny. This news made her both mad and glad. She was glad, especially if this woman had been the mountain midwife Bernice had spoken about, and mad that she hadn't gotten a shot at her before she died.

Dechtire still didn't know who her birth parents were. Little did she know that if they had been aware she was there, she would be in grave danger of losing her life.

Phillip and Afton had spent the entire night talking by the lake. Despite having had no sleep, she felt pretty good. It helped that she had a little more understanding about the lives of those around her, as well as her own life. Maddie and Nola May prepared a breakfast fit for royalty. Clayton was even able to join them at the table. Afton truly felt that she was surrounded by family.

She spent most of breakfast watching Silas. She now knew what had taken place in order for him to be there. She understood that he took after his grandfather when it came to communicating with animals. Lilly Dale had known all along that Miss Betty was her mom, so she must have had the gift of intuition in much the same way as Joetta had. Silas possessed it as well. He had definitely been aware of the times when Afton was in harm's way. He was special, there was no denying that.

After breakfast, she and Silas took Clayton outside so he could breathe in some fresh mountain air. His lungs were clear now, and the swelling in his extremities was all but gone. Nola May gave his room a thorough cleaning, Maddie tidied up the breakfast dishes, and Phillip joined them outside. He played a couple of songs on the wooden flute. It was December 7th, and Afton still had three more weeks off from work. She told herself not to think about that yet. She needed to simply enjoy this family while she could.

"You should get Clayton back inside now," Phillip suggested. "Those dark clouds are rolling in pretty fast. It looks like we may be in for an early snow."

Now that Afton stopped and took notice, it was getting colder very quickly, and the dark clouds looked like an ominous army preparing for battle. Silas stayed behind and helped Phillip bring in extra firewood and do a few other chores. When they finally came inside, it was close to noon and they looked half frozen. Phillip told them that the temperature had dropped at least thirty degrees since breakfast.

Afton caught the look that he and Maddie exchanged. Could they sense something worse than a snowstorm approaching? She fixed some hot chocolate on the wood cookstove that was now cranked up, but she still felt waves of chills come and go each time the wind howled through the holler. There were other signs as well, like uncomfortable moments of silence that stretched a little too far before someone would finally speak up.

Something or someone was coming, of that much Afton was certain.

In town, it hadn't taken Roy and Claire very long to learn that someone had been asking a lot of questions—a young beauty with long dark locks and eyes even darker. That was, according to the town drunk. Every little town had at least one. This one was about the only person willing to run his mouth. And for a fifth of Jack Daniels, he would spill his guts.

Dechtire decided she needed to go to this "Robinson Holler" and check it out for herself. She figured Afton had high-tailed herself back there. Clayton, on the other hand, was from Kentucky, so with any luck he had returned home to either recuperate or be buried. She hoped for the latter of the two. Nevertheless, she had made up her mind … she knew that, soon enough, she would be on her way.

Silas paced back and forth with Dalton and Graham hanging on tight to the collar of his T-shirt. Everyone felt the tension thickening. Finally, Silas spoke, breaking the silence. "The dark-haired girl has made up her mind. She'll be coming to Robinson Holler soon."

"Afton," Phillip said, "you and Silas need to go—"

"No!" she told him firmly. "I will not leave this family again. I will stay here and stand my ground with the rest of you. There has to be a way for us to get through to Dechtire. She's acting on vengeance and it will not bring her any peace. If she knew the whole story, perhaps she would understand."

Clayton stood in the doorway looking at her. She could tell he had an idea. There was still some time before the storm arrived and before Dechtire would get there, and Clayton made it clear what he thought they should do.

Afton and Phillip left the holler and drove into Bottom Creek, where they believed Roy and Claire to be living. In 1985, the Tug River had flooded Elkhorn Fork where Roy, Claire, and the elders of both sides of their family lived. Roy and Claire had been married the year prior. They wanted to separate themselves somewhat from the watchful eyes of the elders, so they had gone to Bottom Creek to look at property. The two wanted to build their own cabin and have the privacy to do as they pleased. According to rumors, this often involved using drugs. They were gone the day the flood waters washed away most of Elkhorn Fork. None of the elders survived.

The drive to Bottom Creek allowed her and Phillip the opportunity to discuss what they would do if they couldn't find Roy and Claire. Their options were limited. Once they arrived, they discovered that each house they came to appeared to be abandoned. Afton was starting to doubt that they would find them. Finally, they saw smoke coming from a chimney. It was a small cabin on a knoll about a quarter mile from the creek. If it hadn't been for the smoke, she doubted they would have even noticed it tucked neatly behind a row of pines.

They knew it was the place when they spotted a tattered flag with a faded raven in the center. It was being tossed roughly in the wind that had steadily picked up throughout the afternoon. They parked Phillip's truck on a side road. She felt a rush of adrenaline— or maybe it was pure nausea; she couldn't be sure which.

Phillip's hand lightly touched hers. "Are you okay, Afton?"

She nodded her head yes, but her stomach was screaming no. Moving slowly and quietly, it would be about a ten-minute walk.

Would their plan work? She was beginning to wonder, but it was too late to turn back. Before she realized how close the cabin was, they were almost on top of it. Voices could be heard inside, and she hoped it would only be Roy and Claire. They hadn't counted on any others.

Maddie and Nola May were working in the kitchen. Having been shooed out of the kitchen earlier, Silas busied himself playing with Dalton and Graham. He wanted to help but wasn't quite sure how to yet. Maddie worked with a mortar and pestle, making a paste out of juniper berries. Nola May heated the other oils and butters they would need to finish the body lotion they were making. It would come in handy if the legends turned out to be true.

Clayton had been lying in bed for almost two hours. Looking at him, one would assume that he was sleeping soundly, but it was more than just a sound sleep. It was much deeper than that. Over the years, he had found that he could slide into a meditation so deep that he could travel. His physical body would remain, but his being would seek out whatever he was looking for. Clayton definitely wasn't a typical dowser.

This time, he sought out Phillip and Afton. He needed to be close to them so he could watch and warn. He could be another set of eyes, in case things got out of hand with Roy and Claire. The gifts that Clayton held had gotten him out of plenty of jams working as a warden in the prison system. He hoped they would be of value now.

Silas peeked in on Clayton and found him to be asleep, or so he thought. Maddie and Nola May were still deep into their work in the kitchen. Silas had been thinking a lot about something that Miss Betty had told him when he was younger, and he now felt compelled to seek out answers. He slipped out of Miss Betty's cabin and quickly disappeared into the woods. He had some friends he needed to talk with.

In Bottom Creek, Phillip pointed out the side window of Roy and Claire's cabin. The curtain was askew, hopefully enough for them to get a good look inside. The property was littered with trash, mainly liquor bottles, beer cans, and the occasional potted meat can. They made their way to the window and peeked inside. The voices they heard were coming from an iPod lying on a cluttered coffee table. It was playing the Steve Miller Band's "The Joker." The music and the wind whistling through the trees seemed to collaborate as they vibrated against the glass, creating an eerie yet hypnotic melody.

There was movement inside the cabin. It was definitely Claire and Roy. Afton recognized them from Joetta's funeral. Claire appeared to have aged in the short time since then. She was about five feet six with dingy blond hair that was most likely from one of those do-it-yourself dye kits. Her jet-black eyebrows would have agreed. She was also unhealthily slim.

Roy didn't appear to be in much better shape. He was a bit shorter than the frail Claire. He had the tanned skin of his ancestors, but he lacked the long dark hair of his elders. In fact, he was almost completely bald. His movements were here, there, and everywhere, like a nervous squirrel. When he stopped long enough to light up a cigarette, his hands shook uncontrollably. He started cursing when the lighter didn't work. He spoke with such venom it made both Claire and Afton jump.

She could tell he was a man that felt slighted by his height and was determined to take it out on anyone he felt was weaker than him. This made him feel the bigger man. He made Afton cringe. Phillip could see her distaste for Roy; it was written clearly on her face. She had to look away to compose herself. She had to be ready for whatever she saw when she laid her hands on him. She already had a feeling that it would be nothing short of evil.

Silas soon found the friends he was looking for. He sat on a log and talked with the forest animals. The evening air was frigid as it bit into his skin. He wouldn't be able to stay very long. It was too cold, and he would be missed at the cabin before long. The animals quickly understood what Silas wanted. He started back to Miss Betty's cabin with hopes of being helpful.

Maddie and Nola May were finished with the lotion and were putting it into a Mason jar when they felt a blast of cold air as Silas opened the cabin door.

Nola May turned and regarded the child sternly. "Silas Wade, where have you been? We hadn't even realized you were gone. What if something had happened to you?"

Maddie shot him a look of disapproval that needed no words.

"I'm sorry," said Silas. "I just needed to talk to some friends."

The women knew the friends he referred to were the animals. They didn't reprimand him any further.

Claire cleared a spot off of the filthy coffee table so Roy could set a small tray down. There appeared to be drug paraphernalia on it. Afton could see a straw, razor blades, a baggie containing a white powdery substance, and a pill bottle.

Roy said something to Claire, and she stepped out of the room, but quickly returned carrying a fifth of tequila and two shot glasses. They were preparing to get wasted and do who knew what. She and Phillip looked at one another and knew they had a long wait ahead of them. If they ended up passing out, they would not need to use the valerian root tincture they had brought with them.

Roy and Claire did two shots of tequila each, then snorted the contents of the baggie.

Roy dumped a few of the white pills onto the tray and started chopping them up with one of the razor blades. That went on until dark. The temperature had dropped below freezing, and the first snowflakes began to drift from the sky like wisps of goose down from a ruptured pillow.

Claire was the first to give in to the drug-induced stupor. Her body slowly melted into the deep cushions of the stained couch. Roy stood and took two steps, but staggered forward and banged his shin on the coffee table. He managed to spit out a few curse words before falling to the floor. Minutes later, they could hear his snores.

Clayton was now in Afton's head, along with Phillip's, telling them it was safe to go inside. To their surprise, the door was unlocked. She guessed they weren't accustomed to uninvited guests. She first took Claire's hand, then grasped Roy's. Afton didn't want to chance doing one at a time and then have one of them wake up. She hoped she would be able to look inside both of their lives at the same time.

The visions came like a blow to the head and she gasped. She had to stay calm no matter what she saw. First, she glimpsed Claire as a child being beaten by her father, then as a teenager stealing beer from a store. She saw her on the morning of her wedding. She was crying before the ceremony. She saw her the day she thought her daughter was dead. She cried not only out of sadness but because of the beating she would later receive for failing. The years were clicking by and the tears turned to anger as she took her hatred out on anyone she came into contact with.

Roy's wrath started filtering in along with Claire's. He had been mean from an early age. The crimes he committed escalated quickly from killing pets to killing and mutilating drug dealers who tried to cross him. He was not capable of remorse. His only goal was to find his daughter, if she was out there alive somewhere. He fantasized about how he would drain the life from her and, in the process, gain any powers she might have. Afton wanted to break free of their thoughts, but something was pulling her in deeper. She felt like she was free-falling from a high cliff, and all that awaited her were jagged rocks below. She wanted out, but couldn't loosen her grip.

Clayton spoke. *Afton, you can let go now. You have the information you need. You can feel your grip loosen. Claire's hand will drop from yours and then Roy's. Just let it go. Do it now!*

Phillip took Afton by the shoulders and steered her out of the cabin. They were in the concealment of the pines before she realized they were outside. Her insides were shaking. She had to stop. A wave of nausea was followed by forceful vomiting. What she had seen and felt had done something to her. She felt poisoned by Roy and Claire's visions. Her head felt as though it was spinning like a top. She needed to close her eyes for just a minute and clear away the ugly images.

When she opened her eyes again, Phillip was carrying her through the woods and back toward the dirt road. Afton tried to protest, but she was so weak she couldn't make the words form, much less get them out of her mouth. She felt her body relax against Phillip's chest. The rhythm of his heartbeat in her ear was more healing than any drug.

Once they were back at the vehicle, Phillip buckled her in and jumped behind the wheel. He drove as fast as the snow-slickened roads would allow. When they were a few miles away from the cabin, her numbed mind began to thaw. She processed the images, the thoughts, and the heinous acts that her mind had witnessed. How can one absorb such things and not be permanently affected? Would she be able to "unsee" what had been seen? She hoped so.

"Phillip, please take me home," she muttered.

The mountain man failed to pull his gaze from the frozen road ahead of him. "Do you want to go back to Clay County?"

"No, I want to go to my home in Robinson Holler."

Relief shone across Phillip's face. "Yes, Afton, I'll take you home. You rest now."

As they drove into the night, Afton drifted in and out of strange dreams that were mixing the real with the unreal. Each time she opened her eyes, she could see that the snowflakes were getting larger and more dense. They raced into the headlights, making it impossible for her to focus. She hoped that Phillip wasn't having the same problem.

When she closed her eyes again, Afton could see the Village of McKinley. It looked as it had for the past four decades, only this time she really noticed things that had been there all along. Every barn had one of those signs on it, a hex sign. That doesn't sound right, she thought to herself. I think Grandma Ruby called them talismans. At that moment, they reminded her of painted quilts, much like the quilts that the women would get together and make. Each square told part of a story, and once all the squares were pieced together, the story seemed complete.

Silas peeked in on Clayton again. Something wasn't right. Clayton's eyes were still closed, but his body twitched and beads of sweat covered his face and arms.

Silas ran to the kitchen and called out, "Come quick! It's Clayton."

Nola May and Maddie were right behind him. The two women checked Clayton from head to toe. Maddie told Silas to run and get a cool, damp cloth. He came back in a hurry, and Nola May dabbed the sweat from Clayton's body. The twitching was slowing to an occasional jerk.

"Clayton is somewhere else," Maddie told them. "He's trying to wake up so he can come back to us, but something's preventing him from leaving."

Nola May stared at Maddie for a long moment before running off to the kitchen. She returned with a pitcher of ice-cold water and told the others to stand back. She emptied the contents of the pitcher abruptly onto Clayton's face. Everyone stood frozen in place as they waited to see if anything would happen. It did. Clayton's eyes shot open, as did his mouth as he desperately gasped to take in a breath.

After a few minutes, he was able to talk. "I was with Phillip and Afton at Bottom Creek. Afton had a hard time breaking free of Roy's and Claire's minds. I talked her away from them, but then I was pulled in. Silas, thank you for checking on me. I hate to think what could have happened."

Silas shivered at the thought.

"How did things go for Afton?" Maddie asked. "Was she able to see what they had in mind?"

Clayton seemed to finally have his wits about him as he answered. "Yes, she got more than she counted on. If we can show that to Dechtire, her vengeance will be for Roy and Claire, not us."

Nola May spoke up. "That's all well and good, but are we to forget what Dechtire did to Joetta, and the fact that she almost killed you, Clayton?"

Silas slowly came forward. "I know something we can do," he said. "Miss Betty kept things from the five babies who were born in 1966. She buried them out in the woods. Those things are special and they'll be of help."

Maddie was intrigued by the boy's words. "What do you mean, she kept things?"

Silas wasn't sure how to explain it, but he tried his best. "I remembered something that Miss Betty told me a couple of years ago. It came back to me earlier, and that's why I had to go into the woods and talk to my friends. She told me about the 'Granny Bottles' that held something special from the five babies. She said that they had to stay hidden, unless a time came when there was no choice but to use 'em to get rid of the bad ones." His youthful face was dead serious. "This is that time, don't you think?"

Chapter 16: Naked Creek

Soon, they had all moved to the kitchen and sat around the table to consider what Silas had just told them. They had no idea where the so-called Granny Bottles were, and they weren't sure how to use them if they did find them. Silas informed them that his friends were looking for the bottles at that very moment.

"Afton will know what to do with 'em," Silas assured them.

They were hopeful that Silas was right as they began preparing a meal in hopes that Phillip and Afton would be back soon. Silas was kept busy by Graham and Dalton. They played hide-and-seek, but the mice seemed to be aware of the tension among the humans. Maddie and Nola May were making some old-time favorites—venison stew, cornbread sticks, and warm apple pie. Clayton commented on the wonderful aromas that wafted through the cabin.

A gust of wind thrust a broken limb against the side of the house and everyone jumped. The storm was worsening, and the snow was piling up.

Dechtire had finally gotten directions to Robinson Holler from a woman on the outskirts of the small town called War. The woman who shared that information looked like she was probably in her mid-thirties. She had fiery red hair that she kept tucked beneath a brown-and-black-checked wool hat with earflaps. She wore men's clothing—which wasn't very odd, considering the wretched storm that had hit that area of West Virginia.

Considering the severity of the weather, Dechtire began to question her own choice of attire. She also regretted not insisting that the direction giver come along for the ride. There was something off about the woman, but Dechtire couldn't put her finger on it. She thought it unlikely that the woman had ever made a trip outside of McDowell County. The redhead had a toughness to her exterior, but Dechtire imagined she was soft underneath. She'd had a slow, drawn-out way of speaking with a hint of a rasp in her voice, and Dechtire was drawn to her voice as well as to the woman herself. She had often been attracted to women, but had never acted on such desires. She had learned long ago not to trust anyone, no matter how strong the feelings. Besides, she had a much more important mission for the time being. Perhaps she would cross paths with the redhead again when the time was right.

As Dechtire drove away, the redhead walked in the opposite direction—which was the actual way to Robinson Holler. She had known as soon as Dechtire started talking that she was a bad one, so she had fed her false information to buy time. She needed to get to the cabin and warn Phillip, Maddie, and Nola May that a stranger was looking for Robinson Holler. That could only mean one thing: that the stranger was searching for her friends.

It took a while before Afton felt fully awake. Phillip stopped and bought them hot coffee at a little mom and pop store. She wrapped her cold fingers around the warm paper cup and waited for the heat to penetrate into her skin. She sipped carefully at first to make sure it wasn't too hot. The warm fluid soothed her throat. She felt as though she had been in a nightmare, screaming to get out.

They were just a few miles outside of war when Phillip made a quick maneuver to avoid hitting something in the road. Afton only caught a glimpse and thought for sure it had been an animal. Phillip pulled over and jumped out of the truck. She followed. It wasn't an animal at all.

Phillip was helping a person to their feet when Afton approached. She assumed from the clothing that it was a man, so she was surprised when the person removed the wool hat. Long, unruly locks of red hair fell down around her shoulders. She brushed snow from her face with the back of her mittened hand. It was not a face that bore a stitch of makeup, nor did she need any. She seemed to be a down-to-earth woman who wouldn't hesitate to get right to the point.

Phillip looked surprised as well, for he actually knew her. "Cardinal, what in tarnation are you doing out on a night like this?"

Before she had the chance to answer, Phillip said, "Afton, this is Cardinal. She's a special friend of Connor's, as well as a friend of mine and everyone at Miss Betty's. Cardinal, I'd like you to meet Afton."

Cardinal looked her over from head to toe before speaking. Then she said rather bluntly, "So, this is the lady who led my Connor to prison. Everyone certainly has her pegged as some kind of treasure. I hope she's worth all the hell that's about to break loose on Naked Creek."

It dawned on Afton then, just how many times she had crossed Naked Creek. It wound in and around the mountains from beyond the Village of McKinley, down into Mingo County. The mention of it took her back to her first day of work after having surgery, and how she noticed the dark clouds that hung low over Naked Creek that morning. Her body shivered hard. She hoped they hadn't noticed.

"You still haven't told us what you're doing out in this weather, Cardinal," said Phillip.

"Well, as a matter of fact, I was coming to warn y'all," Cardinal answered. "A woman with long dark hair and eyes black as a pit stopped me and wanted to know how to get to Robinson Holler. I could tell right off that she was a bad 'un, so I sent her on a bit of a goose chase. I figured y'all were gathered at Miss Betty's, so that's where I was headed when you all but ran me over."

Phillip shook his head and looked over at Afton. "You have to get to know Cardinal. She appears a bit rough around the edges, but the truth is, she has to be that way to survive in this area. There are plenty of drug-addicted men around here, especially close to town. Drugs have a firm grip on that small town, and the addicts will do almost anything to get more. Sometimes women and children go missing. I hate to say it, but they most likely get sold as sex slaves. And there are those that get high and go out looking for someone to rape. That's why Cardinal camouflages her appearance. It's in her best interest to be mistaken for a man."

It seemed such a sad thing to have to live that way. "Why do you stay here then, Cardinal?" Afton asked.

She looked at her as if she should know the answer already. "I do it for you, Afton, and those who are like you. I care about the good people that live in these mountains and hollers. We all have a part in keeping the Cunnin' Folk safe."

Afton was taken aback by the woman's words. She was still naively oblivious to the sacrifice that so many were making for such a few. She prayed that they were worth it.

"Are you coming with us, Cardinal?" Phillip asked.

"I reckon so. I got word from Connor this morning. The paperwork is going through for him to be released. I take it that someone finally figured out he was inside by mistake. I'll be glad to have him back in the Holler again."

She glanced Afton's way. She knew the red-haired woman resented her, but she also knew she would do anything in her power to help her.

Dechtire grew angrier with each passing mile.

She had been lied to. The directions from the redhead had taken her straight to an abandoned coal mine. She backtracked to the town of War. Clean white snow covered the bleak grayness of the town. Dechtire was determined that this time when she asked for directions, she would not be made a fool.

She stormed into the local Stop-N-Shop, yanked the teenaged bag boy halfway across the counter, and demanded directions to Robinson Holler, "Be specific, boy, or you may not live to regret it."

He was very specific.

Silas helped knead the dough for the dinner rolls. Nola May did her best to keep him occupied. She knew how he worried about everyone, especially Afton. The bond between the two had grown strong. Maddie busied herself preparing the venison while Clayton sat in front of the window and stared out into the storm's darkness. What, or who, did he really see as he peered into the night?

"We need to take a short detour to my cabin before going on to Miss Betty's," Phillip told them.

He didn't offer an explanation, and neither Cardinal nor Afton ask for one. Afton had learned from Silas that Phillip had grown up near Delbarton in Mingo County, so she assumed his cabin was there. She had a great deal of trust for this man whom she'd known for such a short period of time. That was unusual for her. When Phillip pulled onto a side road, she discovered that she was getting very curious. Afton wanted to know more about the man who was willing to put his life in harm's way for this strange little group of people.

"Now's the chance to stretch your legs or whatever," Phillip told the two women.

Cardinal and Afton climbed out of the truck and followed Phillip inside the cabin. He quickly disappeared into a back room, and Cardinal headed to the bathroom. Afton stood in the living room and tried to take in all that she could. Beautifully varnished logs created a magnificent backdrop. There were several paintings hanging on the walls, each containing at least one wolf somewhere in the scene. There was a wolf carved from wood on the mantel. It was poised to howl at a full moon that must be somewhere above the carving, just out of sight. When Cardinal returned from the bathroom, Afton took her turn.

Phillip appeared from the back room with a large satchel in hand. She was curious about what was inside, but did not ask. The bag was large enough to carry a bow or a gun or any number of other weapons.

He didn't waste any time. "Okay, let's load up. We've lost time to make up. Afton, will you grab some water from the fridge?"

She opened the small fridge and was surprised at how empty it was. He had spent so much time at Miss Betty's, looking after Silas and everyone else. Was he regretful? If so, he didn't show it.

Chapter 17: Wise Old Owl

Clayton suddenly stood up. "I think someone is coming."

"I don't believe it's Afton and Phillip, though," Silas added.

Nola May grabbed the juniper lotion that she and Maddie had made to protect against a skinwalker's bite, and had each person apply it to any exposed skin.

She said, "This may be silly, but I'm not willin' to take a chance. We know Roy and Claire can't skinwalk, but we don't know what Dechtire is capable of. The best-case scenario is we all end up with softer skin."

Dechtire had just pulled up in front of the Robinson Holler sign. She sat and studied it, trying to decide which path to follow. Instinct led her to choose the path that would take her straight to Miss Betty's cabin. She grabbed her coat from the seat and stepped out into the dark, snowy night.

Snowflakes swirled frantically around her, and the night was so quiet she could hear the large flakes landing on the tree limbs and ground. The moon was hidden deep within the thick snow clouds, but Dechtire could navigate just fine without the light of the moon to show the way. Her dark eyes glistened with hate and an intense focus on the task at hand.

The lights from Miss Betty's cabin came into sight, and she slowed her pace as she went over in her mind what she intended to do. She heard a man's voice, which startled her, but she saw no one. She listened for the sound of someone moving through the woods, but there was none. The voice was in her head. She placed her hands firmly against her temples, hoping to stop the unwanted chatter inside her mind. It continued. Dechtire shook her head furiously from side to side but could not shake the unwanted visitor trespassing inside her head.

It took a moment, but she finally recognized the mind invader as Warden Tolley. But she knew she was no match for the intense concentration of the skilled silent talker. He told Dechtire not to be afraid because he only wanted to tell her the truth about the Cunnin' Folk, as well as about her parents. She desperately wanted answers— that was all she had wanted her entire life. She stood perfectly still in the darkness and opened her thoughts, waiting for the unknown.

Clayton silently told her that her birth parents had had only one purpose for her, and that was to steal for themselves any powers she possessed. And the only way they could accomplish that was to kill her in the process. The midwife who had delivered her was trying to save her life. He tried to convince her he had no reason to lie. He told her that he could have kept quiet, lying in wait for her, and killed her for what she had put him through. But there had been enough killing. It was time to put an end to the mess. He told her that Afton and Phillip would be back soon. If she needed proof that what he was telling her was true, she would have it.

Dechtire felt he was close by now. "Okay, I'll wait for a while," she told him. "But you better not be pumping me full of crap, old man, or I'll finish what I started."

She walked toward the small barn. Somehow, she already knew that she would find blankets and a place to rest there. Had Clayton put that in her mind as well? She made herself as comfortable as she could and fell into an unusually sound sleep.

Afton's stomach lurched when they pulled in and saw a strange vehicle parked near the Robinson Holler sign. She instinctively knew it belonged to Dechtire. Phillip passed the car, then drove up the lane and parked the truck near Miss Betty's cabin.

Silas appeared on the porch almost immediately. Relief that they were back safely showed on his youthful face, along with something else. That something else was fear. They quickly left the truck and went inside. After they said their hellos, Nola May introduced Cardinal to Clayton. Then they all sat down and ate the wonderful meal that had been prepared.

It was clear that business would not come until after dinner. It was good to be back, and Afton wanted to enjoy the meal with everyone there. Each dish had been prepared with much thought. She hoped there would be many more shared meals together. She felt blessed to be among these people. She was in awe of each of them. One by one, Afton looked at them. Every one of them had a specialness. She was sorry when the meal eventually came to an end.

Clayton started, "I was able to get into Dechtire's head when she arrived," Clayton explained. "I told her about her birth parents and their intentions, as well as the reason Miss Betty switched her with the other baby when she was born. I nudged her to the barn, where I had already set up a place for her to rest. I tried to clear her mind so she could sleep, and thus far, I believe it's working. It will be up to Afton and Phillip to see that she gets the proof she needs to put an end to this once and for all."

Before either of them could respond, Silas chimed in. "Afton, I remembered about the Granny Bottles Miss Betty saved. The bottles were from when you all were born. My animal friends are in the woods looking for them. Miss Betty buried them, but I'm not sure of the exact spot. You read Miss Betty's book, so you should know what to do with the bottles. They hold something from each of the 1966 babies. You do know what to do, don't you?"

Afton's heart sank. "Silas, I read Miss Betty's book, but I'm not sure that I recall anything about 'Granny Bottles' in it."

His response held a note of near panic. "You have to use them to get rid of the bad people! Miss Betty told me they were the only way. Afton, you have to remember!"

Maddie reached over and gently laid her hand on Afton's hand, patting it ever so lightly. "Afton, it may not have been written down in the book. It may be something that will have to come from within you. I trust that when the time comes, you will know what to do. Miss Betty would have written it down if she thought it needed to be."

Afton felt her insides turning cartwheels. Was Maddie right, or was she just trying to give her confidence? She knew one thing for sure, and that was the fact that Silas was confident those Granny Bottles held the answer to this conflict. Would it actually come to a war? Dechtire was in the barn, only yards from the cabin. Something was about to break loose, of that she was certain.

The following morning, the sky remained dark and unruly. Heavy clouds hung motionless over Robinson Holler, and the darkness brought a gloom with it like none Afton had ever felt. Today would be the day. She didn't know what the outcome would be, but either way, it would come to an end.

Her insides were no longer doing flip-flops, and her anxiety had now been replaced by finality. She was calm and prepared to do what needed to be done.

The dark clouds began to shed their moisture and an icy rain was locked in on Bottom Creek. Roy and Claire were finally coming out of their drug-and-alcohol-induced stupor. Claire knew that last night had been the build-up to something big that Roy had planned. She also knew it wouldn't end well if left up to Roy. Claire had never told Roy, but occasionally she did have a "feeling" about things, and there had been a few times when that feeling had been right on the money. Fear had kept her from divulging that secret.

The cold rain played havoc on Claire's frail, thin frame. It was much more than being cold; it was a bone-deep chill. That day, Claire was having another feeling. She felt as if she would never be truly warm again.

Roy started to grumble, so Claire quickly dressed and steered clear of him. She knew from experience that it was best to give him plenty of room the day after a binge. She started a pot of coffee and sat down to wait. She watched as the last of the brew went into the pot, drip by drip. Claire hoped that if she drank plenty of the piping-hot coffee, it might warm her insides just enough. Roy staggered into the kitchen. He opened his mouth to gripe, but took one look at his wife and changed his mind. They silently sat and drank their coffee, then Roy snorted the last couple of lines of meth.

Roy and Claire's relationship was peculiar, for lack of a better word. Deep down, Claire had blamed Roy for their daughter's stillbirth. He had beaten her on a regular basis, and being pregnant had not been cause enough for him to interrupt that routine. Roy had been raised by a heavy hand, and it was the only way he knew to be. She had hoped that once they were on their own and away from the elders, things would change.

Claire, for whatever reason, loved Roy—perhaps because he was all she had ever known. She had always done whatever he told her to do, but decades of abuse had made Claire a hardened, bitter woman. Most days she would just as soon spit in your face as make eye contact with you. She hated people, and the thought that her daughter was alive and someone else had raised her filled her with venom. She longed to release that poison on anyone who was in any way connected.

Roy had gathered everything he thought they might need, everything they could possibly use to exact revenge. As Claire watched him, one of her feelings came over her. She felt that it was possible that neither of them would ever see their home again. She was fine with that as long as she got to see her daughter at least one time.

Roy wouldn't be satisfied with that, however, because he felt he was destined to be immortal.

Claire knew different.

Maddie and Nola May insisted that Phillip, Cardinal, and Afton also rub the juniper lotion on themselves. Clayton had gone over and over what he thought they should do. Some things he told Afton silently.

It was midmorning and there was still no movement from the barn. Clayton wanted to take Afton and Phillip outside at eleven a.m. Maddie, Nola May, and Cardinal were to stay inside and out of sight, unless they were told otherwise. Silas had gone into the woods shortly after daybreak to look for his animals and the place where the Granny Bottles were hidden.

Silas was deep in the woods when he heard a swooping sound coming toward him. Frightened, Graham and Dalton scurried into his pocket. One last swish of outstretched wings and it was upon him. A large, barred owl with all-knowing eyes gently perched on Silas's shoulder. Its talons could have crushed his young bones with little effort, but instead they applied only enough pressure to secure its position. The regal bird made several garbled sounds deep down in its craw. The boy had no trouble understanding what the owl was saying.

"Show me," Silas said.

The barred owl took off and Silas ran fast to keep up as the bird weaved in and out of the branches. After a while, it finally landed above a fallen log. Silas knew without a doubt that was the spot where Miss Betty had buried the bottles.

He pulled a stubby shovel from the pack on his back and began to dig. A few minutes later, he hit something solid. It was a small wooden chest with strange markings on it. He instinctively knew to open and retrieve only the two bottles marked Roy and Claire. Knowing that Afton and Clayton would be in danger if anyone discovered the burial spot, Silas carefully reburied the box—then ran as fast as his legs would carry him back to the cabin.

Chapter 18: Get Out of My Head

Roy and Claire's old Suburban was loaded. Roy was behind the wheel, and he had the radio blaring. The heat was cranked up all the way, but it put out very little warmth. It would be a long, cold ride to Robinson Holler.

Claire had layered on just about every sweater and jacket she owned. She still looked harshly thin, as though the smallest rush of wind would lift her up and carry her away. The cold had already set in, and no amount of clothing was going to help now. They drove away from their ramshackle home at Bottom Creek. Claire watched it disappear in the side mirror as she caught one more glimpse. Roy was oblivious to the idea that they might never be coming back.

Clayton walked ahead of Afton and Phillip as they headed to the barn. Once there, they stood outside the door and listened for movement inside. Only quietness echoed back at them. Clayton knocked twice and opened the door. Dull light from the outside shone into the small structure.

Dechtire was sitting cross-legged on a bale of hay. She neglected to look up when the door opened. It wasn't until they stepped inside and stood before her that she moved at all. And then it was to smooth out the wrinkles on the skirt of her dress. She finally looked up and stared into their faces. Her eyes were so black, Afton could hardly tell where the pupils stopped and the irises began.

Clayton spoke out loud. "Dechtire, you already know Afton, so I won't bother with formalities. This, on the other hand, is Phillip. Phillip, this is Dechtire."

Phillip simply gave a half nod and chose not to speak.

Dechtire stared at him for a bit, then switched her gaze back to Clayton. "He must be related to the Whelan inmate. He has the same mongrel eyes. You claimed these two would have proof for me if I needed it. Well, I reckon I'll need some of that proof … proof that my parents are, as you say."

Clayton looked at Afton and Phillip and spoke silently, *I hope the two of you are ready.*

Dechtire's expression darkened. "There will be none of that," she ordered sharply.

"Okay, Dechtire," agreed Clayton. "I'll say what needs to be said out loud."

He looked at Phillip, then Afton. The look said it all; no spoken words were needed for the two of them.

"Afton will hold Phillip's hand, but she will also need to hold your hand," Clayton explained. "That's just how it works."

Afton stepped cautiously toward Dechtire, who continued to sit motionless on the hay bale. She could see hell-fire burning behind those ebony eyes of hers. She took Phillip's hand and then reached for Dechtire's. The dark-haired woman recoiled just the slightest bit before allowing Afton to touch her. The air inside the barn was cool, but Dechtire's skin was scorching hot. The heat from her hand was bound to leave a red mark on her skin, but she couldn't think of that now. She had to focus. Afton closed her eyes and allowed Phillip's thoughts to become her own.

Once the thoughts were clear, she spoke. "There was a split among the Mingo and Irish people, who fell in love and married, back in the early 1960s. There were those who believed all people were the same and should be treated as such. They believed that the color of your skin should not determine your rank in the tribe or community. Dechtire, your parents came from the line of elders that did not feel the same. They believed you had to marry within the tribe. Yes, there were already those who mixed, but they were accepted because of their rank. All marriages were prearranged in accordance with the laws of the elders. Your parents' marriage was arranged when they were only children. The elders believed their union would be special because they had gifts, and that their children would have gifts."

Afton let Phillip's hand slip from hers. She felt like someone had knocked the breath from her lungs. Phillip reached out to steady her.

Dechtire was livid. "Is that it? There has to be more! Surely you don't believe that's all I need to know."

Afton interrupted her rant. "Yes, Dechtire, there's much more. Everything I just told you comes from Phillip's memories. He is a mixed, so he knows what went on. I had to tell you the backstory before I could tell you about your parents, Roy and Claire Youngblood."

Dechtire was visibly moved by the simple fact of hearing their names spoken. She had never known their names, so it was a huge moment for her. Afton realized that she should have waited until after she told her what her parents had planned for her before she revealed their names. She was connecting to them through their names alone. Afton gave her a minute to process that information.

Phillip gave her a look that said, *You should take a break. You're looking weak.* He was no silent talker, but he had a way of getting his message across with no more than a look. Afton returned the favor as she looked at him with a *No, I'm fine, and I don't want to disconnect what we have going with Dechtire. Just stay close and trust me.*

This time she took Dechtire's dominant left hand. She knew it would hold the secrets of anything bad she had done in her past. Afton didn't know what her response would be if she saw her hurting Joetta or Clayton, but it had to be done and the time was now.

She asked Dechtire if she was ready. She simply shrugged, so Afton proceeded. She took her left hand and prepared herself for the heat that would follow. But the burn never came. This time it was cold, as if she had just stuck her hand through the ice of a frozen pond. Afton gasped. Phillip started toward her, but she caught his eye and shook her head no. She continued holding Dechtire's hand until the coldness eventually became tolerable.

Afton cleared her mind of her own thoughts so that she would be open to receive Dechtire's memories. It was just a trickle at first, but before long, images began to gush in so fast she had a hard time keeping up. Slow down, slow down, she thought. Finally, the reel of the woman's unnerving horror show slowed to a manageable speed. She witnessed the birth of Dechtire. She felt Miss Betty's presence, then saw her hands passing Dechtire into the hands of Bernice, the woman who would raise Dechtire.

Several years slipped by with nothing unusual occurring. Around age eight, a man entered Dechtire's bedroom during the night. It was her father, Big John, and she didn't feel threatened because he had never before given her reason to. He lay beside her on the bed and waited until he thought she was asleep. He gently slipped his hand down the front of her white panties with the Winnie the Pooh design. Dechtire wasn't asleep, but she kept her eyes tightly shut, frozen with fear. She didn't know what to do. She wanted to scream, but nothing came out. He groaned and grunted like a hungry beast as he fondled her. Dechtire swung her elbow back and caught him in his eye. She mumbled as though she was dreaming. Big John whimpered like a wounded pup and slipped quietly out of the room. Dechtire was determined he would never touch her again. The next morning, Big John told Bernice he had run into the door frame on his way to the bathroom during the night, which explained the black eye.

Afton could see three older children; two girls and a boy. Dechtire didn't resemble anyone in the family. After Big John abused her, he urged the older siblings to torment her. They treated her like an outcast. Dechtire felt she was not part of that family, so she created her own world. She read every book she could get her hands on and read article after article on the Internet. The knowledge she accumulated led her to the certainty that she was not the child of Bernice and Big John Massey.

Next, Dechtire was on a field trip when she was about nine. The class went to Delbarton to see a Native American pow-wow. She was immediately drawn to the people there. She spent that day eavesdropping on their conversations. They had no idea that one of the young students was listening. Dechtire knew she was somehow connected to the people from the pow-wow. They had been talking about skinwalkers, and it had intrigued her to no end.

She kept up with her grades in school, but every spare minute was devoted to studying the legends of the Mingo-Irish mix. She knew without a doubt that somehow there had been a mistake made and she had been sent home with the wrong family. But she played her role in that family and tried not to draw attention to herself. Dechtire believed with all her heart that she would someday escape her tormentors and locate her true family.

The day was drawing near and she could feel it. She had learned from all her studying that skinwalkers were almost always men. There was an exception, though, and it could happen if a female was to take a life. It was only then, if the gene was in her bloodline, that she might start to "turn" during puberty. The thought of killing someone didn't seem to faze Dechtire in the least. She only wondered which member of her hideous family would be the one to die. That answer came when she was twelve years old. Bernice, Big John, and the two older sisters, Rachel and Jenny, were gone. Rachel and Jenny needed dresses for an upcoming dance, and they would be gone most of the day. That left Dechtire home alone with her older brother, Little John, age fourteen, who spent most of his time alone in the workshop in the barn.

He told Dechtire he wanted to show her the project he had been working on. She was curious, so she went along. Once they were inside the barn, Little John locked the shop door and tried to rape her. Dechtire had told Afton that story the night she had drugged her juice and burned her arm with the raven pendant. But seeing it for herself was different. Dechtire was strong, and she fought hard. She got her hands around a ball-peen hammer and landed it perfectly against Little John's temple. He dropped like a head-shot hog. Dechtire remained in survival mode while she cleaned the hammer and wiped off everything she had touched. She moved Little John's body, so it lay just below the big anvil that was mounted to the workbench. She even untied his shoelace, so it would appear that he had tripped and cracked his head. After she finished in the barn, she rushed back to the house. She laundered her clothes and put them back on. Dechtire sat back and waited for the family to return home and find their precious son dead in the barn. It worked without a hitch. Everything she had told Afton that night had really happened. She had killed her brother and had probably caused the deaths of other family members as well. This was a cold-blooded killer she was dealing with, and there was never one sign of remorse.

The visions skipped ahead to working at the prison. Dechtire sensed that Joetta had suspicions about her. Dechtire spoke briefly to someone about Joetta, but Afton couldn't see who it was. She went through Joetta's personnel file and saw that she, too, was from McDowell County. She wanted Joetta out of the picture, but the visions didn't show her actually causing Joetta's death. She saw Dechtire talking to the inmates before the class she'd taught. She had instructed them to start a fight and, if possible, kill Afton in the process. That didn't work, so she paid her a visit. If it hadn't been for Clayton coming to her rescue, she probably would have died that night. Then she saw Dechtire in the pharmacy, pouring a white substance into a container. That must have been when she used the graveyard dust on Clayton. Once again, the picture was not perfectly clear. However, she could see her face full of hate, and could feel it as well. Afton's body trembled; her grip on Dechtire's hand began to slip, and she struggled to keep hold. She could sense her laughing on the inside. It gave Dechtire great pleasure to cause her such distress.

In the next vision, Afton found herself in a place she didn't recognize. It was a huge barn, and she could smell the hay and the horses. She followed a staircase up to the small apartment above the barn. The furnishings were sparse and had apparently been provided by the landlord. She knew this was Dechtire's apartment. This was where she had been living while working at the prison. The frantic sounds of neighing and stomping in the stalls below made Afton jump. She rushed back down the stairs in time to see Dechtire with a large scythe in her hands. The horses were rearing up and screaming. They feared Dechtire and with good reason. She swung the scythe with the precision of a seasoned farmer. The first horse's head left his body and thudded to the barn floor. Blood spewed from the headless carcass for several moments before it, too, crashed to the floor. The next horse tried to back away, but he could not escape Dechtire's reach. The scythe made full contact with the horse's underbelly as it reared on its hind legs. There must have been over fifty feet of intestines unraveling across the barn floor. The horse screamed in agony as Dechtire brought the scythe down upon its head. The animal staggered briefly before collapsing. Both horses lay twitching in a huge pool of blood and guts that was already attracting hundreds of flies. Afton's stomach lurched at the gruesome display.

The vision started to change. Afton looked up in time to see a man standing in the barn's doorway. She wanted to scream out a warning, but she wasn't really there. Nothing she could do could prevent what had already taken place. Dechtire killed the horse farmer. She spun around as though, even then, she knew Afton would be watching. She threw back her head and howled with crazed laughter as she admired the glistening blood that now dripped from her hands.

It was time now for Dechtire to see her parents and what they were capable of. Afton grabbed her other hand and held on tight to both. The woman didn't like what was coming and tried to wiggle from her grasp. She threw the first vision at Dechtire like a fireball. It burned as it made contact with her mind. The vision was of her mom holding the dead baby girl that she believed was her own. And then her dad storming in and slinging threats at the midwife.

She showed Dechtire the years of drug abuse and the drug dealers they had beaten to death or had come close to killing. She saw the elders as they shamed Roy and Claire for not possessing the gift of skinwalking. The elders told them the only way they might gain the gift was if they were to birth a child that held the gift. Only then could they claim the gift for themselves by killing the child. Dechtire knew then that the midwife had saved her from death at the hands of her own parents. Afton took no pleasure in showing Dechtire such horrible things, but she had to know the truth once and for all. Her entire life had been based on lies. She could feel the fire building inside her, and Afton knew she was already planning how she would release it.

She needed to let Dechtire know what Roy and Claire had done to the midwife. Her name was Miss Betty, and she was a good woman. She helped to bring many children into this world. She only wanted to save you from Roy and Claire. They killed her by poisoning her. She suffered a great deal before leaving this world.

Since her death, I've wondered if she would have done the same had she known you would turn out as you did. Miss Betty was a virtuous woman, so I can only imagine she would have done what she felt was right.

Afton loosened her hands from those of the dark-haired woman, and as she did, Dechtire opened her eyes. They stood there in silence, staring at one another.

"Dechtire, there is no one here for you to blame, no one for you to hate, and certainly no one for you to exact revenge upon," Afton told her. "Your anger belongs with the elders who have long since passed. And for the two people known as Roy and Claire. They are the only ones left on Naked Creek that want to cause you harm. They will soon be here in Robinson Holler, and they will bring a terrible wrath with them."

Dechtire regarded her differently now. Her voice was bewildered as she spoke. "Afton, I don't know what to say to you. I have never been capable of caring, kindness, love, or even gratitude. My life has been full of strife. I did what I had to just to survive. I'm not asking you to understand, and I'm definitely not asking you to forgive me. I would have to be sorry for what I've done and I'm not. You showed me what I needed to see. The darkness that grows within me isn't going to accept the light that you possess. That's your gift alone. I wouldn't want any part of it." She stepped back into the depths of the shadowy barn to gather her things.

Afton had seen something else as she had held Dechtire's hands. It was a glimpse of her future. It made her sad to even think about it, so she tried her best to drive it from her mind.

Chapter 19: Bittersweet Revenge

Silas came barreling out of the woods. He was so out of breath, Afton was sure he would pass out.

"I've got them!" he told her excitedly. "I've Roy and Claire's bottles!"

"Here … give them to me," Afton said. Without another word, Silas nodded and did as she asked.

Phillip stepped forward. "Afton, maybe you should let me keep the bottles. I don't want you getting hurt over them."

"Likewise, Phillip. I don't want you getting hurt, either," she told him flatly. "The bottles are mine to deal with."

The three of them went inside the cabin with Maddie, Nola May, and Cardinal. Dechtire remained inside the barn. Afton could only guess that, after everything she had just been told, she needed some time to take it all in. No one felt comfortable with Dechtire there because it meant Roy and Claire were sure to show up, eventually.

"Afton," asked Nola May, "don't you think we should spend some time tryin' to figure out what to do with the Granny Bottles?"

"You're right, but I really don't know where to begin. I've read Miss Betty's book, and it made no mention of the bottles at all."

Once again, reassurance came from Maddie. "Afton, when the time comes, you will know what to do."

She only wished she could share her grandmother's confidence.

Phillip preferred not to leave anything to chance. Afton could tell he was anxious about Roy and Claire's impending arrival. He knew there would be chaos once Dechtire saw them. And the chance that Afton or one of her new family would get caught up in the middle of the conflict was almost inevitable. She recalled what Grandma Ruby had told her at the cabin about a war brewing. Phillip was out the door before she could stop him.

Afton ran after him. "Phillip, wait! What are you going to do? We don't want to rile her up after everything she's learned about her life. She'll go off the deep end and do who-knows-what!"

It was too late. Phillip was already at the barn and pulling the door open. Several beams of sunlight made their way through the clouds, barely illuminating the structure's interior. The two of them stood in the doorway, waiting for their eyes to adjust to the dim light. Afton no longer tried to stop Phillip. It was far too late for that. They glanced inside and then at each other. It appeared that Dechtire was gone.

All of a sudden, a dark mass sped toward them. The sound of beating wings was deafening. Phillip was fast on his feet, but not fast enough to account for Afton as well. A massive flock of barn swallows gushed out of the barn so quickly and with such force, she was knocked off balance and landed hard on her butt. Phillip had ducked and tried to pull her out of the way, but it happened too fast. Afton was fine other than a little dirt on her britches and the wind knocked out of her. Phillip put his hands out for her to grab, gave her a quick tug, and she sprang up like a jack-in-the-box.

"You don't know your own strength," she gasped.

Phillip didn't reply. He just stared ahead into the barn. Her eyes followed his. She could feel a scream welling up in her throat. It was quickly stifled by the palm of Phillip's hand. Afton understood now why the swallows had wanted out of the barn in such a hurry.

Somehow, Dechtire had made her way to the highest rafter of the barn. She was just crouching there on a four-inch beam. There were no bales of hay stacked up, nor was there a ladder. How had she come to be on that beam so high up? It was a small barn, but it was two stories high—and that didn't account for the open rafters to the roof, which put her a good twenty-five feet off the floor.

There was an eerie quietness both in the barn and outside. Not a bird was chirping or moving about from limb to limb. Dechtire sat like a gargoyle perched on an ancient castle wall, quietly waiting for its intended victim to stroll by. She looked different than she had an hour ago. Her face was devoid of expression, and her dark eyes shone like polished coal. Her hands were clasped around her knees, which were pulled tight against her chest. It was as though she had retreated within herself.

Afton felt cold, stale air wrap around her body like a cloak. It tightened around her core as if being cinched. She looked at Phillip with pleading eyes. She couldn't gather the breath to speak, so she mouthed the words help me. A look of terror tore across his face at that very moment. Did he believe he was about to lose her to the evil presence that had taken over the barn?

Phillip leaned down just enough to swoop her up into his arms. He turned on his heels, kicked the door closed behind them, and ran back to the cabin.

They moved so fast that Afton's face pressed hard against his chest. It felt as though his heart would pound right through his chest wall. Just as they reached the cabin, Silas swung the door open for them. Phillip quickly told the others what had happened at the barn and what they had seen. Afton still found herself unable to speak and began to panic. She had no idea what was happening, and it terrified her.

Phillip helped her to the chair in front of the fireplace. The heat radiating from the hearth slowly penetrated the cold shield that had formed around her, and little by little, her body thawed. Silas was on his knees at her side with his head buried in the crook of her arm. She could hear him quietly praying for God to help her find her way back to him. Afton closed her eyes and prayed too.

She could feel the presence of Grandma Ruby, Miss Betty, and Joetta all around her. She remained still with her eyes closed tight. She knew they would be with her only briefly, and she dared not chance missing their message, if there was one to be received.

"The book holds the key to your future," Miss Betty whispered. "Afton, you hold the key to the present."

Grandma Ruby added, "My dear, fair-eyed child, you will see through the darkness and expel it."

Then Joetta spoke softly. "Remember my warning, Afton. You know who tried to hurt you, but there is someone who stays hidden that has a part in it, as well."

Together they said, "Let the light shine child, it's a gift not to be reined in."

When the three women faded away, Afton slowly opened her eyes and realized that she was warm once again. She hugged Silas and thanked him for his prayers. Silas's mice, Dalton and Graham, scurried from his pocket and onto his shoulder. They stood on their tiny hind feet and squeaked their little sounds into his ear. This made Silas beam a big, beautiful smile.

When she asked what they had told him, he just grinned and said, "It's a secret."

The old Suburban that Roy and Claire drove drank oil almost as much as it drank gas. Roy had stopped to add another quart of oil when a feeling came to Claire like a ton of bricks.

"Roy, hurry up! We are close to our daughter! I can feel her. Please tell me you can sense her, too."

Roy had never shown any sign of premonition, intuition, or even recalling his dreams, for that matter. But Claire thought perhaps this time was different because the feeling had been so overwhelmingly strong. Roy just shrugged his shoulders and shook his head no.

Claire thought his senses were dulled because of all the drugs he had used. She had done her fair share, but Roy had always dived in headfirst, like a raccoon in a garbage can. Maybe the drugs had numbed his power. Or maybe he didn't have any power. The only specialties he had ever had as long as Claire had known him were a nasty temper and the drive to go through with whatever urge hit him at any given moment. Sometimes those urges left people dead.

Claire herself had felt dead from time to time over the years. No amount of drugs or vengeance made her feel alive. In the beginning, when they went on their rampages, she would get something of a kick out of it. Now, she only felt empty.

Soon, they were back on the road. Considering their progress so far, they figured they'd arrive at Robinson Holler in less than an hour.

"Grandma Ruby, Miss Betty, and Joetta just paid me a visit," Afton told them. "They each gave me a message. It sounded like a riddle or puzzle to me, though. Why couldn't they be more specific?"

Maddie answered that question. "It's not allowed. They cannot outright give you all the answers you seek, because it wouldn't be fair."

"What does that even mean? It wouldn't be fair?"

Nola May tried to explain. "It would be like interferin' with fate. They avoid that by only bringin' clues. We'll have to figure the rest out for ourselves."

Afton got up and walked to the kitchen. She craved a cup of Miss Betty's special tea. As she walked past the table and chairs, she heard something clank. She felt down to the side pocket of her pants and rubbed her hand against something. She shoved her hand in and retrieved the old skeleton key that Miss Betty had given her on that very first day. Afton held it in her right palm and traced all around it with her left index finger. The key tingled against her flesh, as though charged with a strange energy.

"Miss Betty told me that I held the key to the present."

"What did you say, Afton?" Clayton asked, having overheard her.

She hurried back to the main room and repeated what Miss Betty had told her. She opened her hand and showed them the key.

"Miss Betty said this key would open the three gates that led to Joetta's cabin," she explained. "I saw those three gates one night in a dream. The dream was about you, Maddie, when Joetta's mom was ill and her dad brought you there. In the dream, it seemed to me that you had a hand in causing her death."

"Afton, Joetta's mom was ate up with the cancer and was dying a slow and painful death," Maddie quickly replied. "When I arrived, she was very close to crossing over. I blended some of our herbs to lessen her fear. As it turned out, she breathed her last breath at that very moment. It was as though she had been waiting for me to get there before crossing over. Sometimes when one is dying—and in this case, leaving behind a child so young—they fight till the very end, until they know it's okay to let go."

"I feel guilty for believing you could do such a horrible thing, Maddie. Please forgive me."

"Afton, there's nothing to forgive. You didn't know who I was at the time, and I can only imagine what it had looked like to you. I only wish you had told me about the dream sooner."

"Those gates have been gone for more than a decade," Phillip said. "Miss Betty had me haul them off because they had fallen down and no one used that path anymore. Why would she give you a key to gates that were no longer there?"

Nola May was quick to answer. "Because she knew the day would come when you would need that key and whatever it unlocks."

Afton could only hope that she would figure out what the key unlocked before Roy and Claire arrived. Her thoughts drifted to the barn and Dechtire.

Roy parked the Suburban next to the car that sat empty near the narrow dirt road. It was Dechtire's car, but of course to them it was completely unfamiliar. Roy started unloading his belongings from the back of the vehicle. Claire thought she had seen everything he had loaded, but she definitely didn't remember him loading two gas cans. Claire had hoped they could just grab their daughter and get out, but apparently Roy had iniquitous plans for the remaining Cunnin' Folk.

Silas suddenly made a disturbing announcement. "The bad ones have arrived and they're walking toward us now."

Afton was sitting on the side of the bed holding the two tiny Granny Bottles. How could she use their contents to get rid of the bad ones? She found it a strange and eerie realization that somewhere hidden in the woods were three more of those bottles—one for her, one for Lilly Dale, and one for Clayton. Then it dawned on her what Silas had just said.

She stood and started to walk out of the room, but realized she still had the bottles in her hand. She grabbed a piece of felt off the bedside table to wrap them so they wouldn't break inside her pocket. When she turned them to make sure the bottoms were protected, she noticed a tiny mark. A key had been painted on the bottom of each of the Granny Bottles.

Phillip burst into the bedroom. "Afton, they're almost here!"

There was no time for her to explain to Phillip what she had discovered. She didn't know for sure what it meant, but she did have an idea.

"Is there time for Maddie, Nola May, and Silas to go to Grandma Ruby's cabin, where they might be safer?"

"No," Phillip answered. "And even if there was, they wouldn't go. They are much like you in that way."

She nodded. "Well, at least try to make them stay inside and out of sight, please."

A commotion started inside her head. Clayton was trying to get her attention. *I'm listening ... go ahead.*

He silently said, *You and I need to go out first so I can try to hear Roy and Claire communicating with one another.*

Afton headed for the cabin door. Clayton was already there waiting for her. She looked back at the others and told them that Phillip would let them know what to do. Then they slipped out into the cold. At least the snow had stopped. The mercury definitely had not risen, though. Only silence emanated from the darkness of the barn. She wondered if Dechtire was still perched up in the rafters, waiting.

Clayton and Afton headed for the small patch of woods just beyond the barn where the dirt road came out. They hoped to be able to hear or see Roy and Claire approaching from that direction. Afton could tell by the look on Clayton's face that he was listening for any loud thoughts coming from them. He looked at her and shook his head no.

As they sat in the thicket and waited for the bad ones to come, Afton considered the different paths that had been taken to bring them all to that point in time. Sometimes, the paths we are on seem so clear, she thought to herself. Those are the straight and narrow paths. Sometimes we take many curves and never know what's around the bend. Those are the unsettling times when we take chances on the unknown. Those times are unknown to us, but there's a higher power that knows what paths we will follow, where they will take us, and how it will all turn out. At that moment, she was glad to know that it wasn't all in her hands alone.

There was movement to the side of them. Clayton looked Afton's way briefly, then back toward the noise. He sent her a message: *Claire is anxious about the gas cans that Roy brought along.*

Afton's heart skipped several beats. She wanted to warn the people she had grown to love that Roy and Claire's intentions were more macabre than she could have imagined. She hoped that Clayton had sent a message to Nola May, letting her know what was taking place.

Soon, they could make out their shapes moving slowly just beyond the dirt road. In a couple of minutes, they would be able to see them as they moved in and out of the underbrush. Afton was about to get Clayton's attention when a hand firmly covered her mouth. She thrust her elbow back as hard as she could. She heard a groan and knew she had made contact. Afton turned to find that her "attacker" was actually Phillip. How did they not hear him come up on them? His smoke-gray eyes smoldered a dark charcoal now. She felt bad for having hit him, but there was nothing she could do about it at that moment.

Clayton was deep in concentration, trying to get inside Roy's head and urge him to turn away from the cabin. But it wasn't working. Roy and Claire kept right on coming. The pair was fully in sight. There were no longer trees for them to hide behind. They would actually have to walk past their hiding spot in order to get to the cabin.

In the distance, an animal howled a song of impending agony. Phillip tilted his head as though he was tempted to respond. He made no noise, but Afton was sure that she saw him sniff the air. Roy and Claire were just a few feet from the three. She repeatedly had to remind herself to take a breath.

Clayton continued to try and silent talk. His focus had shifted to Claire. She came to a halt and looked around. Roy stopped and set down the two gas cans he had been carrying.

"What is it, Claire?" Roy asked, annoyed. "Did you hear something?"

Clayton closed his eyes and burned an idea into Claire's thoughts.

"What are we doing here, Roy?" she asked him.

"You know what we're doing," Roy hissed. "It's time to get rid of the rest of the Cunnin' Folk, and if our daughter is here, then we drain her of her powers."

"Then what?" Claire wanted to know. "It will never be enough for you. Will I be the next one you drain, if you think I have any power?"

Roy gave a dry laugh and said, "You? Power? Don't kid yourself, Claire. If I thought for a minute, you had something worth taking, I would have taken it a long time ago."

Clayton had planted the seed. Now he had to wait and see if it would take root.

Roy's attention was drawn by noises coming from the barn. "This way," he whispered. Then the two made a beeline in that direction. At least they were not headed toward the cabin. Not for the time being, anyway.

Roy put his hand on the iron handle of the barn door. He hesitated, but only for a moment, before pulling the door open. Afton expected to hear screams from Claire or screeches from Dechtire, who waited patiently in the rafters. Was she still perched on the crossbeam or had she come down? Was she even still in the barn? Her mind was swirling with every possible scenario she could think of. Why wasn't she hearing the commotion that she was bracing herself for?

Then, without warning, it began. Horrible squealing, shrill and ear-piercing, that sounded like a freight train attempting to stop on a dime. Afton, Phillip, and Clayton rushed from the safety of their hiding place. The urge to see what was happening was too powerful to hold them back.

The barn door stood open. There was just enough sunlight to afford them a view inside. What they saw caught them off guard.

Dechtire was indeed still inside the barn and had come down from the beam. She had apparently landed on Roy's back. They fought savagely, as though only one could possibly come out alive, if even that. Claire was nowhere in the mix. She stood nearby, watching nervously as her husband fought to take the life of Dechtire, their daughter. It seemed that Clayton's thought still burned fresh in her mind.

They were not aware of it yet, but Silas had snuck out of the cabin and was also in the barn. He too, had to see for himself who was getting hurt in the fray. The boy was hidden behind a couple of bales of hay that sat just below the window he had crawled through.

Clayton, Phillip, and Afton stood and watched as the battle played out. They had to jump in at some point to break it up, but they agreed that Dechtire needed time to see firsthand just how far Roy was willing to take things. As for Claire, there was a new fury quickly building behind her deadened eyes. Roy was strong, but Dechtire knew she was in a fight for her life and she was giving it her all. Her long fingernails were sharpened like claws. She struck out and hit her target dead-on, slashing at Roy's throat. She dug her talons into his neck and tore away strips of flesh dripping with warm blood. He jerked to escape the fury of her claws and stumbled back just enough to catch a glimpse of the small boy hiding behind the hay. Desperately, he took advantage of the boy's bad luck.

Dechtire turned her vengeance toward Claire, who stared motionlessly at what was unfolding in front of her. Claire knew now that Roy was a monster. She also knew that she had done enough bad things in her life to deserve whatever she got. Dechtire stepped close enough to look into Claire's gaunt face. Her eyes reminded Dechtire of a hospice patient's eyes dulled by the darkness of knowing they were about to die. There was scarcely a hint of light left in the faded eyes that stared back at her.

Claire's intuition told her that she was not long for this world, but the only thing she felt was relief. She pulled a switchblade from the back pocket of her jeans and waved it at Dechtire. She thought she could speed things along by threatening her.

Dechtire was so amped up with anger that she totally ignored the threat and grabbed the opportunity to seize her revenge. Dechtire easily sidestepped the knife and pushed Claire hard against the barn wall. Claire let out a whimper and blood started to trickle from the corner of her mouth. There had been two iron rods protruding from the barn wall exactly where Claire had hit. Miss Betty had used the rods to hang her mattock on after gardening. Strangely, the tool was absent from the three-inch rods at that moment.

Dechtire watched her birth mother gasping for air as her lungs grew engorged with blood. The gasps turned into wet, gurgling sounds. Afton knew Claire would be gone in just a few minutes. She called out to Dechtire, and when she turned her way, Afton pulled the Granny Bottle with Claire's name on it from her pocket and tossed it to her. Dechtire caught the small bottle and looked at it. Claire already knew what Dechtire needed to do. It would be Claire's only chance to do something good for her daughter.

Claire gathered the last ounce of strength she could muster and spoke. "You must drink it, Dechtire," she whispered. "It's all I have to give you, so please let me do this one thing for you."

Without hesitation, Dechtire unscrewed the tiny lid, tipped the bottle to her mouth, and drank down the liquid. Claire released one final sigh as the last drop of liquid left the bottle. Claire's gift was now Dechtire's.

Nola May, Maddie, and Cardinal ran from the cabin, screaming that Silas was not in his room. Something was wrong, and Dechtire felt it as well. She knew immediately that Roy had grabbed the boy, and she also knew he wouldn't hesitate to kill him—especially if he thought he could gain some special power by doing so.

Clayton fought hard to locate Silas's thoughts. Finally, he heard the boy in his mind and sent him a message. He told him to call out to all of his animal friends to help him until they could find him. There was a faint *Okay* in return.

"My battle's not with all of you," Dechtire told them. "Get me to Roy and I'll do what I can for the boy."

Oddly enough, they believed her.

Afton pulled the other bottle from her pocket and handed it to Dechtire. "Claire had a gift, and she gave it to you with her dying breath. Roy is different, so don't be too quick to drink in the darkness that resides in him."

"They will be at the lake!" Maddie yelled out to them.

So, that's where they headed, all of them. Phillip was in the lead, and no one could keep up with his pace. Afton's neck hairs prickled as another howl sounded. That one was coming from the direction of the lake. She broke into a dead run and soon caught up with Phillip. She was about to pass him by when he caught her arm.

"The howling isn't Roy," he told her. "Don't be afraid."

Afton didn't take the time to ask him whether the howls came from beast or man. She wasn't sure she wanted to know the answer. There was only one thing on her mind, and that was getting to Silas before Roy could kill him.

It wasn't long before Dechtire caught up to them. The lake was within sight and so was Silas. His small body lay motionless on the big rock while Roy towered over him. A fire was burning in a circle next to the rock.

Just then, a figure stepped from behind a massive oak, and Phillip immediately started talking to him. It was his nephew, Connor. He looked different out of his prison clothes, but his smoky gray eyes were the same.

Phillip said, "I need everyone to spread out. We need to surround Roy and Silas. Cardinal, you get closer to Connor."

"Will do!" shouted Cardinal.

"Maddie, you and Nola May stick together."

"Always have," said Maddie.

"Afton, you, Dechtire, and I will fill in the gaps."

They shortened the distance in a split second, or so it seemed.

Roy had a massive rock in his hands, holding it high above his head. He was about to slam it down on Silas when a red-tail hawk swooped in and reopened the blood-crusted wounds on Roy's neck. He fell backwards and dropped the rock, screaming as he clutched at his throat. They were all there in a circle, surrounding the screaming Roy and their precious Silas.

"You sonsofbitches!" Roy half screamed; half cried.

Clayton sent Silas another message. Silas didn't hesitate. He bolted from the rock and into Afton's arms. Dechtire moved in closer and they tightened the circle by joining hands. Afton recalled the dream about the people in a circle by the lake. Had the dream revealed that very moment?

Roy saw Dechtire among the others. "Baby," he pleaded, "I came to get you away from these people. You can finally come home with me and your mother. You belong with your true family."

Dechtire cringed, disgusted by the man's dishonest appeal. "I have no real family," she said bitterly. "And just so you will know, Roy, I am well aware of what you want from me and the only way you can get it. How does it feel to know that your daughter possesses everything you ever wanted? Claire even had power, but you were too stupid to recognize it for what it was. It was a gift, Roy, and she gave it willingly to me."

Hate burned in Roy's eyes. How pitiful he was now. He was alone with no wife left to strike out at. He had no one to inflict suffering on but his daughter. Roy took his chances and lunged at Dechtire. As he did so, she popped the cap on the remaining bottle.

Afton screamed, "No …" Her heart raced. She was certain Dechtire was about to drink it. "Take this!" Dechtire flung the bottle into the fire in one swift move.

"You worthless bitch!"

Roy burst into flames before their eyes.

"Don't watch, Silas!" Afton attempted to shield him from the horrible sight, but it was too late.

"Noooo!" Roy writhed on the ground as he scrambled to put out the flames. But there was no extinguishing the fire until he was dead.

After burning for quite some time, eventually his charred body disintegrated into ash. A gust of wind picked up his remains and carried them far away from Robinson Holler.

Dechtire looked at Afton. "You're right," she said. "I don't want his darkness in me."

The flames from the fire dwindled and a cloud of dense smoke suddenly filled the circle. When the smoke cleared, Dechtire was gone.

Silas looked up at Afton with questioning eyes, but didn't have to ask a thing.

"She is gone from here and she won't be back."

Together, they walked back to Miss Betty's cabin, but this time, they went a lot slower so they could take in the beauty that surrounded them. Afton knew Dechtire had a lot she had to work through. She had to make right all the wrongs she had done—or at least try to do so. It might take her a lifetime of trying.

Dechtire was finished with the Cunnin' Folk. Afton could only hope.

CHAPTER 20: HIDER

Back at Miss Betty's cabin, they all chipped in and prepared a huge supper. They had reason to celebrate and give thanks. Connor and Cardinal were inseparable; they had been apart for far too long.

The dedication of these people was hard to imagine. *These people,* Afton thought to herself. *I am one of them now.*

Maddie called everyone to the kitchen, and they ate, talked, reminisced, and laughed. The night hours clicked by quickly and it was after 2 a.m. by the time they finally decided to go to bed. Most of them slept on the floor, but it was comfortable and felt like home. The time to get up would come soon enough, and the goodbyes would start shortly afterward. Afton didn't like the idea of leaving, but it was going to happen, regardless.

She slipped in and out of one dream and into the next. They all seemed to run together, and they all ended with her leaving Robinson Holler. The sun came up and lit the cabin with its coruscating beams. It had been many days since the sun had shone so brightly. Nola May and Maddie had shared Miss Betty's room, while Connor and Cardinal shared the other. It would be some time before the latter two would be up and about. Afton lay there in her makeshift bed and listened to the morning sounds. Winter songbirds chirped happily just outside the still-frosted window. Silas was playing with Dalton and Graham. Phillip and Clayton were bringing in more wood for the fire. Maddie and Nola May sat in the kitchen, drinking their strong breakfast tea. They were all welcoming sounds to her.

When Afton got up and went to the door, she found that a fresh blanket of snow had fallen. It covered the ground and clung to every limb. It made everything appear clean and new again. The radiant glow of the sun's beams danced on the snow's surface, changing the snow crystals into shimmering diamonds. The quiet whispers of two people in love floated through the air like dandelion feathers once the yellow is long gone.

Cardinal and Connor appeared from their room. Both had the look of fulfillment after months of separation. Silas stopped playing with Dalton and Graham long enough to look up, and he, too, recognized their love. Despite his tender age, he knew more than many adults.

The couple announced their departure shortly after breakfast. They were eager to return to their own home. Cardinal and Conner needed and deserved more privacy than that small, crowded cabin provided them. Afton was forever grateful to them both and knew they would remain friends forever. They said their goodbyes and were on their way.

Clayton remained for most of the day, reminiscing about the "good old days" he had spent with his grandmother, Mommy Bud. Then it was his turn to say goodbye. When Clayton left, he took Nola May along to drop her at her home. Clayton was returning to the prison, back to being warden to the two hundred plus inmates in Duck, West Virginia.

He told Afton to take as much time as she needed before coming back to work. Back to work. Those three simple words felt like a billy goat had just rammed her in the gut. It was inevitable; she knew she had to return to the Village of McKinley and to work. What about Silas, though? Was it right of her to assume that Phillip would continue to look after him?

Maddie interrupted her thoughts. "Afton, you look as if you're a million miles away."

"No, Maddie, my thoughts are right here. I feel torn about leaving this place and going back home and back to work."

"Why would you feel guilty? You've always known the Village of McKinley as your home. You have your house there where you were raised by Ruby. And your job at the prison. Perhaps there's something else that you now long for …"

"I've never known anything else. I don't know why I'm worrying so much about Silas. I know Phillip will take care of him."

"And me and Nola May will help," Maddie added.

"I know you will. Silas is so fond of everyone here. He is blessed to have you all."

"You know, someone else he is quite fond of is you, Afton. You won't be too far away. We can always visit."

"You're right, Maddie. I can come down on my long breaks, and maybe you all could come to see me."

Afton had convinced herself that it would all work out, but something was still gnawing away at her. What had Miss Betty told her during her last visit or dream? She had said she held the key to the present, and the book held the key to her future. Afton's first thought had been the gate key, and that had been wrong. It had been the Granny Bottles with the key painted on the bottoms. What if she couldn't figure out the book?

"Afton, it's getting late," said Phillip. "You aren't going to leave tonight, are you?"

"No, I think I'll wait until the morning."

Phillip smiled. "Good. I wouldn't want you on these roads late at night. Sleep well."

"Thank you, Phillip, for everything. Good night."

Afton pulled back the heavy quilts and settled in for the night. She was glad to be spending her last night there off the floor and in a real bed. Maddie had the other bed. Phillip and Silas were camped out in the living room again. Silas didn't seem to mind a bit. She wondered if Phillip was comfortable. That was her last thought before a deep slumber carried her off into a world of dreams.

She felt something cold on her face. When she opened her eyes, Afton discovered she was outside in the dark of night. Her thin cotton gown was no match for the biting winter wind. Dime-sized snowflakes were coming down hard, and they stung her skin as they landed on her face.

The moon was full. It allowed her to see the individual flakes of snow as they drifted to the ground. They sparkled in the moonlight. On the earth, several feet in front of her, she saw a different color. It was dark crimson, and it glistened as it began to crystalize and freeze. Afton followed the crimson trail with her eyes, through the powdery snow until it formed a complete circle around her. An old wooden sign stood just beyond the circle. She strained to read the faded words: Givers to the right and Takers to the left. What did it mean?

Afton closed her eyes and tried to remember why the words on the sign seemed familiar. Then it finally dawned on her. Grandma Ruby had always told her that folks could be divided into two groups: Givers and Takers. Did Afton actually know what she had meant? Had she taken it literally? Some people take things from you and some give things to you?

No. Even back then, she knew she was referring to energy. Maybe good and bad. There were people in this world who took from you without asking. They stole your energy and left you dark and empty. The Givers did the opposite: they emanated good energy. You could feel it as it made its way inside you, leaving a warmth that glowed like embers. Those kinds of people always gave freely and asked for nothing in return.

Afton opened her eyes again. The sign was still there, but now there were people standing on either side. To the right were Grandma Ruby, Miss Betty, Joetta, and Afton's parents, Ida and Ora. Her memory of her parents had faded like an old photograph, but she recognized them in an instant. Her heart leapt. She caught movement and her eyes shifted to the left. She saw Roy, Claire, Darcy Doyle, and a couple of other inmates from the prison who had died. There were several more people standing on the left side of the sign, but she had no idea who they were. Afton was completely surrounded by the dead. They were separated in front of her by the sign and behind her by an old tree. Somehow, she knew Grandma Ruby would have referred to that tree as a "Spirit Tree."

Afton wanted to reach out or run to her family, but she didn't. Grandma Ruby's eyes warned her it was best to stay within the circle. She was safe there. That was Grandma Ruby's way of reminding her about the Givers and Takers. She needed to be aware of the living and of which group they belonged to.

The people began to fade until, eventually, they were completely gone. The sign and the crimson circle vanished as well.

The snow stopped and then disappeared. Suddenly, the moon was replaced with the bright, warm glow of sunshine. Afton no longer felt cold. She was filled with a light that lifted her mood and spirit.

It was springtime now. The ground that had been a crusty blanket of snow was now covered with lush, green grass. Buds were on the trees and daffodils and hyacinths were blooming. The little purple flowers released a wonderful lavender aroma. The smell was refreshing as she drew in an extra-long breath and held it as long as she could. Spring had always been her favorite season. It held the promise of new beginnings. Grandma Ruby had always become childlike with enthusiasm when springtime approached. She would spend most of the day outside planting flowers and working in the garden. If what she was experiencing was a dream, then Afton believed it meant that life would go on past that harsh winter that had held so much pain and darkness. Spring would come again and bring with it new life.

The scene changed again. Now it was summer. The grass crunched beneath her bare feet and the air around her felt like a heat wave. She saw a thermometer nailed to a fencepost with its reading sitting dead on 90 degrees. Tension hung heavy in the air. She knew this would be a trying time. Tempers always rose right along with the mercury.

Afton awoke to the sound of Silas's laughter. She reflected on the strange trio of dreams that were so fresh in her mind. Were the dreams a message from Grandma Ruby and the other Givers who had been a part of her life?

Life seemed to be a string of puzzles waiting to be finished. She hoped she would not grow weary trying to piece it all together.

Afton climbed out of bed and headed toward the laughter. Maddie was in the kitchen preparing breakfast. Silas was laughing at something Phillip had told him. It was good to see the child laugh. He deserved to be happy. She hoped he would remain that way.

He looked up at her and the laughter died on his lips. "Maddie is making a special breakfast for you since you're leaving us today."

That all but tore Afton's heart in two.

"Silas, you know I'm not leaving forever," she promised him. "I'll come see you all on my long weekends, and maybe sometime Phillip could drive you up to see me. Would you like that?"

Silas answered with enthusiasm, "Sure I would, Afton!"

Maddie called from the kitchen. "Come get it while it's hot."

She had made silver dollar pancakes. Special recipe that had been passed down five generations back. Rich, golden maple syrup that had come from that very holler, and warmed to perfection. There was fresh sausage, bought from a family from two ridges over. Maddie only bought pork from them. The sausage had just the right amount of sage. Made for some fine sausage gravy. Cathead biscuits that lived up to their name. Bacon had been smoked low and slow. Eggs, soft fried eggs from her own hens. And fried taters and onions in her grandmother's cast-iron skillet.

Afton was anxious, but that didn't stop her from enjoying the meal. Good quality food; the country way of showing love. Maddie wasn't one for skimping on that ingredient.

Silas managed to engulf two triple stacks of pancakes and a half dozen strips of bacon.

Phillip and Connor ate two plates of food that were so overloaded they couldn't hold another crumb. They all ate their fill and enjoyed it.

The entire house was filled with the smell of hickory-smoked bacon and fried onions. It was full of something else, as well. Love.

Once the feast and wonderful fellowship were over, there was a quiet time of contentment.

Everyone seemed to be doing okay with Afton leaving. She was the one having a hard time with it. She knew it was what she needed to do, but something didn't seem right. She believed it to be more than feeling guilt for leaving. Something seemed unfinished.

After breakfast, she packed her belongings, which didn't take long at all. Phillip and Silas were outside, and Maddie had finished cleaning up after breakfast and was waiting at the kitchen table for her. She had fixed them each a cup of tea. Afton joined her at the table.

"You know, dear, sometimes those dark clouds only seem to be gone," Maddie began. "Sometimes they're just hidden behind a veil. They will eventually show themselves again. You may have to catch them with their guard down."

Somehow, Afton didn't believe she was talking entirely about clouds. "Maddie, are you trying to tell me something in a roundabout way?"

"Probably just the ramblings of an old lady. I just don't want you to get too comfortable. Life can surprise you at times and it isn't always good. But, then again, I reckon you've already been through a lot of the not-so-good."

Afton started to tell her about the strange dreams she'd had, but decided against it. She wondered if perhaps she had experienced the seasonal dreams the previous night as well.

The goodbyes went fairly fast during her second departure from Robinson Holler. She wasn't sure if that helped or made it harder. Nevertheless, Afton was on her way back to the Village of McKinley by ten a.m. The drive was uneventful, and she arrived home a little after one o'clock.

She decided to unpack before fixing a bite for lunch. By two o'clock, she was sitting in Grandma Ruby's thinkin' chair, eating a sandwich and drinking a glass of ice water. Afton hadn't thought to stop and buy milk. Before it got too late in the day, she called Clayton's office at the prison. She half expected his secretary to pick up, but wasn't surprised when he answered.

Clayton answered the phone with a question. "Hello, Afton. Can I assume you're back home now?"

"You would assume correctly. I take it your dowsing abilities are working well, since you knew that it was me calling."

He laughed a bit and said, "Yes, I suppose all is working well. Can I expect you to return to work in the morning?"

"Yes," she assured him. "I gave George a call already and let him know. He seemed glad to hear I would be back."

"Everyone will be glad to have you back on the job," Clayton told her. "I'll see you in the morning."

"Okay, Clayton. Bye."

Afton had one more phone call to make. She dialed Miss Betty's number. Silas answered on the second ring. She told him she was just letting them know she had arrived home safely and hoped to see them next month when she had her next long weekend off. "Oh," she blurted before the call ended. "Tell Phillip I said hello."

The boy chuckled. "I'll be sure to tell him."

The day slipped by rather quickly. Before Afton realized, it had grown late, and she felt herself become sleepy. She needed a good night's rest, and it felt good to be back in her own bed. She slept soundly, without any dreams—none that she could recall, anyway.

Afton's return to work after four weeks off went pretty smoothly. She thought the fact that Dechtire was no longer around to make trouble might have had something to do with that. It was also nice to have Clayton nearby. They would take their lunch breaks together from that day forward. It continued like that through the remainder of the winter. There were a couple of heavy snowstorms and a few run-ins with inmates, but nothing she couldn't handle.

Spring made its return not long after Saint Patrick's Day. The grass started to green up and flowers pushed their way up through the rich West Virginia soil. Before she knew it, spring had passed and summer had arrived.

Soon, it was time for the summertime family weekend at the prison. Afton usually worked both the family picnic that was held in midsummer and the one in late September. The family members and friends that were coming to see their loved ones had to be searched, regardless of age. The searches took place in one building, then visitors were chaperoned to the main yard, where huge canopies had been set up for the occasion. That day the sun was out and shining brightly, so the shade beneath the canopies would be welcome.

Afton would work her way to a tree off to the side, where she had a better vantage point to observe everyone. She looked up at the rooftops and saw that the extra security officers were in place with rifles in hand. She grabbed a walkie-talkie and headed toward her shade tree. Afton's eyes always seemed to be drawn to the very young visitors running around in the midst of so many predators. She wondered how many had already been violated. Were the children even aware of where they were, and why their dads, uncles, or grandfathers could not leave?

The morning had mainly consisted of requests for sunscreen and first aid for one bee sting. Lunch would be served shortly. Afton was watching a child toss a ball between her mom and what she assumed to be her inmate dad. The game had been going on for about ten minutes when the inmate leaned down and picked the little girl up.

The inmates were allowed to hold their young children, but Afton had an uneasy feeling about this one. She looked around to see if any of the officers were watching. No one else appeared to notice, and now the inmate was on the move. The mom remained where she was. Afton immediately walked away from her shade tree and in the same direction as the inmate. She stayed a hundred feet or so off to the side to avoid drawing attention.

Her first thought was, Clayton, where are you? Would he be listening?

She kept the inmate and child in view. Where was he taking her? If he wanted sunscreen for her, he was walking away from the nurse's station. The inmate looked back briefly but kept going. He was headed toward the smoking area behind the weight room. Afton's heart felt like it was about to explode, it was beating so fast. She quickly walked to the other side of the building. She heard Clayton telling her he was there, and she was relieved to hear his voice in her head. Her pulse immediately started to slow. She knew her feeling had been right, and she wasn't alone.

She peeked around the corner of the building in time to see the inmate pass the little girl over to another inmate who had been waiting. Afton opened her mouth to protest, but quickly closed it when she saw a shadow moving on the ground in front of her. She looked up in time to see two armed officers move across the rooftop and take aim at the two inmates. Clayton appeared from behind a tree. He must have been there the entire time.

Clayton's voice rang out. "Gently put the child down and place your hands behind your head!"

The first inmate attempted to grab the child back, but one of the armed officers prevented that by shooting him with a rubber bullet. The inmate fell to the ground and rolled in the grass, screaming. He would have a sore chest for several days, but he would live.

The other inmate refused to put the child down. "No," he growled defiantly. "I intend on having her!"

Clayton was definitely speaking to him, but she couldn't hear his words and neither could the officers. Finally, the inmate gently put the girl down on the ground. He turned to run, but the officers fired, peppering him with their rubber bullets. He hit the ground and wailed at the top of his lungs from the pain.

The little girl was sobbing and scared half to death. She was younger than she had originally thought, maybe five years old at the most. Afton walked toward her, and when she looked into her eyes, she stopped crying. The little girl reached for the nurse and said, "Up."

Afton picked her up and she buried her head in her shoulder. It turned out that the mother had brought her daughter to the prison not only to see her boyfriend, but to allow another inmate have his way with the child to pay off a debt. It sickened Afton to her very core. The state police and Child Protective Services were notified. The little girl's name was Violet. She cried as Afton passed her over to the woman from CPS.

Violet reached for her and cried. "No, don't let Vio go!"

A wave of guilt washed over Afton. She wished she could take Violet back into her arms and protect her forever. But all she could do was pray she would go to a safe and loving foster home. Clayton caught up with her after things calmed down. He knew what she was thinking and, in his special way, told her that she had helped save the little girl.

The events of the day brought an early end to the prison picnic. Afton hoped that the prison officials would take the incident into consideration before allowing any more family events. She was all for human rights and rewards for good behavior, but inviting the innocent into a prison full of pedophiles was too much temptation, even for the best behaved.

Before clocking out, she stopped by Clayton's office and asked if he wanted to come over for supper. This was not unusual for her to do, and they did not talk about their visits with the other employees. Gossip ran rampant in most workplaces, and the prison was no exception. But she and Clayton were family; they both felt that way.

When Clayton finally arrived, she greeted him with, "We're having brown beans and cornbread tonight."

"Sounds great. I was thinking maybe you were still worried about Violet."

"You've grown to know me too well, my friend. Of course I'm worried about Violet."

Clayton tried to put her mind at ease. "I thought you would be and so was I, so I checked with child services before I left. They were able to place her with a foster family with an excellent reputation and many years of experience. They assured me that it was one of their best homes."

"Thank you, Clayton. That really does make me feel better."

After dinner, they sat out back and enjoyed the breeze that blew in from the woods.

"Have you talked to Nola May lately?"

"I spoke with her last night for a good while," said Clayton. "She sounded good, and she told me everyone else was doing well. She and Maddie have their hands full, trying to tend to all the women who refuse to go to the hospital to deliver their babies."

"Did she mention Silas and Phillip? I've put off going back to see them. I don't want to stir things up if Silas has settled into life there with Phillip."

"Don't you mean life without you?" Clayton asked. "Afton, he misses you badly. They all miss you."

"Once I returned here to the Village, I found it easier to just stay put. I miss everyone there terribly. I believe I've put off going back for selfish reasons. I think it would be too hard on me to have to leave again."

Clayton looked into her eyes. "Thank you for being honest with me and for being honest with yourself too. Sometimes you need to put others ahead of your own needs. I'm going to Robinson Holler this coming weekend. I'll leave Friday after work, and you'll come with me."

"You didn't put that in the form of a question," she said with a laugh, "but I'll answer it, anyway. Yes, I'll go with you. We can drive Hazel if you like. You can just leave your truck here."

Afton was angry at herself for not keeping her word to Silas about visiting regularly. She had been a coward. All she had done was send a handful of generic cards saying hello and "hope all is well."

Silas—and Phillip—deserved better than that.

It was Thursday. Only one more day, and Afton and Clayton would be on their way to Robinson Holler. She finished the task at hand, which was to take off the orders from that morning's doctor call visits. The phone rang, and she answered it.

"Medical, may I help you?"

There was a brief pause, then a familiar voice came on the line. "Afton, are you okay?"

"Silas, is that you? Is something wrong?"

He paused again before answering. "I just had a feeling that you were in trouble. Please don't be mad that I called. Phillip told me I couldn't bother you at work, so I waited until he went out to do some chores."

"Silas, you won't get into trouble for calling. Tell me what's going on. What has you so worried?"

Silas whispered, "I gotta go. Phillip's back."

"No, Silas, wait. You won't get in trouble."

But it was too late. He'd already hung up.

She glanced at the clock and saw that it was time for pill call. "Crap!" she said out loud. "I'll call him back as soon as I get home."

Pill call took an extra fifteen minutes. Anytime she was in a hurry, something odd always seemed to come up; it never failed. That day was no different. Halfway through pill pass, the electricity went out and she had to rely on the dim emergency lights and a battery-powered lantern to finish up.

Finally, Afton was ready to give her report and clock out. Then the night nurse called and told her she would be a little late because her babysitter had had a flat and was late arriving. She had to remind herself to just take a deep breath. It'll be okay, she told herself. Relief will be here shortly.

"Hey, Afton, you working late?" It was George.

"I just have to stay a little longer because my relief is running a bit behind."

"I've been wanting to talk to you," he replied, "so maybe now is a good time."

Just then Shelby, the night nurse, walked into Medical. "Sorry I'm late, Afton. It was one of those things that was out of my control."

"Don't worry about it. Unexpected things happen to all of us. George, can I catch up with you tomorrow and we can talk then?"

She didn't give George the chance to protest before she started giving Shelby her report. She quickly clocked out and headed to the parking lot.

Afton felt strangely anxious the whole drive home. She couldn't imagine what had gotten Silas so worried. He had called, so she felt that was a sign that meant he didn't resent her for not visiting. It puzzled her, though, that he didn't want Phillip to know he was calling. Perhaps Phillip was the one who resented her. He had his own life and home in Mingo County, but lately he was playing dad to Silas. That had to be difficult for a loner like Phillip.

It was after six o'clock by the time Afton got home. She glanced over at the thermometer on the porch post and saw that the mercury was sitting on 90. It felt more like late summer than July. She hurried to the door and found that it was slightly ajar. She stood there for a moment with her hand on the doorknob. She was trying to remember if she had pulled it all the way closed when she had left for work that morning. She was sure that she had, so she shook away the thought and went inside. Everything seemed to be in order.

Afton fixed herself a glass of ice water just in case her phone conversation turned out to be a long one. She reached for the phone but froze before her hand could reach it.

Lying next to the phone was a photo. It was one that she had never seen before and had certainly not posed for—not knowingly, anyway. It was a picture of her asleep in bed. She went to pick the photo up and realized how badly her hand was shaking. Someone had come into her home while she slept and taken a picture of her. The partially open door came immediately to mind. Someone had been in her home, and apparently more than once.

Afton went from room to room, looking for anything out of place or disturbed. It all looked as it had when she'd left that the morning. Her mind was racing, trying to figure out who could have done it. Was it a recently released prisoner, or had she been wrong about Dechtire coming back?

She rechecked all the windows and doors to make sure they were locked up tight. Anxiously, she slid down into one of the chairs at the kitchen table. She drank almost the entire glass of water in one long swallow. Who would have thought that being scared could make one so thirsty? Once again, she reached for the phone. This time, she actually dialed Miss Betty's number. She wondered if she would ever stop calling it Miss Betty's number and start calling it Silas and Phillip's number?

"Hello," came Silas's young voice. "Is this Afton?"

"Yes, Silas, it's me. Our call was cut short today, and I just wanted to give you a call back so you could tell me what you wanted earlier." He seemed hesitant to start talking, so she continued. "So, how are Maddie, Nola May, and everyone doing? I miss you guys a lot."

He cleared his throat nervously. "But you haven't been back to see us."

There it was. The dreaded statement she had feared that she would eventually hear.

"I'm not going to try and make excuses, Silas," said gently, "because there's no excuse good enough to give you. I was afraid to come back because I knew I wouldn't want to leave. I didn't know if you all even wanted me to, and I knew it would hurt if I came back and found that you were all doing just fine without me. It was selfish of me, Silas."

Silence came from the other end of the line. Then Silas spoke again.

"Afton, were you hoping that I wasn't doing okay?"

"Oh, Silas, that's what it sounds like, doesn't it? No, I want you to be doing great. It's me that hasn't done well without you. I miss each and every one there. It seems so silly now that I've said it out loud. I'm glad you're okay, and I'm truly sorry that I haven't been back to see you. Can you please forgive me?"

"Of course I do!" Silas replied. "That's not even why I called you today. I called because I'm worried about you. Afton, I think there's someone near you, but you aren't aware of them. The person—I think it's a man, but I can't be sure—is hiding."

A chill ran through her body as he spoke those words.

"Silas, is Phillip or someone there with you?"

"Phillip's outside. Do you want me to fetch him?"

"Yes, Silas, please get Phillip to come to the phone."

A few seconds later, Phillip picked up the receiver. "Hello?"

"Phillip, this is Afton. I was just talking with Silas about the bad feeling he was having. He told me that he could sense someone watching me without my knowing. He thinks the person is hiding."

"It could simply be that Silas is missing you," Phillip replied. "Try not to worry too much about it."

"No, Phillip, Silas is right. Someone has been watching me and coming into my house. Whoever it is even took a picture of me while I slept."

That startled him. "Wait a minute, Afton. Back up and start from the beginning."

"I don't know what to say, other than Silas is right. He called the prison today to tell me, but you were coming back into the house and he was afraid you would get mad at him for calling me at work, so he hung up without telling me anything. When I got home this evening, I found my front door cracked open, and I also found a photo of me. The photo was lying on the table next to the phone. Someone had taken it while I was in bed asleep. I called Silas to see what he wanted to tell me, and that's when he told me about his feeling. Phillip, someone has been in my home." Afton felt a little unsteady after telling Phillip everything. She waited anxiously for his response.

Finally, Phillip responded to what she had just told him. "Afton, there's something I need to do. I'll have to call you back."

"Wait a minute, Phillip. Don't hang up on me without telling me something."

"I don't want to worry you unnecessarily," he assured her. "I need to check with Maddie and Nola May about something first."

"Phillip, please at least tell me who you think it might be."

She knew he was reluctant, but eventually he told her. "Okay, there are Cunnin' Folk that we refer to as 'Hiders.' These Hiders do just that—they hide behind a veil of darkness that they create with their mind. It keeps people like you from seeing them or into them so you won't know what they're thinking, planning, or what they've done in the past. They also keep silent talkers like Clayton out of their heads so they can't be influenced by them. I believe, after hearing what you told me and the fact that Silas has a feeling, that you have a Hider stalking you."

She suddenly felt dizzy, like the walls around her felt like they were closing in. "Okay, call back when you can." Her trembling hand returned the phone to its cradle.

Afton made her way to Grandma Ruby's thinkin' chair, lifted up the false cushion seat, and retrieved Miss Betty's book from its hiding place. She sat in the chair with the book in her lap for a long while before she opened it.

Maddie had warned her not to get too comfortable. Had she gotten comfortable with life and let this so-called Hider slip into her personal space … the space she had vigilantly guarded for so long? Afton felt violated as anger started to build within her. Sleep steered clear of her that night, and she managed to keep drowsiness at bay. She couldn't afford to sleep for fear someone would simply come in and snap her photo, or do something much worse.

The sun came up and found her still sitting in the chair. She ate breakfast, showered, and left for work. She was bound and determined not to stop living because of this Hider.

Clayton stopped Afton before she could get to the medical unit. "Phillip called me last night and told me what was going on. I called you immediately after talking with him. When you didn't answer, I called you silently. You didn't answer either way."

"I'm sorry, Clayton," she apologized. "I didn't mean to worry you. I must have blocked everything out because, honestly, I don't remember the phone ringing or you being in my head."

Clayton had a puzzled look on his face. "Have you ever blocked things out like that before?"

Afton thought for a minute before answering. "Maybe when I was little, after the fire. Why are you asking?"

"It may not even be possible, but it makes me wonder if you possess some Hider traits of your own."

Chapter 21: Home at Last

Afton left Clayton on that thought. She needed to get to work and was glad there wasn't doctor call that day. There was more than enough going on in her head already.

Sick call went by fairly quickly, as did the morning pill call. She settled in to do a couple of hours' worth of paperwork and filing. She was finished with everything by lunchtime. Clayton peeked into the unit to let her know he had a meeting to attend so he wouldn't be joining her in the break room for lunch. She was fine with that because she really didn't feel up to being in a small room full of other employees.

Afton found herself wandering up to the fourth floor. She stood at the window where Inmate Doyle had fallen to his death. The window had been replaced with some kind of shatter-proof material. She closed her eyes and could still see his expression as he seemingly floated to the ground below. It was followed by the loud thud of his body upon impact. The audible sound of bones breaking and his skull cracking was unforgettable.

The first time Afton had seen the visions of an inmate had been years ago.

She had only been working at the prison about six months at the time. A call came over the radio for her to report to the ball field for a possible broken leg. She arrived at the scene to find a young inmate who had tried to steal home plate. He had slid into the bag with such force it snapped the femur in his left leg. When she touched him to assess his injury, the visions hit her hard. She saw his plans for how he would strangle his ex-wife, tie up his daughters and put them in the trunk of a car, then take them to a campsite he had set up in a secluded area, where he would torture and kill them.

The inmate knew that Afton was seeing his plans. Had that insight or his broken leg sent him into severe seizures? He had a death-grip on her hand, as though he was trying to take her with him. The inmate's head had slammed repeatedly onto the hard ground, causing a fractured skull and a bleed to the brain. By the time he was transported to the closest hospital, he was brain dead.

Life support was removed the following day. Afton assumed his ex-wife had made that call. She wondered if the decision had been difficult for her … or if it was more of a relief. He died within three hours. Now she couldn't remember his name for some reason, and that bothered her. She was usually extremely good with details.

The Friday alarm check sounded and brought Afton back to the present. Goose bumps covered her arm, and she had an uncomfortable feeling that she was not alone. She tried to shake off the chills and the feelings she was having.

It was time to head back to Medical. She took one last look out the window and saw that the inmates were starting to mill around in the big courtyard. They were splitting up into small groups to play their various games.

One of the other nurses was scheduled to come in at one o'clock that afternoon, which should ensure her departure on time. Afton was looking forward to getting away from there for the weekend. She needed to hear for herself what Maddie and Nola May knew about the ones known as Hiders.

On her way back to Medical, she stopped and unlocked the medical request box and removed the forms. There were only three; two were nurse sick calls and one was a medication review. None were urgent in nature. She decided to go ahead and have the officer call those three inmates to Medical. She figured she could get those done by the time the next nurse came in to relieve her.

Inmate number one complained of cold-like symptoms. After checking him out, she prescribed the usual nursing protocol medicines and sent him on his way. Inmate number two complained of a toothache. Upon examination, Afton discovered that a filling had come out of one of his back teeth. She gave him the over-the-counter medicines that were allowed and placed his name on the dental list. She went ahead and completed their paperwork and placed their charts on the cart for review.

The next inmate request stated that he wanted to discuss his medications. That was not unusual. Sometimes the inmates didn't feel comfortable questioning Dr. Gray and preferred to talk to one of the nurses. She called him in and proceeded to get a current weight and a set of vital signs. Afton touched his wrist for a pulse and saw a glimpse of him when he was filling out the request. He appeared very anxious and kept looking around as if he thought someone was watching him.

Could this be my stalker? she wondered. No. She knew that wasn't possible. Whoever it was had possessed the freedom to invade her home.

He opened his mouth with some hesitation. Then he said, "Nurse Sullivan, I think I saw something I shouldn't have."

Her mind went straight to the photo of her sleeping. He can't be the stalker because he's in prison, she thought. He's locked up 24/7.

"What do you mean?" she asked.

After some hesitancy, he continued. "I don't want to get in trouble."

She assured him that if another prisoner had done something wrong, that inmate would be shipped out. He looked up at her and started to say something, but the nurse assigned to night shift stepped through the door and the inmate immediately clammed up.

"So, I'm to take my blood-pressure medicine in the morning?" he asked, completely changing the subject. "I wasn't sure about that. Thank you, Nurse Sullivan."

Concerned about the inmate's behavior, Afton finished her work and gave verbal shift report to her relief, a young nurse named Becky. She was turning out to be a good hire. Another year of experience and she would do quite well.

Afton clocked out and headed toward Clayton's office. She wanted to make sure he would be getting off on time. She could hear that he had someone in the office with him, so she hung back a bit to wait. She heard two male voices, but couldn't be sure who the second person was. She thought it could possibly be George, but they were not nearly as soft-spoken. She jumped when the door opened. It had been George.

As he walked by, he paused for a second. "Have a good weekend, Afton. While you're in Robinson Holler, put some flowers on Joetta's grave for me."

She thought it strange that Clayton would have told him about their trip, but she decided it was no big deal. She knocked on the door before going inside.

"See you at my house around four o'clock?" she asked him.

Clayton smiled. "Yes, you will. Are you finished for the day?"

"Yes, I didn't think Friday would ever get here. See you in a couple hours." Clayton gave her a wave as she closed his door.

Afton hurried down the three flights of stairs. The hairs on the back of her neck stood on end again. She had the eerie feeling that someone was still watching. She hadn't told Clayton about the inmate who had tried to tell her something, but she would do so as soon as he got to her house. If it happened to be one of the inmates who were allowed to leave the grounds for work release, he would be back at the prison now because they only worked half days on Friday.

She slid behind the wheel of Hazel. Afton had decided to drive her that day so she could stop on the way home to top off the gas tank and have all the fluids checked for their trip to Robinson Holler. As the gas station attendant took care of the gas and fluids, she went inside to get a snack. It had hit her after she was in the car that she still hadn't eaten lunch. She grabbed a bag of popcorn and a Coke and settled up with the cashier before heading home. The uneasy feelings from the past couple of days were replaced with excitement about seeing Silas and the others.

Arriving at home, Afton felt as though she had a renewed energy as she walked across the yard. The grass crunched under her feet, but she didn't think anything of it at the time. Her mind was focused on packing.

She threw a few things together. She still had an hour before Clayton was due to arrive. Not sleeping at all the night before had finally caught up with her in a big way, so she decided to lie down for forty-five minutes. Afton set her clock so she would have a few minutes to pull herself together before Clayton arrived.

She stretched out on the bed and drifted in and out of sleep for the first fifteen minutes or so. Her mind finally surrendered, and soon, she was sound asleep.

Afton opened her eyes and discovered that she was standing in the middle of a yard.

It was her yard, and she wasn't wearing any shoes. The grass felt dry and brittle against the soles of her feet. In the distance, she could hear someone calling to her, but she didn't want to answer. She just wanted to stay where she was in her own yard. Whoever it was, they wouldn't give up. They continued to call out to her. Finally, she threw her hands up in frustration and yelled back at the voice.

"What do you want?"

Silence fell over the dry little yard. She was glad. She didn't want to be bothered at that moment, but the quiet didn't last. A wind pounded its way through the woods, sounding like a train that was building up steam. She thought it must be another big wind blowing in like the one in 2012. It had done a lot of damage to homes and took down hundreds of trees across West Virginia and into Virginia. It had a name—derecho, she thought.

A large, dark cloud moved quickly across the sky and seemed to come to a halt as it hovered above her. She no longer heard the effects of the big wind, but could feel the darkness from the cloud as it attempted to creep into her very being.

An alarm sounded. Afton opened her eyes to find that she was in her bed and drenched with sweat.

She felt as though the dream had left her somehow drained of life itself. She took a quick cold shower and dressed in a lightweight sundress and sandals. She twisted her damp hair up in a bun and slid a bobby pin in to secure it. Afton checked the time—four o'clock on the dot. Clayton would be there any minute. She grabbed the tote bag with her clothes in it and decided to go ahead and put it in the trunk. She would roll down the windows, too, so the car could air out.

She stepped off the porch and onto the grass. It crunched. That brought the dream she'd just had flooding back. It also brought back the memory of the trio of dreams that had dominated her sleep the night before leaving Robinson Holler. Her body felt like it was stuck in quicksand. There she stood in her yard, and the grass was dry, just like in her dreams. From the corner of her eye, she could see the thermometer on the post sitting on 90 degrees, just like in the dreams. A chill ran over her skin as though someone was standing next to her waving a large fan.

So many thoughts spun in her mind. She needed to focus and grab one. The one that stuck was Clayton asking her if she had ever blocked things out. Afton closed her eyes and blocked all the excess noise out. She needed another thought, so she focused on Maddie. This time, what she brought back was her explaining that the dark cloud was like a veil and Afton might have to catch it off guard.

She had to think about that one a bit. What next? She looked up and saw the dark cloud was still right over her. Afton thought of what Grandma Ruby had told her about Givers and Takers. She wondered if that applied to dark clouds as well. The cloud in her dream had left her feeling drained—the way one would feel around a Taker, someone who sucked the life out of you and left you empty. It was a veil, not a dark cloud. She had to focus hard enough to push that veil to the side and see who was behind it. So she stood, focusing on the dark cloud, not knowing what to expect next. She heard tires crackling on gravel and turned to see Clayton pulling into the drive. That broke her focus. She looked up and the dark cloud had dissipated into several little clouds.

Clayton got out of his truck with a puzzled look on his face, no doubt trying to figure out what she was doing. Afton explained the dreams, the things Grandma Ruby had told her, and the last thing Maddie had said to her. She didn't expect him to understand completely, but she needed him to at least consider what she was telling him.

Afton locked up the house and Clayton moved his bag over to her car. They drove away from her little home and headed to Robinson Holler. She still felt on edge and found her mind continually drifting backward to the day's events. She was missing something. She could feel it as plain as day, but she just couldn't put her finger on it.

Clayton was the first to break the silence. "Would you like to stop and get a bite for supper? There's a diner just up ahead."

"Yes, that sounds great. I think a break and some food is just what I need to clear my head. It aches from all the clutter that's moving about in there. Do you ever feel that way?"

"I'm a silent talker, but there's a whole lot of commotion in my mind sometimes that's louder than you might think."

They laughed as Afton turned off the road and into the parking lot of Bones Diner. Inside, there were plenty of booths open. There were only three other customers; an elderly couple in one booth and one other gentleman sitting on a stool at the counter. Clayton ordered the special, which was a bacon cheeseburger and fries. Afton ordered tomato soup and a grilled cheese. Soup was her medicine; it had a calming effect on her.

They ate every last bit of their food. It was actually really good; she guessed that surprised her. They paid the check and headed to the parking lot. Afton hadn't noticed on the way in, but there was a cemetery on the other side of the diner. She pointed it out to Clayton.

"Guess that's why it's called Bones Diner," he joked. "It sits right next to a boneyard."

He followed her as she walked over to the little cemetery. The graveyard contained fewer than twenty headstones. As she looked at the name on one of the headstones, it hit her like a ton of bricks.

"Clayton, did you tell George we were going to Robinson Holler?"

Clayton looked surprised at the question. "No, I didn't tell anyone at work. I'm like you when it comes to sharing the details of my personal life. I tend to keep it to myself."

"Clayton, we need to go back."

"Go back where?"

"To my house. I have to check on something."

Afton jumped behind the wheel and gestured for Clayton to hurry and get in. She pushed Hazel as hard as she thought old car could handle. Clayton remained quiet. She knew he was trying to get into her head to see what was going on, but she blocked him out. She had to.

It was dusk when they neared her house. Afton pulled off the road before they got there and cut the engine. She told Clayton to stay in the car. She didn't know if he would listen or not, but she didn't wait to find out.

She headed through the woods as quietly as she could. The house was just a couple hundred feet away. There was a light on in her house … a light she was positive she had not left on. Afton reminded herself to stay focused and block everything out, even Clayton trying to poke his way into her thoughts. She crept up to the back door and looked in. Before her eyes, there in her little kitchen stood her nurse manager, George Samoht.

Catch him off guard and the veil will be pulled aside and his true identity will be revealed. Isn't that right, Maddie? she thought to herself.

Anger started bubbling up inside her as she watched that man invading her space. Afton clenched her fists, not noticing that her nails were digging so deeply into her palms that they were drawing blood. Her focus was so powerful, it spun George around and slammed him up against the wall. His eyes were wide with surprise and pain. He had definitely been caught off guard.

Without losing focus or taking her eyes off of George, Afton walked into her kitchen and stood before that poor excuse for a man. A man who preferred to create a dark veil to hide behind, rather than face his prey, eye to eye. He opened his mouth to speak, but Afton's intense focus snapped it shut. She wasn't ready to hear his excuses—at least not yet.

"George Samoht, nurse manager, my supervisor … you are the Hider. You are a person that chooses to sneak around in the cover of darkness and snap photos of me while I sleep."

Afton's concentration had never been so dead-on. She was not able to rein in her anger. A bright yellow Fiestaware teapot flew off the shelf and crashed into the side of George's head. Bright-red blood trickled down his temple.

"Afton, stop!" shouted Clayton from the doorway. "You're going to kill him!"

She shot Clayton a look across the room and the expression on his face changed. It told her that he was disappointed that she would sink so low. That was enough to bring her back from the darkness that she was embracing as her own.

"Clayton, this is the Hider," Afton said, in as calm a voice as she could manage through her anger. "He's the one who's been breaking into my home."

"Okay, Afton. I'll tie him to a chair," Clayton replied. "You need to slow your breathing and your pulse before you blow a gasket."

He yanked George from the wall, pushed him into one of the kitchen chairs, and secured him tightly with a length of rope. Where he'd found the rope, she had no idea, but George certainly wasn't going anywhere now.

Afton placed her hands against her temples. She could feel the throbbing in her head through her fingertips. When she took her hands away, she saw where her fingernails had drawn blood from her palms. A lifetime of pent-up anger had been let loose all at once. She was thankful Clayton had come in when he did, because she believed she could have easily taken George's life at that moment. But that wasn't her, nor was it what she wanted.

They heard noises outside. Much to their surprise, they discovered it was Maddie, Nola May, Silas, Phillip, Connor, Cardinal, and a woman Afton didn't recognize.

"What on earth are all of you doing here?"

"Silas was sure that you were in trouble, so I decided to come," Phillip told her. "And there was no stopping the rest of the family."

Afton's eyes were drawn to the stranger and then back to Phillip.

He immediately knew the question she wanted to ask. "Afton, this is Sally, my niece—Connor's sister. I believe her concern has a lot to do with Clayton."

Afton was still confused.

"I've been going back to Robinson Holler every other weekend since Christmas," Clayton explained. "I knew you would return when the time was right for you. In the meanwhile, I've become quite fond of Sally and I believe the feeling is mutual. If I have my way, we will be spending the rest of our lives together as husband and wife."

Sally blushed at Clayton's confession. She ran into his arms and hugged him tight, as if she never wanted to be apart from him again. They made a beautiful couple; her tall, slender build was a perfect match for Clayton's six-foot-two stature. She had long, dark, straight hair and big, beautifully kind, brown eyes. Afton's heart filled with joy for the two of them.

"So this is the Hider?" Maddie asked. "Is he a stranger to you?"

"No. As a matter of fact, he's my boss, George. What I don't know is why he would have any reason to stalk me. We've worked together for years. I thought we were friends."

George finally chimed in bitterly. "Friends? You've got to be kidding. You treat me as if I don't exist. You and your perfect nursing skills. Well, it wasn't so perfect back when you had only worked at the prison for a short while. You probably don't even remember, but you were called to the ball field for an injured inmate. The inmate you 'took care of' that day was my half-brother, Billy Call. You didn't follow procedures to protect him when he started seizing. He ended up brain dead. The decision had to be made to unplug his life support. Where was your perfection then, Afton? It was your fault. You could have held him down or ordered the guards to hold him down."

Billy Call was the first inmate who caused her to have visions. Afton had put her hands on him, and in a flash, she had witnessed the horrible things he had done and what he was planning to do to his wife and daughters upon his forthcoming release.

Grandma Ruby had assured Afton that she was not killing people. She had told her that what she possessed was a gift. She was stunned. All those years had gone by with George secretly blaming her for Billy's death.

"George, I did everything I could for Billy. Did your brother have a history of seizures? There had been nothing listed in his chart to indicate any such problems."

George thought for a minute before answering. "When he was a kid, he suffered a few seizures, but that was all in the past. Billy had been fine for years."

"George, the pain from the broken femur must have triggered the seizure," she told him. "I had no way to stop it. I don't know if you were told the entire story, but I ended up with a concussion myself trying to help Billy. There was nothing anyone could have done to prevent it. Your brother was having a massive grand mal seizure. I know you must have loved him, but you need to tell me one thing, George. Are Billy's wife and daughters okay?"

George dropped his head and stared at the ground before responding. Apparently, he had been aware of the abuse that Billy had inflicted on his family. "Yes, they're fine. She moved on with her life and remarried and had a son. Her new husband is good to her and the children."

"That's good, isn't it? George, when I touched Billy, I saw the horrible things he had done in the past, and I saw what he had planned for his wife and children." Afton searched George's face for understanding.

George nodded his head as tears streamed down his face. "Afton, I didn't mean to cause you so much trouble. When I first met Dechtire, I was drawn to her. I hid so I could watch her. I knew she wanted to find the people who had kept her from her parents. I told her I could help her, so I hired her. I'm the one who told her where Joetta was from. It's my fault that Dechtire poisoned her." He looked over at the big prison warden. "I was jealous of how quickly you took to Clayton, so I told her that I had tried to save her job, but Clayton had the final say. She tried to kill Clayton too. Everything bad that's happened has been my fault." An expression of deep misery haunted his face. "Please, Afton, can you take this veil of evil from me, once and for all?"

"I'll try to do as you ask," she replied, "but I can't promise it will work."

Once again, Afton's focus was heightened as she stared into George's eyes. She could feel the heat rising in her core. She grew almost feverish and wondered if perhaps her blood would actually come to a boil. As soon as she had that thought, she could see steam rising from George's flesh. She heard the sound of wind as it made its way through the woods. It slapped against the limbs, bending them just shy of breaking, and then the wind was upon them, instantly cooling their skin.

Afton shivered as the mercury dropped. The steam that rose from George's skin was now freezing like thin ice in midair. It crackled all around him, and with one final gust, the ice shattered and fell to the ground. The veil of darkness had been broken, and the rope fell away from George's body as if by magic. George was free of his dark companion. He would never again be able to "hide."

They all stood around George as he slid to his knees, sobbing.

Fortunately, he hadn't actually hurt anyone. Yes, he had led Dechtire to believe certain things, but he could not control her, no more than any of them could control Roy and Claire. He had invaded Afton's space and taken a photo of her while she slept, but he hadn't harmed her in any way. They all agreed that putting an end to his "hiding" was enough. The Cunnin' Folk had no problem in forgiving him.

George told them that it was time for him to retire from the prison and get to know his nieces and his new nephew. Afton reached out to him and they shook hands. As his hand grasped hers, she clearly saw that he had no harmful intentions in mind for anyone from that point onward.

Then George Samoht quietly left them.

Now, there they all were in Afton's little home. They celebrated late into the night. There were many things for which they needed to give thanks. Phillip got out his Native American flute and gladly played all of their requests. A long summer shower watered the dry lawn during the night and softened the hard grass. By morning, the brown, brittle blades had turned a lush green again. Grandma Ruby and her green thumb may have had a hand in that.

Afton made sure she was the first to get up. She had an important chore to do.

A few months earlier, she had run across an antique door lock in the outbuilding, and she wanted to try something. She gathered a few tools and took a chance, changing the front door lock over to the one she had found. When everyone else got up, she called them all out front. They didn't have a clue what she was up to. She pulled the old key that Miss Betty had given her from her pocket and handed it to Clayton.

"This is for you and Sally. I have a feeling it's going to fit in the old lock I just installed. That tiny apartment of yours is no place to make a home with Sally."

Clayton looked down at the key, then looked at her, and then at Sally. Afton smiled and nodded that it was okay. Hand in hand, Clayton and Sally approached the door and the big man slid the old key into the lock. When he turned the key, it clicked and everyone cheered.

"Afton, you can't possibly be serious," said Sally. "This is your home."

Afton's reply was to the point. "I have no need for two houses. My real home is in Robinson Holler, and that's where I intend to live."

Clayton and Sally graciously accepted her gift, and the two were married that afternoon.

As Afton sat back and watched the couple dance their first dance together as husband and wife, she knew in her heart that she had done the right thing. Maddie and Nola May prepared a wedding feast. They also danced, as did Connor and Cardinal. That left her, Phillip, and Silas to enjoy the show. Someone put on an old 45 (where had they found that?, she wondered), and the song "Feeling Good" by Nina Simone started playing. It was one of her favorites.

Afton was delighted when Silas took her hand and said, "Come on, Afton … dance with us."

The three of them danced together, and when the song ended and another started, Silas excused himself to get something to eat. She and Phillip continued to dance. It all felt so carefree until the Percy Sledge song "When a Man Loves a Woman" came on, and then Afton didn't know how to move to the slow music. She began to walk away, but Phillip took her by the hand, pulled her closer, and placed her hand on his shoulder. With one of his hands resting on her waist and his other hand in hers, he taught her to slow dance. The heat of his body pressed against Afton's and the earthy smell of his skin stirred emotions she had never felt before.

The next day, Afton packed her personal things from the house and cleared out her belongings from her locker at the prison. Maddie and Nola May rode back with Connor and Cardinal. Afton gave the keys to Hazel to Sally and told her she would need a dependable ride while Clayton was at work. The dark-haired woman knew there was no need to protest.

Sally smiled her beautiful smile. "Thank you so much, Afton. I'll take good care of her."

Clayton slid his arms around his wife and picked her up. She squealed like a teenage girl. They waved goodbye as they stood on the front porch of their new home.

Afton slid into the passenger side of her jeep and Phillip took the wheel. Silas was buckled safely in the backseat. As the miles clicked away, she knew she was finally headed home for good. Phillip reached out and took her hand in his. Afton laid her head back against the headrest and closed her eyes. A peace like she had never known washed over her and she slept all the way to Robinson Holler.

Her first night back, she decided to stay in Grandma Ruby's cabin. Nola May and Maddie were spending the night at Miss Betty's, and Afton wanted them to have a bedroom, as well as Phillip and Silas. There was no longer a need for anyone to be crowded or to sleep on the floor for fear that "bad ones" would come.

She felt safe as she went through the cabin and opened all the windows. A gentle breeze was blowing, and it brought with it the music of the summer hot-bugs and peepers. She was about to go to bed when there was a knock on the door. She opened it to find Phillip standing on the porch.

"Do you have everything you need?" he asked.

"Almost."

Phillip looked so concerned, so eager to please. "What is it, Afton? I can run back to Miss Betty's to get whatever it is."

Afton could feel her face blushing as she reached for his hand. No longer did she feel the need to keep people at arm's length. She was ready to let someone in, and that someone was Phillip Whelan. He smiled warmly and his eyes lit up as he stepped across the threshold and into her waiting arms.

"Phillip, I've avoided touch for so long because it so often brought only bad visions with it. That's changed now—you changed it. I want to touch and I want to be touched."

"Afton, I've waited a long time for you to say those words to me," he whispered in her ear. "I've been in love with you since you returned to Robinson Holler the very first time."

Phillip lifted her up into his strong arms and carried her to the bedroom.

That night they did much more than touch. They made love. Afterwards, they held one another close, and talked into the wee hours, drifting off to sleep just before sunrise.

Not long after, they started making plans for their wedding. They wanted to keep it small, but include all their families and special mountain friends.

They held the ceremony outside. Flowers adorned the entire shape of the lake and up around the rock, where Phillip played his flute. Afton wore an ivory gown, which had been made by piecing together both of her grandmother's wedding gowns. The long veil and short piece that covered her face, down to her nose, was trimmed with intricate silk flowers. She was a vision to behold.

Silas walked Afton from the lake's edge to the rock. Phillip gasped when he saw his soon to be wife. And Afton did the same, only quieter, when she looked up and saw Phillip waiting at the rock altar. He wore a freshly ironed, crisp white dress shirt. He had the sleeves rolled up to just below his elbows. The sight of his tanned, muscled arms brought back their one night in bed. They had decided to wait until they were married before lying together again. He wore a pair of tan work pants that were snug in all the right places. They both were barefoot. Everyone in attendance was.

After saying their I do's, the reception lasted all night. There was dancing, singing, and music. The mountains held many talented musicians, and they played guitars, fiddles, and banjos. Phillip even played a few songs on his flute.

It was bound to be the most perfect celebration of love the mountains had ever hosted.

Miss Betty's cabin became home for Afton, Phillip, and Silas. Her Grandma Ruby's house was left as it was in hopes that someday, years from now, it would be a home for Silas and the family he would start.

Maddie and Nola May each had their own cabin on adjacent ridges. Afton felt they were always watching over them. Grandma Ruby would eventually stop visiting her dreams, but Afton knew that she, too, was keeping watch and smiling at the happiness she had found. This new chapter in her life, with this unique group of people, was a good one. The necklace Silas had made for her now hung in the kitchen window, and as she washed dishes, the breeze would make the pendant spin and the raven would chase the wolf. But no matter how fast it would go, it could never catch him.

Miss Betty's book was never too far away. Afton would refer to it often over the years. She had been right: it did indeed hold the answers to her future as a Cunnin' Folk Appalachian Granny. Grandma Ruby had been right as well: she had a gift, and living there in Robinson Holler allowed it to flourish. Sometimes, she pictured Miss Betty, Grandma Ruby, Joetta, and her mom sitting together around a new quilt as they made each square extra-special. They were all special women, and that she knew for sure.

They would have many a celebration in the Holler, and Afton would be surrounded by the people she loved—Phillip, Silas, Maddie, and Nola May.

The Tolleys continued to drive Hazel to all their reunions. Clayton kept the prison running smoothly, and the inmates in order. His gifts were often put to the test, but his abilities outweighed anything the inmates tried to get away with. He and Sally had a daughter, Cordelia Rose, named after Mommy Bud. They never missed a gathering.

Connor and Cardinal had a daughter named Lilly Dale, a namesake of Miss Betty's daughter. They were living in Phillip's cabin, so they were close enough to visit on a regular basis. Silas grew up to be the best veterinarian in the area, which covered all four of the surrounding counties. It kept him busy, but he always made time for their unique family, especially after a special young lady named Violet found her way to Robinson Holler. She was that same beautiful Violet, who Afton had handed over to child services years before, only now she was a lovely grown woman with hair as bright as spun gold.

The lush, green mountains that surround Robinson Holler were more unique than one could imagine, and the special people who made their homes there were the best. As for those dark clouds that hung low over Naked Creek for so many decades … they moved onward and left behind nothing but clear blue skies overhead.

In the depths of Calhoun County, WV, there's a knock on the door of a secluded cabin. The door slowly opens to a raven-haired woman standing on the porch.

The woman asks, "Is this the home of Ora and Ida O'Sullican? My name is Dechtire, and I'd like to talk to you about your daughter, Afton."

Acknowledgements

I want to thank Steve and Heather Ventura for their fervent enthusiasm in publishing this new version of *Dark Cloud on Naked Creek*. I am forever grateful to Thomas Tessier and his encouragement for this story to be read. Thanks to Ronald Kelly for agreeing to be my early editor, and blending his familiar Appalachian voice with my own. My never-ending gratitude to Bella Gentile and Cathy Moriarty for loving the novel and characters as much as I do. Many thanks to the entire team at Brigids Gate Press. Much appreciation goes to cover artist, Lynne Hanson, for seeing my vision through to completion. I must thank my self-proclaimed, number one fan, Steven LaCroix, for his constant backing over the years. Many thanks to my friends, Owl Goingback, Bob Ford, Linda D. Addison, Patricia Gomes, Jeff Cilione, and Wayne Fenlon for their support. Special thanks to Zack, Elijah, and Jonnathas—for being my family. And to my Appalachian Mountains, may you continue to surround and stand guard over me for decades to come.

About the Author

Cindy O'Quinn is an Appalachian writer. She grew up in the beautiful mountains of West Virginia. She writes fiction, nonfiction, and speculative poetry, which all lean heavily into the horror genre. It was with Cindy's fifth Bram Stoker Award® nomination that garnered her a winner of the prestigious award. Her poetry has been nominated for the Elgin, Rhysling, and Dwarf Star awards.

Also by Cindy O'Quinn

Fiction:
"Quondam," *The Nightmare Never Ends*
"Lydia," from the Shirley Jackson Award-winning anthology, *The Twisted Book of Shadows*
"The Thing I Found Along a Dirt Patch Road," *Shotgun Honey Presents: Recoil*
"A Gathering on the Mountain," *The Bad Book*
"The Handshake," Sanitarium Magazine, and Northern Frights, Women Issue
"Perfect Seed," SFPA Halloween Recordings
"Advent," *Eerie Christmas.* Later re-released as "The Fizz," In Northern Frights

"The Patch," Northern Frights
"Black Cats and Bone Dust," *Vinyl Cuts*
"Hank." *Something Bad Happened*
"Vine House," *Something Bad Happened*
"A Wayfaring Woman," *Brigids Sisters*
"At the Foot of Jones Mountain," *Bestiary of Blood*
"Swimming in the Aftertaste," *Bestiary of Blood* *
"Rolling Boil," *Discontinue if Death Ensues: Tales From the Tipping Point*
"Everyone," *Discontinue if Death Ensues: Tales From the Tipping Point*
"Like-minded," *A Quaint and Curious Volume of Gothic Tales*

Nonfiction:
"One and Done," *Were Tales: A Shapeshifter Anthology*
"Waiting on a Diagnosis," *You're Not Alone in the Dark*

Sudden Fictions Podcasts:
"Storm Surge"
"Give Me Shelter"

Poetry Collections:
Return to Graveyard Dust
Foundlings **

Individual poems published:
75+

*Wayne Fenlon
** Stephanie Ellis

MORE FROM BRIGIDS GATE PRESS

Extinction Hymns

Eric Raglin

A vengeful owl haunts the man who poached her. A desperate entrepreneur holds a ghost hostage for profit. An addict finds hope and terror in an imprisoned angel. A father and son search their dying world for something to eat other than human flesh. Eric Raglin, author of *Nightmare Yearnings*, returns with his second collection of horror and weird fiction. Strange, terrifying, and tender, these eighteen stories explore what happens when extinction comes for us all.

COUNTRY ROADS

Colin Leonard

Something is outside; in the fields, by the ditches, on the roads. Something old and cruel and vicious.

When Luke Sheridan moves out of Dublin city to rural Kilcross with his wife and baby, he imagines the worst part will be his extended commute to work. They can look forward to enjoying the countryside and being part of a small community. After all, his old friend Declan Maguire lives in the house next door and is a Garda in the nearest town.

But Declan's devilish attitude towards drink, drugs and women means trouble is never far from his door. And worse, gruesome murders and the appearance of sinister figures at night mean the countryside is becoming a very dangerous place to live.

Country Roads—don't go outside alone.

Food for Thought

Ariana Ferrante

Limos is the goddess of starvation. Whatever she touch withers and wastes, crumbling to dust. She aids those seeking destruction, plaguing fields with famine and waters with drought. When mortals see her, they yearn.

Her opposite, harvest goddess Demeter, makes life flourish wherever she goes. She supplies mortals with fruits and vegetables, piling their tables with sustenance and satisfaction. When mortals see her, they are contented.

Given their opposing natures, The Fates themselves have decreed Limos and Demeter are never to meet, promising only ruin and mutual destruction should they ever unite.

But when Demeter arrives at her doorstep, begging for her assistance, Limos can't help but fall victim to the same yearning her mortal worshippers feel …

CLAY BOY

Craig E. Sawyer

Caleb Jenkins is a bullied middle schooler that everyone calls Clay Boy, due to the way he uses clay therapy to cope with the tragic murder of his mother at the hands of a serial killer. While at school, he discovers a playful video on how to create an imaginary best friend called a tulpa, but the more he interacts with his mental creation the more real and self-thinking it becomes, eventually convincing Caleb to sculpt a body for it to inhabit in order to unleash the hate that both share upon his bullies and the entire community of Wheeler's Cove, Tennessee.

Visit our website at: www.brigidsgatepress.com